PRAISE FOR
WILLA & HESPER

"A debut novel for those who loved *Everything Is Illuminated*, but updated with a queer-young-romance twist. The title characters in Amy Feltman's *Willa & Hesper* find solace from their breakup in the rabbit holes of their European Jewish background."

—*New York Times Book Review*

"Feltman slices directly to the core of heartbreak's ugliest moments: the temptation to fall back into patterns, to keep running from intimacy and risks. She evocatively captures the tension between aching to move on and to not give up, and how the shattering of one relationship fractures others. Feltman stays away from happy ending conventions and skillfully weaves glimmers of hope and healing throughout, making for a keenly perceptive novel."

—*Publishers Weekly*

"After crystallizing in the thrill of a new relationship, Feltman adeptly captures each progression of the stages of heartbreak. This is a cathartic breakup read if there ever was one."   —*Refinery29*

"A haunting story of aching love and grief, desire and hope . . . There is no love like a young woman's love—strong and fine and grasping and consuming; it leaves a mark. *Willa & Hesper* is the story of such a love, and so, of course, it is also the story of heartbreak and longing, searches for identity, struggles to make sense of the world and of each other."

—*Nylon*

"I'm always here for portrayals of 21st-century queer life, and *Willa & Hesper* looks to be an excellent addition to the genre."

—*Literary Hub*

"From *Willa & Hesper*, readers may see how relationships between twentysomethings, even when brief, have the potential to inspire unimaginable self-discovery . . . Feltman's novel is as titillating and tense as the experience of young adult love." —*Booklist*

"Writing in alternating first-person chapters, Feltman renders each perspective with moving fidelity to her characters and their interior lives. The result is a deep and intimate portrait of two queer women in their midtwenties who come of age in New York while navigating—or refusing to navigate—their relationships to privilege, family, identity, and faith. What could be a novel about an intense attraction that falls apart is, in Feltman's hands, a bigger story about how people change us—and how we welcome or resist that change. A moving glimpse into 21st-century queer womanhood." —*Kirkus*

"*Willa & Hesper* is a novel with a beating heart, a love story that is also an intricate love affair with time, history, religion, and inheritance. In fresh and captivating prose, and spanning three vibrantly rendered countries, Amy Feltman's debut enthralled me."

—Chloe Benjamin, bestselling author of *The Immortalists*

"A lyrical, timely story about love, heartbreak, and healing. *Willa & Hesper* explores religion, queerness, what it means to live in today's world in a female body, and the meaning of family in tight, absorbing prose." —Crystal Hana Kim, author of *If You Leave Me*

"Amy Feltman's debut novel is a joy to read, thrumming with inventive, playful language and filled with characters so finely drawn that they'll feel all too familiar. With a sharp eye for detail and a lush sense of place, she has written an unforgettable story about love, grief, identity, and belonging."

—Angelica Baker, author of *Our Little Racket*

"*Willa & Hesper* crystallizes a truth that haunts any of us who yearn to fall in love—our ability to be close to another person is always shaped by our secrets, our memories, our familial past. This debut is tender and tough, startlingly intimate, yet attuned to the larger troubles of our current political moment."

—Naima Coster, author of *What's Mine and Ours*

"This is the queer, coming-of-age, complicated love story I've been wanting to read for years. I wish I knew Willa and Hesper when I was in my twenties, though I still don't know whose side I'd take after their breakup—both are strange and smart and compelling."   —Katie Heaney, author of *Never Have I Ever*

"At once bittersweet and sharply funny, *Willa & Hesper* is a lovely meditation on how the trauma of the past intertwines with the future, fashioning our worldview no matter how hard we resist. Both protagonists are urgently, imperfectly real, and you will miss them as much as they miss one another once their story is done."

—Julia Fine, author of
What Should Be Wild and *The Upstairs House*

All the Things
We Don't Talk About

All the Things We Don't Talk About

Amy Feltman

GRAND CENTRAL
PUBLISHING

NEW YORK   BOSTON

Grand Central Publishing
Hachette Book Group
1290 Avenue of the Americas, New York, NY 10104
grandcentralpublishing.com
twitter.com/grandcentralpub

First Edition: May 2022

Grand Central Publishing is a division of Hachette Book Group, Inc. The Grand Central Publishing name and logo is a trademark of Hachette Book Group, Inc.

The Hachette Speakers Bureau provides a wide range of authors for speaking events. To find out more, go to www.hachettespeakersbureau.com or call (866) 376-6591.

Library of Congress Cataloging-in-Publication Data

Names: Feltman, Amy, author.
Title: All the things we don't talk about / Amy Feltman.
Other titles: All the things we do not talk about
Description: First edition. | New York : Grand Central Publishing, 2022.
Identifiers: LCCN 2021025309 | ISBN 9781538704721 (hardcover) | ISBN
    9781538704714 (ebook)
Classification: LCC PS3606.E45 A78 2022 | DDC 813/.6--dc23
LC record available at https://lccn.loc.gov/2021025309

ISBNs: 9781538704721 (hardcover), 9781538704714 (ebook)

Printed in the United States of America

LSC-C

Printing 1, 2022

To Christine

All the Things
We Don't Talk About

1.

It started with a gun that didn't go off. It never went off, because it was spotted in a backpack and confiscated. Later, Morgan would think they'd heard a scream, but they hadn't. All of the students in the high school were evacuated and stood in single-file lines on the quad, but soon the single file disbanded. They thought about looking for Tiana and Aiden, but then remembered the three of them weren't really friends anymore. Not the kind of friends that would be able to acknowledge this, or try to mask it with chatter, anyway. Morgan looked at the ground. Dampness from the grass soaked through the hole in their shoe.

At first a blanketed hush fell over the groups, but it didn't last. Sadie ended up next to Morgan in the crowd, where they could hear occasional laughs, some even spirited. People had located the thing inside them that allowed them to move forward, except Morgan hadn't, and they kept their hands inside their puffy khaki pockets. Policemen went inside and checked for bombs. It looked so cinematic, Morgan thought, with their dark uniforms and solemn faces. If it were a movie, Morgan would've seen their stern, glassy eyes in a close-up before they burst through the front doors. Sadie said they looked like a drawing of electrons bouncing from one atom to another. This was the first thing that Sadie said to Morgan that wasn't directly related to homework.

"It's okay that you're freaking out," she said.

Sadie's voice was so beautiful, deep but honeyed, that it took Morgan aback whenever she spoke.

"I'm not," Morgan protested, but their own voice was weak. It was the herbal tea of voices.

"I actually think it's really fucked up that no one else is," Sadie said.

Morgan didn't know her super well, so they tried to observe her acutely then. They were the two financial aid kids; Sadie's family lived in an apartment complex near Morgan's favorite deli, the one where you could still buy an individually wrapped Swedish fish. They'd recognized each other at orientation on the first day of high school. Sadie had unfashionable shoes. Sadie had a body that Morgan tried very hard to never think about. It was hard to look at her directly.

"You don't seem spooked," Morgan said. Their word choice was painfully geeky.

"Boo," Sadie said. She poked them. Morgan felt the contact between their bodies travel all the way down. "I am. But I have three brothers, so I know how to pretend. You can't get by without a little armor."

Morgan tried to respond but ended up gagging. "Sorry but I'm probably going to throw up," they said, the flutter and pull familiar. Sadie led them around the perimeter of the parking lot. Morgan vomited in front of a tree that had been planted in memory of a teacher who'd died slowly of cancer. It was the same kind of cancer that had killed Morgan's grandma. Morgan tried to tell Sadie to leave, but she seemed completely unfazed. She looked out into the parking lot like a captain—evaluating the weather, steering a ship into the harbor.

"You didn't have to stay," Morgan said.

"I only do things I want to do," Sadie said. She gave them a stick of cinnamon gum.

"What's that like?" Morgan asked.

"Kind of spicy," Sadie said.

It took them a second to realize she meant the gum. Morgan smiled. They backed away from the clumpy vomit on the grass slowly, pretending to be very absorbed in the movement of clouds.

"It would be kind of ironic, right? If we died at *this* school after working so hard to be somewhere without a metal detector."

Morgan nodded, but didn't know what else to say. Sadie led and Morgan followed down the pebbly path that eventually fed into the soccer field. "How do you like it here?" Sadie asked.

"I don't especially like it here," Morgan said, and Sadie laughed. It wasn't exactly true, but they thought it would sound good. They couldn't realistically imagine a high school that was better, but they could certainly imagine one that was worse. Morgan had started here in sixth grade, minnowing and retreating from different social circles along with fellow latecomers Tiana and Aiden. Now, on the high school food chain, Morgan was just liked enough to be rendered completely invisible in a crowd. They lent people pens but spent lunch in the library.

But then they felt guilty, lying to Sadie. Maybe she could tell they were lying, trying to impress her with wit. She was probably tired of people trying to impress her. "I was homeschooled until sixth grade," Morgan said. "People weren't as mean about it as I expected, but it's . . . kind of cliquey. Hard to break in."

Sadie nodded. "Yeah," she agreed, and the pause that followed felt significant.

"What about you?" Morgan asked.

Sadie paused. "Do you want a real answer or a cotton candy answer?"

"A real one," Morgan said.

"Every time I walk in there," Sadie said, "I feel like I'm one test score away from losing my financial aid and it makes me *itch*. It feels like everybody else has been here since kindergarten, or at least since middle school. At my last school, we didn't have textbooks for everybody. We had to rotate." She shook her head. "But then, on top of that, everybody I talk to thinks I'm trying to steal their boyfriend. Like I would even have time to steal somebody's boyfriend." She tilted her head toward the sky. "I don't want to die here surrounded by people who think I'm some lascivious bitch."

"I know what you mean," Morgan said. "Not— I mean, nobody thinks I'm a lascivious bitch."

"How can you be so sure?" Sadie asked.

"I'm not," Morgan said, and they both laughed. "The first part, though. Walking on the tightrope, trying to keep your grades up—it's a lot of pressure. It makes you tired."

"It does," she said. "It makes you fucking tired."

Sadie's eyes glinted bluer in the light, like the color of Neptune in science textbooks. "You know what I worry about sometimes? That I'm going to be thinking about something really stupid when I die. Or, like, I'll have a horrible song stuck in my head, and the last thing I'll think is . . . *it's the remix to ignition, hot and fresh off the kitchen.*"

"If I'm there when you die, I'll make sure you have good music," Morgan said. "But only if you don't tell anyone that I threw up before."

"Worried about your reputation as Mr. Tough?" Sadie said. "You seem like you could *really* hold your own in a fight."

Morgan forced a laugh. "Yeah. That's it."

"I mean— Sorry, I know you're not a mister," Sadie said.

Morgan had always wondered how fast news of their nonbinariness traveled. Most people seemed to approach Morgan with a new, *so you're specialer than I thought* energy for a few weeks after Morgan strategically told a motormouthed lab partner they used *they/them*, actually, and then had been asked to write a personal essay about it for the school literary magazine. But their moment passed, and then they had a new lab partner, and a new issue of the magazine came out, and the only debris of the conversation happened in grammatical acrobatics.

"Maybe we should get back," Morgan said.

"I didn't mean—"

"Oh, I know. I don't want to miss World Civ." They tugged on the strap of their backpack and felt the weight of the textbooks inside shift. "Thanks for the gum."

Sadie busied her fingers into her hair. "Okay, yeah. No worries."

"I'll see you," Morgan said, an emptiness mushrooming over their anxiety. The walk back toward the front door felt interminable, knowing Sadie was watching. It was their fault, obviously, for taking a joke too personally. This was how many friendships started to unravel or, more often, stopped from beginning to ravel at all. In class, their teacher gesticulated wildly across a smudgy whiteboard. The only thing Morgan could think of was Sadie with a gun pressed to the front of her pretty forehead, R. Kelly blasting through the loudspeakers overhead. *Say cheese*, they pictured the school shooter whispering before Sadie crumpled to the floor.

There were offers of therapy in the guidance counselor's office, but Morgan didn't see anyone else going, so they didn't go, either. Ethan, the would-be gunman, was expelled. After World Civ came gym. They swatted tennis balls into the air and plunged through the world with rackets outstretched. Around Morgan, everyone seemed hesitant, maybe a little nicer to each other than they would've been, but generally unaffected. Part of them wanted to bolt. Dad's office, on the Upper West Side, wasn't so far away: $2.75 and forty-five minutes. Probably if everyone's lives had been threatened, Morgan wouldn't be reprimanded for missing gym. (But their scholarship, they thought; a constant refrain.)

But: Dad. He worked in a strange office, over a basement location of a sports club that smelled like chlorine even though there was no pool. The office itself was in a converted theater with tall windows. Morgan's dad was the IT director, which sounded fancy, but Morgan didn't know what he did all day besides stare anxiously at screens. They hired him without a college degree and kept him despite the fact that the company seemed to be perpetually on the verge of collapse. Instead of a holiday party, everyone got a white chocolate snowman. Every year, Morgan tried to train themself to like white chocolate, but it just tasted like sweet wax. Every year, Morgan felt guiltier about this job that their dad visibly hated, but they needed insurance, a new roof, the medical bills from Grandma Cheryl dying were still arriving in thin menacing envelopes, and even with aid, Morgan's tuition was nine thousand dollars a year.

The place where Morgan's dad worked offered an incentive to buy out your vacation time with 1.5x the pay, and he took it.

Morgan knew the expression that would be on Dad's face if they showed up unannounced, the kind of grimace that might accompany a mild electrical shock. He hated being surprised. It was Grandma Cheryl who'd explained to Morgan words like *autistic* and *burnout* to describe what was happening to Dad, or at risk of happening. By now these weren't terms that needed names; the ingredients that made Dad different from other parents Morgan knew. He was sensitive to bright light; there were certain foods too wet to consume, like slinky red peppers from the jar. He was more interested than the other parents Morgan knew, too— wanting details about the route Morgan took between classes, the exact time it took from point A to B. Together, there were things that they did: watched old VHS tapes, constructed puzzles with thousands of tiny pieces on the dining room table, drove to the lookouts by the Palisades and stared at the ripples of water. But they didn't broach feelings.

What would they have said? Morgan could easily imagine Dad, nodding slowly, ticking the boxes that Morgan was upset (shaky voice, posture like a wilting tulip) and reacting the way his therapist, Dr. Gold, had taught him. But Morgan knew what Dad would think, even if he said otherwise: *But nothing happened, did it?* All around Morgan, sprightly green balls hurled against rackets. White sneakers squeaked in a chorus. Morgan could picture it all: the swoosh of the 1 train as it reached up into the brightness at 125th Street and plummeted back underground. Dad's office. The smell of the clementines the receptionist, Crystal, ate at the front desk. *Morgan?* he'd say, a tremble in his lip. He'd think: *Why did you spend $2.75 to come here when nothing happened to you?*

Morgan was notoriously bad at tennis but just once, just once, their racket smashed into the ball at the perfect velocity and time, and the ball skyrocketed to Jimmy Lee, and Jimmy Lee was so befuddled by Morgan's success that he stood, motionless, and Morgan got their first point. "It's a modern-day miracle," Jimmy Lee said, but the gym teacher gave Jimmy Lee a look and said it was time to go in and change. In the locker room, surrounded by bodies more confident than Morgan's, they kept their eyes to the ground. Jimmy Lee apologized as the two of them returned to the gym. On the other side of the room, Morgan had felt Aiden and Tiana watching them with a combination of worry and pity, and Morgan glanced back at them with a nervy half-smile, trying to gauge whether to say something. The moment passed. That was always the way.

Aiden and Tiana had also been new in sixth grade, and the three of them clung together like undercooked noodles at the bottom of a saucepan. Initially they'd been friends by default—nobody wanted to sit at lunch alone—but it turned out the two of them were easy to talk to. They all liked watching YouTube videos of mundane, wholesome things: unboxing Amazon electronics like extension cords, babies sucking wedges of lemon, parrots getting misted by a spray bottle. Somewhere in the middle of eighth grade, Tiana's rainbow-elastic braces came off, and Aiden grew into his gangliness and made the soccer team, and their social status climbed without any warning to Morgan. When Tiana and Aiden ended up dating, Morgan wondered how they could've missed it: the ease with which Aiden stretched his arm over Tiana's shoulders, how she used to complain about being cold so she could borrow Aiden's gray, worn-in hoodie. Morgan felt stupid, and young. At school, people called them *Tiaiden* and they were voted cutest couple at the end of middle school. They were both still nice to Morgan, and maybe the two of them were the reason nobody paid any negative attention to Morgan either way, but weekends were suddenly vacant besides numbly scrolling through pictures of everyone else's candescent friendships.

Grandma Cheryl loved those weekends. "Extra time with my favorite grasshopper," she'd say brightly, stretching out on the sofa with her glass of ginger ale and shuffling her deck of cards for a mega-game of Gin Rummy or Crazy Eights. It was like the homeschooling days, the two of them deciding whether to head to the zoo or the park, or ride their bikes along the pretty part of the parkway, maybe picking up a McFlurry to share on the way home. She never made them feel pathetic for being friendless at the crest of high school. *What do you want to be when you grow up?* Grandma Cheryl would ask, making the cards go *riffle-riffle-riffle.* The sounds tingled down the back of Morgan's neck. Sometimes they'd say the most absurd answer they could: *A trapeze artist! A firefighter! A drill sergeant!* They never told her that they wanted to be a filmmaker, plotting every frame as meticulously as threading a needle. She wanted Morgan to have a practical job, something that meant they would never need to worry about their next paycheck, or how her slow scourge of cancer was going to bankrupt their family. She'd tried to steer Morgan into math and science, even as a little kid—*the physics of puddle jumping!*—but nothing stuck. They could only imagine a giant lens, zooming in to capture those droplets of water in midair. But the last thing they wanted to do was disappoint her, or worse, make her worry about the future that she wouldn't get to see.

Plenty of time, Grandma Cheryl would say in the silence of Morgan's omission. Patting Morgan's hand with her scaly fingertips, she'd say: *You'll find your way, Grasshopper, just like I did, and your dad. We always land on our feet.*

She told Morgan stories about growing up in Iowa, how the tornado alarm would ring out by the elementary school and she'd scuttle down to the basement to wait to see whether they'd have a home after the storm hit. Morgan helped weed the garden at her instruction—by then she was too weak from the chemo to bend down without ushering in a burst of nausea. Grandma Cheryl was always cold, clutching her favorite red cardigan to her even though it didn't fit her frame anymore. They tried to learn Spanish together using a series of Rosetta Stone VHS tapes, and inevitably, Grandma Cheryl would fall asleep in the middle of the lesson, leaning back to "rest her eyes." Sometimes Morgan worried she would die right there, in their living room, and her last words would be *Do you want to join me at the discotheque?* But she died the regular way, choking on her own liquidy lungs in a hospital room. When they got home, Dad put the red sweater on Grandma Cheryl's chair in the kitchen in its new permanent spot.

Grandma Cheryl would've known what to say about the almost-shooting; she would've known how to make Morgan feel better and how to tell Dad so he could process it, too. Morgan didn't know how to start. By the end of the day, they didn't even want to get on the bus, just run home until their ribs cracked open. But Morgan followed the steps of every other day. Latch, key, backpack on the floor, shoes off, lights on. They got into bed before Dad got home, and stayed there.

2.

On his phone, Julian had an app that tracked crimes within a certain radius, where golden spots of activity would dance around Morgan's school. This time the school itself shimmered. Julian was sitting in a meeting surrounded by his colleagues when his phone buzzed. Underneath the table, Julian scrolled through updates, his breathing catching on the word *shooter* and releasing on the words *no shots fired*. Data soothed the panic that thrummed at the base of his throat. It was a fancy school that, even with financial aid, cost more than Julian had ever spent on anything. It was a fancy school that was supposed to shelter Julian's only child from this kind of threat. Julian allowed himself one true indulgence in life, taking the Metro-North train rather than the subway to work, which, even with his sunglasses and noise-canceling headphones, was sharp with noise and unpredictable smells and movements that made his insides twist. Otherwise he devotedly saved every possible penny, rather than wade into the innumerable tangles and stressors surrounding using Zoe's family trust fund, to get Morgan into this private school up on a sloped hill.

Julian, too, had gone to the private school on the hill. He'd also been homeschooled through sixth grade, then transformed into a financial aid kid, with a bulky backpack and ill-fitting chinos. His mom never stopped working to afford the tuition; she did taxes for their neighbors and made beaded earrings out of fishing wire that she sold at flea markets. Her fingers were often bleeding, just a tiny bit. Julian had needed special attention, and their local school district had some of the worst test scores and student-teacher ratios in the state. Morgan had followed the same trajectory because of future opportunities, Mom explained. She'd been the one to decide. She'd done it for Julian; now she and Julian could provide for Morgan. They didn't need Zoe's money. The thought of it, Mom said, repulsed her. Dumping money into a checking account like it made her a parent.

Attending the school wasn't only about statistics and getting Morgan primed for a full college scholarship. Morgan—gentle Morgan, who as a child didn't like to pull dandelions from the earth because it looked like it hurt them—had every marker of a bully's target. Morgan radiated self-consciousness; their willowy frame now bent in an effort to shrink their new, towering-above height; chin-length hair and wide-set eyes that were striking, but also unmistakably feminine. Which was maybe the point. Morgan had written an essay about being nonbinary in the school literary magazine and left it on the kitchen table for Julian to find. Julian understood the essay as he read it, but neither one had ever referenced Morgan's identity afterward. Julian wondered if Morgan would get negative attention for it, but they remained vague. Vagueness was its own shelter, Julian knew. That was all Julian wanted—for Morgan to be safe.

Please be safe, Julian thought, frantically scratching up his arms with his fingernails.

He felt the familiar *ping* of oversaturation with light, with sound, with the rough texture of his chair cushion. Thick bars of fluorescent light burned his eyes. On average, these meetings lasted for thirty-six minutes. Julian pictured Morgan and in his mind's eye they are still five or six, crouched underneath a desk, huddled with their chin wedged between their knees. They'd been so small, once.

Every day, parenthood broke Julian a little more—with love, with stress, with challenges that he didn't understand. He expected there to be a plateau once Morgan hit the teenage years, but now there were new sadnesses: *lasts.* The last time Morgan crawled into Julian's lap or wandered into the bathroom to say "I love you" while Julian shaved the beginnings of a beard into the sink basin.

It was normal, developmentally, to be embarrassed of parents. The Internet assured Julian of this. It had been a while since Morgan settled in to watch *The Princess Bride* or *Ghostbusters* with Julian without a halo of shame. Julian didn't want them to be ashamed of their rituals, which he'd spent so much time building to distract Morgan from Zoe's absence. Carrot cake for their birthdays, s'mores over an easily extinguished fire in the backyard for optimal crisping in the fall. Now each tradition also came with a tug of awareness that soon Morgan would be leaving; and another tug, one that Julian wasn't proud of, that looked forward to the ease of caring only for himself, or maybe finally getting a shiny-coated dog to take on his walks, or a dove that would perch on his shoulder and eat millet straight from his hand. The truth was, being around another person, even one that he loved more than he loved anything, was exhausting.

He thought about texting, but then he thought: no. If Morgan wanted to tell Julian, then Morgan could tell him. Julian liked to keep all bad experiences hidden in a dark, impermeable cave that he never went back into, except during his therapy appointments. Maybe Morgan had a cave, too. The last thing you wanted in a cave was a visitor.

Thirty-six minutes had passed since the start of the meeting. Thirty-six minutes, Julian reminded himself, was an average. Now it had been thirty-eight minutes. Julian thought of birds. He tried to name as many as he could: Palestine sunbird, house sparrow, southern masked weaver. He thought of feathers, how quickly they scattered when the wind picked up. He thought of his expression, how easily people misinterpreted him, how he needed to come up with something to say for filing out of the room when Eric would make some quip and leave a smile hanging so long Julian felt like time had stopped altogether. All he could think of was Morgan. The meeting ended. Eric said, "That was a rough one, huh?" and Julian said, "Ten minutes longer than the average," and Eric laughed, his jowly face aflutter. "You're too much," he said, and Julian thought: *Too much of what?*

Tell me you're okay, Julian texted.

Morgan wrote back right away. *I'm okay, Dad.*

Julian couldn't figure out what the sound was, the crunchy staccato sound that filled his ears. It took him almost a full minute to realize it was the sound of his teeth, chattering. He kept his texts open, scrolling so his screen didn't flush black. *I'm okay, Dad. I'm okay.*

In the morning when Julian came downstairs, Morgan was already awake, forking clots of scrambled egg into their mouth and drinking a cup of coffee. "No orange juice today?" Julian asked, sliding into the other chair. Five minutes for morning talk.

"I thought I'd try a different acidic drink today," Morgan said.

Julian inspected Morgan for signs of distress, but they looked the same as they had before yesterday. Their eyes looked vaguely tearful, but nothing dramatic. What did Julian expect?

Sometimes this happened at work, overseeing the files and networks of all those clueless assistants. He just had a whistle in his head that told him, *Maybe Mary downloaded something with a virus*, and followed the whistle to its source. Usually the whistle was right, but with the backups, you could time-travel to Mary's previous day, with minimal damage. This would be different. Julian pressed his thumbnail into a napkin, running through a list of words he wouldn't say.

"We have oat milk," Julian said. "And sugar. Some people prefer it with sugar."

"I've had coffee before, Dad."

Morgan put their fork down on the plate, and Julian felt the beginning of a conflict starting to crest between them, and so he rushed forward into the first thing that he could think of that wasn't on the list, which was how almond milk was actually terrible for the environment. Better than regular milk, better than keeping cows pregnant and swarming with hormones for their entire lives, but almonds took acres of land to harvest. Once he hit a stride, it was easy. He turned the channel to the part of his brain that churned about climate change and recited facts about the future scarcity of water. The reality that would be a perpetual drought. One match and an entire forest aflame, carrying gas masks in our backpacks. Morgan raised their hand at the words *gas masks*.

"I'll drink it black, Dad," they said. "I have to go. Climate change isn't going to write me a note to explain why I'm late to school."

"Let me drive you," Julian said.

"You never drive me."

"We're both breaking our patterns," Julian said, trying to be cheerful. "Come on."

"But you were just talking about climate change," Morgan said.

What aren't you telling me? Julian wondered. Both of them, circling around something unsaid.

"So it doesn't make sense, does it, to drive me when I can ride my bike?" As if on a timer, Morgan zipped their backpack and slung it over one shoulder. The discarded shoulder strap hung loosely, flopping against their back. "I have work after school, so I'll be home after dinner."

"Did you see my email? Did you change your passwords?" Julian burst in as Morgan turned toward the door. He managed a few sentences about updating their VPN, another data breach, the tumbling of personal information as it crossed over to the dark web. Cybersecurity made the skin on his forearms itch, like they'd been overrun with mites.

"I saw. I'll do it, Dad, I will. I'm late, okay? I have to go to school."

Don't go. Don't go to school. Stay here with me, where you're safe. Safer, at least.

Julian felt the words clogging up his throat. "Have a good day, buddy," he said.

For the next two days, Morgan kept their door closed. Julian had to work late both nights but bounded upstairs when he got home. He tried to talk through the wood, through the door that had once been Julian's door; the place where Julian, too, didn't want to talk about feelings with his single parent, although Cheryl had been an excellent mother, and Julian doubted he would be ranked as excellent. Morgan didn't answer. Maybe Julian should break the rule that he'd set about respecting the closed door. No. Once you started bending rules, how would you know when to stop? Unless that was wrong, too. It plagued him, a resting worry that seemed to float along with the blood circulating through his veins: what if he wasn't a good father? Why were the perimeters constantly changing? He could hear Morgan slink through the house in the morning, zipping their backpack with caution rather than gusto. They usually walked with more force. Julian observed this and came to the conclusion that Morgan was avoiding him, but didn't know how to proceed.

On the third day, Julian knocked and said, "Please answer."

"Okay. Come in."

Morgan's room was blanketed with dirty clothes. Julian noticed a familiar scent reminiscent of his own teenage boyhood—cherry licorice and Old Spice—and again he found himself wrestling nostalgia. *Stay in the moment*, Dr. Nancy Gold always said, as if the moment were a supply closet you could huddle inside.

"Is there anything you want to talk about?"

Morgan shook their head. "No. I don't think so."

Julian waited. "What about now?" he asked finally.

"You're not good at this," Morgan said.

Julian nodded. "Okay," he said. He leaned against the bed's frame and waited again. Persistence was the key, he'd read. Persistence and love. "I love you," he said, with great effort. A square of skin on his back tingled. "Can I run you a bath?"

Morgan closed their eyes. "Okay, but not too hot."

"Not too hot," Julian repeated. *What temperature would that be? What if Morgan's conception of hot were totally different from his?* "I'll do my best."

3.

After the almost-shooting, a surge of social media activity. Everyone curled around each other in photos, clamping their fingers over the forearms of friends. Like. Like. Like. People responded with black hearts instead of pink ones.

Days followed and people reached into their backpacks and retrieved other things that weren't guns. Two other actual shootings had happened at schools in Oklahoma and Florida. News anchors pinned ribbons on their lapels and someone started a Kickstarter for grieving families. Morgan ping-ponged between TikTok, Twitter, Instagram, repeat.

Somehow the weekend emerged, leaden and gray-clouded. Dad had some kind of elaborate backup of the company's system to work on and went into the city early; Morgan worked their painfully slow shift at the school library. Their brain felt like slush.

Sadie appeared at the library desk. She leaned very close to the scanner.

"Hey," she said. Sadie's full eye contact was impossible to brush off. Morgan felt their entire body growing taut, clenching. "I actually wanted to say sorry. About last time we . . . I didn't mean to misgender you, or seem like I'm weird about . . . who you *are*. It was . . . careless, and that's not who I want to be. I'm sorry."

Morgan scanned the back office for their boss, Yasmin. She didn't emerge.

"It's okay," they said. "Thanks."

Sadie snapped a ponytail holder against her wrist. "Did you have nightmares this week?"

"Yeah," they said. "Pretty much every night. Did you?"

"They were more nightmares than dreams, but not like . . . *nuclear*. I had a dream about you, actually," she said. "We were in an auditorium, but it was also a coffee shop, and we wanted to get out, but it was super crowded so we were trapped. But you held me by the wrist and you said, *Sadie. I brought you a doughnut*, only I think you were speaking . . . Urdu? But I understood you anyway."

Appearing in dreams had to be a good sign.

"What kind of doughnut?" Morgan asked.

"Glazed."

"Where do they speak Urdu?"

"Pakistan."

"Um, do you want to hang out . . . when I finish up here?" Morgan asked. It had seemed much smoother in their head, and once the sentence was spoken, they felt a flare of panic. But you didn't just *tell* someone that you dreamed of them without an intent, did you?

Sadie tilted her head a little. "Sure," she said.

❧

Sadie left, with a promise to return at the end of Morgan's shift at 3:30 p.m. It was a lie; Morgan got off at three, but the half hour meant they could procure a glazed doughnut for her and return just in time. For the last hour of work, they did little but prepare to talk to Sadie. *What to talk about with your crush?* they asked the Internet. There were a multitude of sites with lists, but most assumed the reader was a woman. *Drop something!* the Internet suggested. *Smile and laugh.* Morgan hated the websites' tone—the bouncy, gender-reinforcing bullshit that didn't include them anywhere. But the forums meant for "regular" guys didn't help either. *Don't ask for a date; go for an "upsell." You know how they ask if you'd like fries with that? Start with coffee or tea, and then you've got her.* The instructions for men were all things not to do: not to hold eye contact for too long; don't just approach without watching first because her husband and kids could be right back. Morgan thought of their mother, Zoe, sitting on a bench, approached by this charming man from Reddit who hadn't seen a partner or a child anywhere nearby. They closed their browser and scuttled to Dunkin'. At 3:29, Sadie tapped on the glass of the library door and Morgan held up the doughnut bag, like a child who'd found a prize.

"Is that for me?" she asked, reaching for the doughnut bag. "A dream come true."

"Literally."

"Literally," Sadie said. The two of them walked along Broadway, following the route of the subway without getting on board. She ripped a piece of the doughnut and handed it to Morgan. "I have four hours before I have to babysit this girl that will only watch *Mary Poppins.*" She sighed, chewing. "Do you want more?"

"No, no. You finish it." Morgan paused. "So . . . why were you at the library today?"

Sadie didn't hesitate. "To ask you out," she said. "Why? You don't want to go on a date with me?"

Morgan thought they might choke. "No, I do. I just... It doesn't seem... plausible. Didn't Aiden ask you out? Before Tiana?"

Sadie shrugged. "I would never want to date Aiden," she said.

"He's not like that," Morgan murmured, protecting him out of habit. Then Morgan realized that they had no idea what Aiden was like when it came to girls. He'd had a habit of fiddling with his hoodie's strings when asked about anything romantic, and Tiana used to raise an eyebrow in Morgan's direction like, *What a clown, he thinks he's so slick*, and they'd all laugh.

"I mean, I guess I don't know anymore," Morgan said. "We used to be friends."

Sadie took this in. Nodding, she said, "To me, all those guys are the same. Their conversations follow this weird pattern, like they think I can't tell they've practiced this with a bunch of other girls."

"Yeah. It's on the Internet. I read it, too, before I came here." Morgan smiled uncertainly.

"You're kidding."

"No. I didn't want to fuck it up. I made up an acronym. SEMI-PCS. Start easy, mutual interest, personal, compliments, share. I mean," Morgan qualified, "I did fuck it up. I didn't start the cycle. But if I had, I would have said something like... doesn't Dr. Gilbert have the worst beard? Does he even have a face under there?"

"So then I disagree," Sadie said, "and tell you, Dr. Gilbert's beard really turns me on. I love how it's like a shield made of wiry copper hairs. Then what?"

Morgan felt their face go hot. "Um... I would die," they suggested. "I'd run into the street and hope for a quick collision."

"Don't die. I hate beards," Sadie said, smiling. "I just wanted to see your face. Now what? Mutual interest? We both like doughnuts. We'd probably both get mono if there were an outbreak."

Morgan shook their head. "I wouldn't get mono. I never share anything."

Sadie held up the empty doughnut bag. "False. You're full of lies, Morgan Flowers."

"Besides with you," they said, and it felt too intimate, so they stared at the traffic forming along the bend of the street. In their pocket, a number marked *unknown* blasted across Morgan's phone screen.

"What's the personal thing?" Sadie said, bringing Morgan's attention back. She touched their hand. Her skin was sticky with glaze. There was a moment in which Morgan could have kissed her, but didn't, and then the light had gone back to red and they waited together, quiet besides the sound of wheels skittering on uneven road.

"Tell me something nobody knows about you," she said. "Something real."

Morgan could feel the muscles in their neck, as tense and thick as a celery stalk. "I let people think my mom is dead, but she isn't," they said. "That's a big secret."

"So...she's fine?" Sadie asked. "Or..."

"I don't know." Morgan felt a scraggly itch in their throat. "She's not here. What about you?" Morgan asked. "Tell me a secret."

A large truck went by, honking loudly. Sadie pretended not to hear Morgan's question. "It's kind of creepy over here," she said, starting to walk toward the subway station.

They talked about easier things again—the mole on Mrs. Dillon's chin, what this year's prom theme would be ("Domestic terrorism,"

Sadie suggested, and even though it felt callous and too soon, it made them both laugh deep into their rib cages). They ended up traversing the sloped hill toward the mall. Sadie pointed out the Applebee's that gave her mom food poisoning. "I got food poisoning there once, too!" Morgan said delightedly.

"You're cute," she said. Morgan felt as if they'd swallowed an entire roll of pennies.

"Is that your secret?" they asked. "That you think I'm cute?"

They regretted it immediately: too much, too soon. They couldn't believe it had even been said, out loud.

Sadie said, "It's not a secret that I think you're cute. My friends make fun of me about it."

"Really?"

"Yeah. You have a total . . . art-house, hoodie-wearing, sensitive doe thing going on." She swept her hair into a top knot. Morgan imagined the camera, close up: the slope of Sadie's neck, the puff of her pink lips. Morgan watched her in disbelief, trying not to get stuck on the word *doe*, which could be a condemnation rather than a descriptor. It was one thing to be a *they*; another to don silks and floral prints. Only at home, in the privacy of a bedroom, did Morgan allow themself to imagine life dressed as Stevie Nicks.

"It's not weird or disrespectful that I compared you to a female deer, is it?"

"No," Morgan said. "I think gender is stupid, mostly. I'm not the kind of person that would be weird about that."

Sadie nodded. "Okay. I didn't want to fuck up."

"I can't believe you had a dream about me." Morgan plodded forward. "And that I knew how to speak Urdu."

Sadie turned to look at them, full-on. "I'm sorry your mom's gone," she said.

Morgan inhaled. "Yeah. Sometimes I am, too."

"Do you want to cry? We could stop by Donnelly's. I could get fries."

"Shut up," Morgan said, a smile twisting over their face.

After fries, Sadie left to babysit and Morgan walked home. The shadowy flatness that usually accompanied them everywhere had receded, like a pincushion punctured. The sudden emergence of happiness—a happiness that felt wiggly, an eel that couldn't be grasped within fingers—was a cousin to Morgan's general anxieties. *But this is good*, they reminded themself. *This is good, this is good.* Sadie. Sadie's mouth and her deep whispery voice and her sharp laugh and her kind tolerance of their unreasonably damp hands. Sadie's T-shirt and the urge to look as she scrunched her body to hop over the divider between the sidewalk and the parking lot and the urge to kiss her until their lips disintegrated into her lips. Morgan craned their head into the sky to look at the stars, but it wasn't dark yet at all. *But so much has happened*, they thought, and it felt true.

Dad stood with his back to the front door. He was doing a three-thousand-piece puzzle of a jungle scene on the dining room table. His face was lacquered with extreme concentration, even though he sang along, quietly, to David Bowie's "Starman" on the record player. Morgan said hi. Even letting this one syllable, *hi*, into the world, post-Sadie, made their mouth stretch into an incriminating smile. They felt the smile tunneling from the inside out.

"How was work?" Dad asked. He looked at Morgan. "What time is it?"

"I think it's like . . . seven-thirty. Work was fine. I took a walk afterwards."

"What route did you take?" Dad asked, putting the piece down to fully absorb Morgan's navigational choices. Dad loved routes. He said often that he "ardently" missed the days when shortcuts were like treasures you discovered along the way. Dad asked more questions: about Morgan's supervisor Yasmin, and whether they'd had to shelve upstairs or downstairs. Dad cared about things that Morgan didn't even care about, and it was their life. But it was nice, even if it was annoying.

"You're almost there," Morgan volunteered, gesturing at the puzzle.

"No. I probably have about ... a fifth completed. Definitely not almost there."

"I'm just saying that to be supportive," Morgan clarified. They stood from their seat and lingered. "I think I went on a date," they said. "Today. After work. With a girl from school."

"Mmm–hmm," Dad said. Morgan watched Dad try to ferry two puzzle pieces together, then put a piece back down with the other greens, a pile of verdant leftovers. Morgan waited for something. They didn't know what. Dad seemed noticeably less enthused about this than about Morgan's work anecdotes.

"You stopped talking," Dad pointed out after a minute.

"Her name is Sadie," Morgan added.

"A popular name for a dog," Dad said. "Though originally, a nickname for Sarah, in the Bible."

"She's neither dog nor biblical figure," Morgan said, feeling the little flame of their happiness fight against its first flicker of wind. "She's really smart and funny and cool. I think she likes me." Vulnerability flushed their face pink. "Dad? Do you want a sandwich?"

"Okay," Dad said. "Do you want to help me with the puzzle?"

"Okay," Morgan said. They cut the crusts off of both peanut butter and jelly sandwiches, careful not to let their thumb indent the main sandwich arena. David Bowie's voice echoed, galactic in their small, badly ventilated house. Scabs of wallpaper threatened to flake from the walls; Grandma Cheryl had never gotten close to fixing their fixer-upper all the way. From the dining room, Dad called to Morgan: "I feel like I'm saying the wrong thing. I'm happy you're happy, Morg."

"It's okay," Morgan said. They brought a plate with four sandwiches for them to share. They wondered whether he was thinking about Morgan's mother, if hearing about Morgan's crush catapulted him right back into his own teenage past.

They thought about asking. Dad wasn't tight-lipped about much; if he found something interesting, he rushed forward with details and tangents galore, a layer cake of trivia and anecdotes until Morgan could barely trace the original topic. But Mom was different. His face looked gray with the residue of old pain when she surfaced. Morgan could even tell when he was thinking of her; he started to twist at the hem of his shirt, flicking invisible dust.

Morgan knew some details, mostly from sleuthing through shoe boxes, sorting the debris of their relationship from the attic. Morgan had been born long enough after senior year of high school ended; to most, Mom probably didn't look pregnant underneath her robe, though Morgan could detect the outline of themselves, just barely. She carried a white rose in front of her stomach in pictures. Grandma Cheryl had bought this house after Mom announced she was pregnant with Morgan. It was all she could afford, a slumpy split-level across from a string of mechanics. The basement flooded in every rainstorm. After graduation, Mom moved into the house with Dad and Grandma Cheryl, and then lived there until she didn't anymore.

Grandma Cheryl hadn't liked Mom. That much Morgan picked up on early: in the silences that she'd let sit after *Your mother*... "She didn't bat an eye if she dropped her phone in the toilet," Grandma Cheryl said once, with a mixture of disdain and awe. Morgan didn't know if that was because Mom was frivolous, unhygienic, bad with technology? Or maybe it was that she was rich. Morgan never knew, only suspected from clues Grandma Cheryl dropped about Zoe's sense of entitlement. Grandma Cheryl would only go a few sentences before she'd fold her hands back into a bridge of knuckles and say, *Let's play a game instead*, and Morgan would deal the cards. And then Mom was gone again, erased from the background of their lives, and would pop up again next month, or next year. Morgan had always wanted to ask more but didn't.

"The truth is, you'll never love anyone the way that you do when you're seventeen," Dad said quietly, chewing through globs of peanut butter.

Morgan felt the muscles in their shoulders tighten. "Should I . . . not love her?" they asked. "Maybe that would be better?"

Neither moved for a second. "No," Dad said, his voice back to its normal flatness. "No, that's not better at all."

❦

The next day, the unknown number called again. And the day after that. Morgan started to feel queasy, watching their phone light up with the efforts of someone unseen, but they couldn't find the courage to answer. What if it was? What if?

After their library shift, Morgan biked home from school the long way in the dark, swiveling to stay close to the side of the underpass. Inside, Dad sat at the kitchen table with his puzzle laid out wide, listening to an audiobook at super speed so that the reader's voice had the frenzy and pitch of a cartoon animal.

"Dad?" Morgan began. "I was wondering about . . . um. Whether you . . ."

Dad looked up from the puzzle pieces. "You're nervous," he said. "Why are you nervous?"

"I was just wondering if you've gotten any calls from an unknown number lately."

"Unknown, or No Caller ID?" Dad asked. "Unknown has to do with a lack of information from the network. No Caller ID is a different story. That means someone has gone to the trouble of blocking your specific number to remain elusive."

Morgan didn't know how to ask *But what if it's my mother?* A cavernous question, one that would replace Dad's congenial mood with something prickly and painful.

"Has anyone called you from an unknown number? Lately?"

Dad frowned. "No. Why would I be getting calls from an unknown caller? Oh, you're talking about you."

"I'm talking about me," Morgan confirmed. "I . . . thought maybe it was . . . somebody trying to reach me." The words sounded so small as soon as they left Morgan's mouth.

"Well, if they're calling you, that's a fair assumption," Dad said.

Keep talking, Morgan thought, but they couldn't. They thought of how slowly Dad walked when he was upset, the hollow click of his bedroom door. The house where Mom left them both. Maybe he pictured her all over, getting water from the sink or stretching in the den, dancing in front of the corner where the Christmas tree lived in winter. Maybe he saw her everywhere.

Dad spent the long pause looking at Morgan, looking at them but looking past them in a way; trying to decipher Morgan's facial expression as if it were an optical illusion. *Say something, say something*, Morgan thought, starting to feel frantic. If they weren't going to tell the truth, they needed to lie more quickly.

"I don't want you to be upset," Morgan said. Dad had already seemed off for the past few days; Morgan could feel something tight in the air between them.

"Why would I be upset?"

"I guess I was thinking . . . maybe it was Mom?" Morgan suggested, their voice faint. The sentence hung there for an awful minute.

Dad focused his attention back on the puzzle. "I have all the corners done," he said after a long beat. "But the bottom third is really . . . tricky in this one, all of the dark green of the leaves in the shadows."

"Do you need more light?" Morgan asked. "It's kind of dark in here."

"No, no. I just need some more time."

"Okay."

He kept his gaze fixed solely on the puzzle. "I don't think your mom would have the foresight to call from a number that would be listed as unknown. I don't think she would know how to block her number, either." His lips pressed together, as if his memories were a noxious smell. "Though I'm not sure that I can rule her out," he said, his voice flat and low. "She can be impulsive." He held the two pieces up in victory. "Ha! I got it."

"Good work," Morgan said.

"You can block unknown callers in your preferences," Dad said. "I'll send you the link. That'll fix the problem, okay, Grasshopper?"

It had been Grandma Cheryl's nickname for Morgan, not Dad's. But it did the trick, a layer of aloe over a sunset sunburn. *My little grasshopper*, she'd said, making a burrito out of Morgan with her arms. Dad made no moves to hug.

Morgan nodded. "Okay," they said.

In the privacy of their bedroom, Morgan lay there in the dark, trying to organize all of their emotions besides *overwhelmed*. Maybe Mom had seen the news of the almost-shooting, Morgan thought. Maybe it had jolted her out of whatever state she'd fallen into, and now she was sorry. She could be.

Or maybe the two of them talked, Morgan thought. There had been a number of phone calls over the years—Dad's voice stringy and shy, with his bedroom door closed—that Morgan wondered about but never asked. That was their family policy. Dad hadn't seemed surprised that Morgan mentioned her, just deflated. Morgan imagined her voice on the other end of the line, waiting for them to pick up. What would she want to say? It could've been anything.

Morgan thought of that last time, in Central Park when they'd foolishly panicked and called Dad to come rescue them just because Mom wandered off for a while. Probably not very long. Morgan was only nine; if they'd known that they would never see her again, they would have waited there in the grass. Every person that passed registered young Morgan with concern, sitting alone among the trees, nervously squinting into the sun's path as if Mom might beam, alien-like, down from the sky. That year Morgan had been obsessed with the solar system, wondering what else could be out there. They'd always been scared, that was the problem—even of hypothetical storms on Jupiter or galaxies they'd never heard of, collapsing into dust. Mom never seemed scared. She probably would've been hanging out with the aliens in their octadome starship, plunging down from the clouds in a stream of sequins and smoke.

4.

When Julian was sure Morgan was asleep, he went for a walk. Julian loved being outdoors at night: the emptiness of the streets, the gentle swish of squirrels as they scampered from underneath bushes. In one direction, their neighborhood was abandoned storefronts and garages, but the walk up the big hill felt like a different city. He turned on his speech-to-text app and started to dictate an email to Brigid, the person he trusted most in this world who was still alive.

Julian didn't know how to talk about what happened with Morgan. Not yet. Instead he told Brigid about Zoe, remembering the sound of her voice on the phone when she'd called last, a few days earlier. Zoe, slurring her *R*s because she was drunk enough to call him. She'd been in a bathtub, she said, and his body remembered how her body looked all those nights and years past, just from the word *bathtub*, as if the word *bathtub* could transport him through time and there he was, wearing basketball shorts and drinking pulpy juice from a mug when Zoe called the landline and whispered *stone's throw*, and he'd known to come outside. Sometimes Zoe slipped old-school Polaroids into his locker, ones of her in only a floral shower cap and fishnet stockings. When he thought back on it, she was so young, playing at being sexy, rooting through images and clichés to what suited her moods.

In high school Zoe was fearless—or, at least, she seemed that way to Julian. She rolled her uniform skirt up so it showed her knees under the canopy of pleats and had the tips of her hair dyed bubblegum pink. Zoe hung around mostly with the art kids, planning and then painting a mural of flowers and trees for the hallway by the science wing, but she always made eye contact with Julian between third and fourth period when he'd pass her. He liked her boldness. He'd heard rumors that she was in a punk band and he could easily imagine her on a stage under a bright spotlight. In the end he joined the art kids with their painting and did the long, slow brushstrokes of the forest's grass and Zoe brushed her arm with his and then smiled. *Your skin is soft*, she said, and he asked, *Doesn't everyone have soft arms?* and she laughed at him. Or with him. He was never sure.

He'd been thinking about those years when Zoe called a few days ago, when she said the words *breakup* and *coming home*. He realized that the home she was referring to was New York and that his response required action. He didn't know what to do with his voice. After he hung up, he washed every dish they had and dried them with all his strength, grabbing at invisible bacteria until he knew, for sure, that they couldn't have survived.

Julian told Brigid everything, with the exception of the shower cap Polaroids. That was private. He didn't say that he still loved Zoe even though he knew she was terrible for him, the equivalent of cradling a poison ivy plant; how he thought often of how she looked when she ran; how she could befriend anyone, anywhere they went, and lose track of them just as easily. He didn't want to think about how she was drinking again, how it seemed possibly worse than she had been before; how devastating it was to have confirmed that he was the backup plan, again, always. Then again, a backup plan is #2, and there are a lot of numbers that follow #2. That's a fact.

He thought of the time Zoe returned, *for good*, she promised, that summer after her father died, how she'd left nine-year-old Morgan alone in Central Park and they'd called Julian sobbing because they thought she was gone forever, and the squirrels were getting too close to the blanket. "Stay on the phone with me," Julian said, nauseously bolting from the office, running down to Strawberry Fields with his work pants chafing, the world getting louder and brighter and full of dangerous veering runners and bikers. Morgan tried to recite the Chinese dynasties to keep calm but failed, crying, and finally when Julian got there, so did Zoe, one hand clutching an oversized, street-vendor pretzel and her eyes as bloodshot as eyes could be, and she had no excuse, and the visit was over and Morgan refused to go to the park for years afterward, not even to cut across.

"I don't know why I think about forgiving her," Julian said to future-Brigid. "When I hear myself talk about the things that she's done...I can't imagine why I still have this urge to put it behind us." But it only took a second for him to figure it out. Morgan could've died in a shooting, and if they'd died, they never would've gotten the chance to talk to Zoe again. Surely Morgan churned with their own list of questions for their mother, just like Julian had.

* * *

Julian thought about his own list, the one he kept for Mom. Cheryl Ruth; she was always trying to get people to use both names instead of just one, but no one ever did. He pictured her with a wide hat, chalky sunscreen across her nose. The red cardigan that Julian kept on her chair in the kitchen. Every time he washed it, the sweater became less close to Mom and closer to the washing machine. It didn't smell like anyone anymore. It just smelled like house.

He had things he wanted to tell her. Mostly about Morgan. How gentle they still were, even now, as a seventeen-year-old; how funny and astute and bewildering they had turned out to be. Julian would want to ask her advice: *How much distance is too much distance? Why don't they ask more questions? Are they depressed? How would I know if they were?* But also the things in Julian's life. How he'd ended up getting promoted to director last year. He had an office with a door and a ledge for sentimental objects and succulents. How he was lonely sometimes, but he was okay, and she didn't need to worry. Julian didn't *entirely* believe in ghosts but sometimes he felt a presence, wrapped around him tightly like that red sweater in February, Mom saying, *Are you okay? Are you sure? What can I do?* and the answer would've been the same as it was when she was alive. Julian didn't know. His own needs were on the other side of a bridge obscured by fog. He had trouble identifying with certainty whether he needed water or food or a nap or a walk. Mom had always been the one who knew.

But he also had questions about her choices. Some of those questions were enormous, sprawling—had she been happy? Would she have had Julian if she'd known that his father would leave rather than deal with his "special needs"? Why did she stay in New York, alone, instead of going home to her family in Iowa? Why did she only have one sweater for all those years? Still, *still*, he thought of these questions and thought *I'll just text Mom* and then would realize again. *Not all questions get answered, Poindexter*, she would have said.

Mom knew Julian better than anyone. As he got older, it had just seemed to be another way in which he stood apart from his classmates: he loved his mom so much. He loved sitting with her in the backyard, scraggly weeds surrounding them while they drank lemonade from bendy straws. She'd studied child psychology and wanted to be a doctor, but social work school was faster and cheaper. They studied together, Julian quizzing her with flash cards for hours. They watched *The Princess Bride* every night in those years; eventually the tape started to wear out. He could spend forty-five minutes watching the individual flecks of glitter sink from the top of the snow globe to the bottom. Maybe these were the moments that gave her pause.

She made appointments they couldn't afford for Julian to see a child psychologist, who diagnosed Julian with Asperger's. Mom talked about this plainly, which Julian appreciated. Afterward he thought of everything he understood about himself and asked: "Is that because I'm autistic?" His sensitivity to sound. To light. To the texture of uncomfortable fabrics on his skin. To being away from routine, from home, from the backyard with the lemonade and the bendy straws. His trouble brushing his teeth when he knew it was time to brush his teeth. His trouble knowing what to say when everyone else seemed to.

"Everyone has their troubles," she explained. "Your highs will be much higher than other people's, and your lows might be much lower, and they'll exist together always." She turned the TV off when someone mentioned anti-vaxxers. *Why are people so afraid of their children becoming like me?* Julian asked. *Only ignorant people hate things that are different*, Mom answered. But she looked sick. *Why are you sad?* Julian asked. These are just facts. He made a smiley face with the crusts of his PB&J and pushed it at her across the table, like what she needed was instruction. She loved him. He rarely went in the backyard anymore. He imagined a thick carpet of flowerless weeds thriving, undisturbed.

Julian walked. Opossums rustled through trash cans and faraway cars accelerated down the highway and then, suddenly, there she was: a carbon-copy Zoe, sitting in a living room that burned with light. For a minute he couldn't think of any words. Long strands of golden hair fell in front of her eyes. The expression of bemusement and boredom. She moved as if she was used to being looked at and didn't even register Julian watching her through the window. *It's the ghost of Christmas past*, Julian thought, although that wasn't quite right. There were only so many varieties of genetic makeup in the world, and only so many expressions of that genetic makeup, and this person was just a similar expression. But he couldn't look away. Suddenly he was sixteen, standing tall in their poorly insulated garage, watching Zoe pull off one sock and then the other before she unclipped her overalls. It was the longest moment of his life, that unclipping, knowing she was watching him react. He could never get his face to look properly happy. The thing about overalls is they crumple around your knees in a puddle of denim and Zoe had to steady herself on Julian's shoulders to waddle out of them. "I've been planning this," she said, and as she kissed him and pressed him against the wall and he felt the warmth of their bodies meeting, he wondered: *If she'd been planning this, why did she wear overalls?* And for the rest of it, the impatient beauty of it, he couldn't stop thinking of the overalls. That was what he remembered, and the crisp little fragments of leaves that had trailed into the garage that stuck to the fabric later. *But your plans don't make any sense to me.*

He knew he should go. He knew that, the minute this teenaged girl spied him peering through the window—frozen on the sidewalk like a mannequin, all the nerves in his feet starting to lose feeling—she would call the police, and no one would be on Julian's side. *Leave,* Julian told himself. *Leave now.*

Deep inside his thoughts, he realized that this girl, this alternate-Zoe, was alone. She was without him, without Morgan. A whole alternate life unfurled, one in which there had never been a Morgan and they'd broken up at graduation like everyone else. Zoe in a white dress, blowing a kiss to a disposable camera before spending the summer in Paris. Julian taking that scholarship from Fordham, moving into a haunted dorm and learning to speak ancient Greek with other sandy-haired trivia enthusiasts. A life that led them away from each other. No conversations involving the word *acid reflux* or *sleep training*. No conversations at all. Just a girl, stretching her arms overhead in the middle of the night, and a person miles away who had once known the small sounds her body made when she was hungry for him.

Zoe's twin fluttered her eyes open and made direct eye contact, and smiled.

His body reacted to that smile like it was an electric fence. He ran, his maladroit feet catching on every uneven hunk of sidewalk. He kept looking back over his shoulder, as if it were Zoe's twin following him and not the other way around. He found he could not get up the stairs in his house. He found he was lying in front of a wicker chair, crying while his mouth leaked drool, and there were many miles to go before he slept.

❧

There was a routine in place. The alarm went off and he gave himself seven minutes to snooze. Hot shower. Instant oatmeal in a white bowl. One and a half minutes. Clothes picked out the night before. Then, waking Morgan. Shoes laced. Walk to the train station. It was an eight-minute walk, crossing over several lanes of traffic with the same weary homeless woman sitting outside yelling about how her roommate had stolen her nail polish and it was *disgusting* to use someone else's nail polish. Unsanitary, she yelled into the air, day after day. Every day, Julian wondered how long ago she'd had a roommate, and a nail polish supply from which to steal. Twenty-seven minutes to Grand Central. It was finely calibrated. By the time he woke up, it was too late; it was all too late; the day was ruined before it had even begun. The choices were intolerable: go to work now and scrounge his way through a workday on no sleep at all, or stay home and lie about being sick. What counted as sickness, anyway? Julian didn't have a fever, he was un-contagious; he was just unable to form words or find his way toward the door without fumbling. Clumsiness rang through him like an alarm. The alarm said, *You aren't like other people.*

"Dad?" Morgan asked from the top of the stairs. "Are you okay?"

"S'okay," Julian managed. "Tired." He was too tired to move from the carpet in the living room. *Your highs will be higher, and your lows will be lower,* his mom explained. This is what lower felt like: a distancing from all the possibilities you previously took for granted. When he saw Morgan's feet by his hands and felt the soft pull of Morgan's teenaged, never-worked-a-day-outside-in-their-life hands against Julian's dirty hair and sweaty scalp, he felt the tears prickle again. But they were internal tears; he knew his face remained stoic. Morgan, well trained by Cheryl, brought Julian the smooth blanket he favored; a plate with white bread dressed in a coat of peanut butter and jelly. "Here we go, okay?" Morgan asked, helping get Julian upstairs, to the rocking chair, in the dark. The chair lulled him to comfort, a slow swing back and forth. The blanket was soft. The dark felt good over his eyes.

I would die if something happened to you, Julian thought, but he couldn't say it. "I'm sorry," Julian said, which is what he always said. And Morgan said nothing, neither accepting the apology nor validating that there was something to be sorry for. The peanut butter stuck to the roof of his mouth, as familiar as a prayer.

Sometimes it took days to recover. But this time, Julian felt the baseline starting to build its way back up within a few hours. He couldn't have spoken the wide-reaching sentences that he usually could—especially when it came to trains or the rich tapestry of aviary species—but it was enough to sit in the den on the wicker chair and watch *Ghostbusters*, as usual. *Shame doesn't solve anything,* he thought, that old guilt wafting back into his thoughts. Shame wouldn't give Morgan a neurotypical parent. Besides, the therapist inside Julian's head said, what was so important about having a neurotypical parent? It didn't mean you were good at being a parent, or easy to love and be loved. He could think of a dozen examples of neurotypical people who were miserable despite the fact that an entire civilization had been set up for them: their brain chemistry and sleep schedules and communication styles. Julian thought about reaching for his phone but found the idea of stroking all the spots on the screen to spell out words to be enormously ambitious. Brigid had replied to his last message. *She'll try to connect with you soon*, Brigid wrote. *I can guarantee it. It's important that you stay well.*

Stay well, as if it were a choice he could make. Brigid's intentions were kind—she had, more than once, used the phrase *deeply value our correspondence and friendship*—but she didn't understand. Even if Julian were to live his entire life at home, sidling from upstairs to downstairs with his plush blanket and his pancaked sandwiches, he still wouldn't be sure that he was *well* or that that wellness would extend to tomorrow. He let the sounds of a movie he'd memorized years ago rush over the din of his thoughts, like a waterfall burying a pebble.

When Morgan returned from school, they stepped in front of the TV and asked, "Thumbs-up or thumbs-down?" In the doorway, Morgan looked so tall, like a real person that Julian might see skateboarding or handing him a plastic menu at the diner by the racetrack. Not like a person who once fit into a bassinet next to Julian's bedside table. Julian gave a thumbs-sideways. Morgan nodded and left to retrieve a glass of water, which Julian sipped carefully, then greedily. Morgan sat at Julian's feet, since there wasn't really enough room for them to share the small couch in the living room anymore. When the movie was over, they watched the credits, Morgan's knees curled up to their chest, the point of their chin resting narrowly between their knees.

"Dad?" Morgan asked, their eyes straight ahead. "Can I do anything?"

"No." Julian paused. "Talk to me," he said, sinking deeper into the cushions as Morgan detailed their day. Their Spanish lesson was on the imperfect versus the preterite; it was humid outside during lunch. Morgan always pronounced the *h* in *humid* extra, the way that Julian's mom had because she hated when people said *yoo-mid*, and it broke his heart a little. When Morgan got to their recap of World Civ, they mentioned Sadie three times. The third time, Julian understood that he should ask more about her, and when he did, Morgan's ears flushed an impertinent pink. He watched his only child fumble through describing the person with whom they were newly in love.

"She sounds very good," Julian said, with every bit of energy he could muster.

"Everybody in our whole school wants to be with Sadie," Morgan said. "It doesn't make any sense why she'd want to be with me."

"That's how I felt about your mom," Julian said. A second later, he realized he had mentioned Zoe, which he hated. It made Morgan eager for information that wouldn't do anyone any good. Their eyes were wide. Julian wondered if Morgan could sense that his filter was so depleted that he could only answer honestly to any question they posed. Lying took energy. Julian could barely keep his jaw closed. He would have to work from home tomorrow. Maybe he would be back by the weekend.

"Really?"

Julian nodded. "Really."

"But then you ended up together, for a little while," Morgan prompted. "So it does happen sometimes."

"Many things happen sometimes," Julian said.

"Right."

Julian's heartbeat snared. "Like maybe someone brings a gun

to your school and you have to be evacuated but you don't ever tell your dad and you avoid him for six days rather than talk about it."

Morgan let it sit for a minute. "I don't know how to talk about it," they said. "I feel stupid saying to you, this thing happened and it made me feel all these emotions but I can't tell you what they are because I don't know myself."

"That happens to me all the time," Julian said.

"It does?"

He nodded. "It's not stupid. Just part of being human."

"But what if I never feel like . . . the same again?" Morgan asked. They tucked their chin tight against their chest. "That sounds melo-dramatic. I just mean . . . what if I'll always be different now?"

Julian reached for their hand and Morgan let him, just for a minute. "You will always be different now," he said, and neither of them said anything after that.

5.

It was an incontrovertible truth: her bromeliad plant was dead. Zoe had promised to care for it, these weeks when Brigid had been away on business. Brigid should have known better than to believe her. Outside, soft sounds of the Lisbon night—the tram scuttling up their modest hill, tourists clinking their wine-glasses rapturously—wafted through her open window. Brigid sat motionless at the kitchen island, nursing a cup of chamomile tea, eyeing each crisped leaf with dread. The apartment was silent, Zoe-less, and Brigid tried to divert the whirring of her brain with plans for product expansion. She couldn't focus on any of it, not with Zoe's latest relapse looming over her.

One more minute, and Brigid would scoop the plant remains into the bin. She would move forward, as she always had. *Chin up, soldier,* her mother liked to say. Of her four daughters, Brigid put on the bravest face in moments of adversity. She was the strong one, unafraid to hop onto an unbroken horse or climb a tree that stretched its gnarled branches into the sky. Being the strong one,

Brigid had realized as an adult, was something of a curse. Even alone, in the complete silence of the apartment where Zoe was not, and would not be, she couldn't bring herself to cry properly. She sipped the grassy tea, now far beyond the pale of tepid, veering dangerously into *chilled*. It was over now. This time, yes. It was over.

Brigid had had enough, she was sure, only she hadn't thought the feeling of over-ness would render her so nauseated and numb. Here she was, a woman in her forties who had only really loved this one person, a love that blistered and then popped and blistered back again. She knew, of course, that the only way a blister healed was to remove the source of the friction. She'd known for the better part of a decade. They'd tried in Copenhagen. They'd tried in London. They'd tried in Paris and Berlin and finally here, in Lisbon, in this apartment that Brigid had filled with terra-cotta pots and greenery, cooking rich pasta dishes with truffle and pecorino for Zoe to inhale, waiting until Zoe was asleep to scour the bathroom to see if she'd hidden vodka in the Lysol wipe containers, inspecting the pill bottles to make sure the capsules matched the innocuous descriptions on the outside. Promises were made, and promises were kept, for a time, but Brigid couldn't sleep without checking. She needed to know when it was coming for them.

Had she known this time? Maybe she had. Zoe had been forgetful, her skin smelled a bit acrid, she'd disappear with the excuse that she was going for a run, but her workout clothes sat untouched in their drawer, neatly folded from Brigid's last laundering. Brigid knew the signs, but she also wanted to believe that she was too vigilant, too suspicious. You could make yourself see anything. There had been a little speck of something, perhaps water damage, at their place in London and if Brigid looked at it for too long, she could swear it was alive. Rapt attention transformed one thing into another. That small brown spot, like a freckle on the ceiling, and suddenly she thought it was a vicious spider, spinning its web, plotting to lunge down to reach her face while she slept. Monitoring Zoe's sobriety felt like that brown spot.

Brigid did what she did best: she called a meeting at work. Her botanical cosmetics company had been growing steadily, expanding into France and Switzerland in the past year, and now there was a flagship store in the works in Paris. She told the C-suite that it was time to expand further—what about Belgium? The Netherlands? Italy? She told herself that the timing was auspicious. She felt soothed imagining the multitude of spreadsheets. Everything neatly arranged in tiny boxes. Sortable. There would be meetings and a flurry of phone calls and conference rooms filled with tiny jam jars and buttered croissants. There would be business trips, as many as she cared to go on; blazers, trains, hotel room keys. Her brain whirled with all of the newness ahead, and she found herself smiling hugely in the dim buzzing light of meeting room A, knowing that soon she could be away, away, away.

Brigid reached for the phone to tell Zoe about the upcoming trip. *I told them two weeks was a long time, but it's non-negotiable*, she practiced internally. Leonor, the new assistant at the design firm, answered brightly, and then there was a long pause. *But Zoe hasn't worked here for weeks, I'm sorry*, she said, and Brigid's mind went static, and then she realized she wasn't very surprised at all. *My*, Leonor added, *did she make an impression.*

Brigid came home with more energy than she knew what to do with. *Chin up, soldier*, she thought, rummaging through the refrigerator manically. She didn't need to dwell. She needed to use her sage before it wilted. She needed to cook. You couldn't dwell when you were cooking. Standing at the kitchen island, she rolled a rope of dough and dusted it with flour. There were steps to follow, herbs to julienne. The cutting board hopped with the force of her raising and lowering the knife, shredding greens into shards.

She made gnocchi with sage and brown butter, a rocket salad with clumps of goat cheese, and they ate on the balcony. The breeze had an unseasonable warmth across the back of Brigid's neck. They chewed, salted, drank lemon water in small round glasses. *Tell me the truth*, Brigid thought, but Zoe just complimented the meal. A silence levitated between them. Brigid broke first, telling Zoe about the business plans and her work trip next week, and Zoe only nodded.

I'll miss you. All by my lonesome, she said, squeezing Brigid's hand. Zoe was practically batting her eyelashes. Brigid thought: If Zoe had been sober, she never would've said that. Zoe was full of quips, sarcastic dodges of emotion. They squeezed lemon over their pasta and watched the sky flush rubicund. Zoe's eyes were watery with tears.

☙

There was only one person Brigid wanted to talk to. Well, besides Zoe.

Brigid checked her phone for New York time. Across the Atlantic, it was 4:30, a time when Julian would absolutely be at work. Past his lunch hour, which he took at 2:00 p.m. promptly, and too close to the end of the day for her to call. She thought of him, at the desk that he'd covered with small succulents, sunglasses on to shield the bright, undimmable lights in his small, gray office. He would be stressed about a call. The time.

It wasn't an emergency, really. She was crushed, she needed a friend, but did that constitute an emergency? How many times had she crawled through this exact range of emotions; and each time, an additional gauzy layer of shame that she'd decided to do this, once again; that she'd lurched right back into the cycle, hoping for something different against the odds. Slowly she'd whittled down her circle of support, unable to stand the syrupy pity or barely tempered irritation from her mother or her three sisters. "On or off?" they'd ask now, as blandly as asking how many sugars for her tea. *On* meant they'd ask a follow-up question about Zoe; *off* meant the next question would be about work. But Julian was different; Julian understood. He'd been under the same gauzy layers, too, for even longer than Brigid.

Brigid had saved the very first email Julian wrote her in a special folder on her phone, and she pulled it up to reread when she wanted to feel less alone, even though she'd probably memorized most of it at this point. *Dear Brigid, I'm not exactly sure how to begin this message.* In it he explained that he was Zoe's ex-boyfriend, though *boyfriend* seemed a paltry, misleading term for what Julian was: the father of her child. The child that she'd abandoned, Morgan, who was a teetering toddler with fine auburn hair and wide-set eyes who loved imitating the sound of dogs panting.

Brigid had long since noticed Zoe's C-section scar, a slash across the creamy expanse of her pelvis, and waited for Zoe to bring up her child. Sometimes she even ran her finger along the scar, in the early days, hoping to prompt a conversation. But when Zoe didn't elaborate, Brigid assumed the worst: a mother who'd lost her child.

In the darkest part of herself, Brigid thought, *At least you got to be a mother.* Brigid felt queasy with jealousy at how easily her sisters had gotten pregnant, when her own attempts had led nowhere. Brigid's own longing woke her up at night. She could sometimes feel the weight of a phantom infant, pulling at her arms.

Hearing this news about Morgan, alive and halfway around the world, revealed a different kind of worst. Later, Brigid was ashamed by how quickly she'd pretended that this was a reasonable part of Zoe's past—an air bubble trapped underneath an expanse of carefully laid wallpaper. She knew where Zoe would end up if she brought it up, slouched at a bar, her eyes rolled back in her head. Slow, shallow breaths. Could she do that to Zoe? Could she do that to herself?

She stayed quiet. She kept rereading.

The first half of the email was logistical, explaining how Zoe's father, Harris, had hired an investigator to find her after her disappearance from New York; how he'd located them in France and sent over a thick binder filled with details about Zoe's life with Brigid. *I know so much about you,* Julian wrote. *I thought you should know. The entire endeavor with the investigator leaves me feeling very uneasy, since it's an invasion of your privacy. A metaphorically sour taste in my metaphorical mouth. (I generally don't eat sour foods.)*

She found it charming, this double clarification of the sourness and mouth as figurative. She found the latter half of the email charming, too—questions about her upbringing, how she'd gotten interested in dressage, what it had been like to grow up bouncing around boarding schools and moving every few years with her father's change in government positions. In retrospect, she supposed most people would've found it creepy. At the time, and now, she was warmed by his attention, and surprised at this person spelunking right into her life, wanting to know about her horseback riding out of genuine curiosity. For better or worse, her life was telegraphed across the Internet, and anyone could've pieced together a timeline if they'd been motivated to do so; and yet it seemed impossible that someone who wanted nothing from her would care enough to ask about so many insignificant shards of the mosaic of her experiences. She answered every question. At the end of the email, her pulse quickening, Brigid typed impulsively: *I've never been a jealous person, and I found your letter delightful. Please keep in touch, if you'd like. —B.*

And he had. Julian was unlike her sisters, who seemed increasingly only to care about their own families or the rubble left over after their respective divorces; unlike her parents, who heaped praise about her success and composure until it felt like a glass cage; unlike her employees, who nodded like synchronized swimmers at her every idea. He cared more about *things* than people: urban planning, computer security, deep analyses of films from the '80s. She'd also loved *The Princess Bride*, growing up— her sisters had teased her by calling her *The Princess Bridge*, which further discouraged her clumsy attempts at feminine clothes and agreeability. Their friendship began because of Zoe, but it didn't stay that way, and Brigid had never been more grateful for someone to talk to when things went sour. They had a code: *Would you care for an olive?* If the other person wasn't in the right headspace to talk about Zoe, they said *No thanks!* and if they were, they'd say: *I'd love an olive.* It worked out.

Zoe loved olives. The brine, the slickness. She could eat a whole jar.

Why stop when you can keep going?

* * *

Would you care for an olive, Julian? Brigid texted.

I'll call you as soon as I'm on the train.

"I'm so sorry," Brigid said when he picked up. "I hope I didn't alarm you. I know it's not our usual time to talk, but—" Her voice caught, and she cleared her throat several times to try to regain composure. The locomotion of her sentences slowed and then accelerated rapidly as she explained about Zoe losing her job, and how Brigid had jumped at the chance for a work trip. "Because I'm an avoidant, cowardly lion of a person," Brigid said, watching herself in the mirror as she spoke.

"Because you don't want it to be over," Julian said. "Well, it does make you avoidant, but doesn't make you a coward. And you, Brigid, are never going to be a lion. Unless you're speaking about reincarnation."

"I'm not," Brigid said, feeling something like a smile happen to her lips.

"I would feel the same," Julian said softly, after a pause. "I have felt the same."

"I wanted to be wrong so badly," Brigid said. "And this— I don't know how many more times I can go through this, Jul. I'm so tired of"—she squashed a sigh—"knowing exactly what will play out when I get home."

Julian considered this. "You're an expert in the field of Zoe studies. You know what's going to play out because you're a prize-winning scientist. You have your hypothesis, you're running the lab, and the results are consistent. Now you're expanding your expertise to include your own recovery." Julian paused. "Wordplay intended."

"That wordplay was quite good," Brigid said.

"Only the best for you, Dr. Holm," Julian said, and she felt, just for a moment, a tiny bit better.

For the two weeks of the business trip, Brigid did what she did best, working past dinnertime and deep into the night. When she returned home to Lisbon, all the lights were left on at the apartment. Zoe was asleep on the sofa, tributaries of dried vomit on her cheek. Brigid checked her pulse; Zoe didn't stir. Quickly Brigid took an inventory of the apartment: the last of her plants had died. Her beautiful plants. She fingered their crisp leaves in each carefully chosen pot until she had to turn away.

The oven was on, a single beet roasted until it was a charred blob, and the sink was full of empty bottles. Tequila, which meant she hadn't been alone; Zoe had always preferred vodka. The kitchen island was covered with discarded discs of cauliflower and what looked like smears of cocaine. Brigid thought about how Princess Diana had loved doing the dishes; how she would come home to her roommates' dinner party and immediately head to do the washing up. She stood with her hands under the tap, willing for the energy to turn the dial for the water to come on. In the end, Brigid shed her clothes and slumped into bed. She could feel the crumbs from whatever Zoe had eaten in bed chafing against her bare knees and ankles. It made her twitch, the scratches of discarded crackers, and suddenly Brigid's avoidance and depressed numbness molted into an anger that made her mouth go dry. *These fucking crumbs are everywhere*, she thought. *These. Fucking. Crumbs.*

Storming into the kitchen, Brigid turned on all of the lights and the tap and squirted an excessive amount of washing-up liquid onto a craggy sponge and scrubbed with a ferocity she did not anticipate. Splashes of water flung over the edge of the sink onto the floor. Brigid's bare feet were damp and her steps were loud and furious. Everything in this apartment was going to be clean again. She would make it clean. When, after a few minutes of loudly sighing and washing up and clattering the dishes into the drying rack, Zoe batted her eyes open and squinted at Brigid, then closed her eyes again, Brigid, unable to contain her anger, felt her voice finally rising to a yell, continuing the conversation that had been swirling through her brain nonstop out loud for Zoe to hear.

Zoe slinked from the sofa with great effort and weaved her arms underneath Brigid's. Their bodies had always felt so well together, Brigid a solid three inches taller than Zoe. Her cheek rested against the top of Brigid's shoulder. Zoe pulled Brigid closer. They swayed in silence and in the silence returned all of the facts of their relationship, their breakup, their trial getting-back-together, which Zoe had ruined, again. They'd danced this dance for almost eleven years.

I'm sorry, Zoe said. *I'm so sorry for everything.*

My plants, Brigid said. *You killed them.*

I know. I didn't mean to.

When you stop dancing, you have to leave.

What if I never stop dancing?

You'll stop, Brigid said, her voice far away. *I know you.*

6.

In the airport, Zoe felt costumed within her body. She lifted her arm and thought, *An arm is in motion.* She lifted her ankle and thought, *I am floating off the floor.* She watched the Departures screen blink with possibilities. New York was leaving in two hours. Her brother Albert was there, unruffled and unsatisfied with his stern wife, Katherine, and their two squeaky girls in matching bows. They sent Christmas cards and signed them *Warmly* instead of *Love.*

New York.

Zoe stood in the gift shop with Brigid's credit card, feeling exhilarated as the air conditioner blew frantically over her scalp. She grabbed a teddy bear holding a heart and bars of soap that were "tropical" scented. She grabbed a sweatshirt that said LISBON and a pair of shoes made of cork. *For Morgan,* Zoe thought, and then felt the jolt that came when she remembered the life that she left, and the fact that that life had continued to unspool. Morgan. She'd line the gifts up, one by one, and let Morgan choose. She tried to picture a body but saw only the navy blue footsie pajamas covered in spaceships.

On the plane, Zoe cinched the complimentary eye mask as tightly as it would go around her head, then inched it back up as she heard the stewardess approach. *Help me*, she thought, sweating instantly at the sound of ice clinking. She kept the teddy bear on her lap. She imagined it, again and again: *I got this for you.* Maybe she'd say, *I saw this and thought of you. You were on my mind. You were never not on my mind.*

"Another vodka soda," Zoe said, nudging the eye mask down until all she saw was darkness.

The woman next to her shifted in her seat. "I think we're about to take off, actually."

Zoe didn't bother lifting up her eye mask. "I could give a fuck what you think," she said.

Zoe went straight from the airport to a building she'd known for many years. She stretched across the front stoop. It had been ages since she'd last been here, to sweet Natalie's apartment building. Natalie, who always welcomed her back, as reliably as peonies blooming in May. Zoe sat, examining the patterns of pruning on her skin. *Maybe I'm possessed*, Zoe thought. Every motion that she made afterward felt predetermined—the puff of her lips into an O, the crackle of her knee joints as she stretched from one step to the next.

"Zoe?" Natalie asked, struggling with a tote bag full of groceries. Thickets of carrot stems peeked out from the top of the bag. Seeing Natalie shook Zoe out of her thoughts. Zoe's brain sloshed, trying to sort out what Natalie saw when she looked at the scene. She'd kicked off her shoes, two discarded, bloodied pumps on different steps. She was surrounded by a moat of precariously balanced luggage; her hair felt oily and clamped to her scalp. Zoe found herself trying to smile and Natalie reached for her arm, tentatively, and then with genuine care. *We love each other*, Zoe thought.

"Of course we do," Natalie said, and Zoe blinked, trying to figure out if Natalie was psychic or if Zoe had involuntarily narrated her thoughts aloud. She was drunk, the urge to spread out wide across the steps of the building overcoming her. A tidal wave of lethargy: *Take me.* Natalie was taking her.

Decades earlier, Natalie's father, Colin, and Zoe's mother, Sally, worked together at Columbia. Sally had been the first female professor of anthropology; Colin was a department head with an infamous mustache. Sally had been poached by Syracuse University when Zoe was five, and they'd stayed until she was sixteen. Upstate New York didn't suit any of them but Zoe's father, Harris, who would have been happy anywhere.

When they returned to Manhattan, the two families picked up where they'd left off. *Thick as thieves*, Colin liked to say. They'd had a new child, baby Natalie, who was "unexpected," a golden gift from her mother's finicky ovaries, seven years younger than Zoe and ten years younger than Zoe's brother Albert. The families shared a cabin in Maine and cracked their lobsters with specially made tools. The summer Zoe returned to New York, she lent Natalie her first tampon and even drew a little heart on its plastic wrapper with a Sharpie. On the Fourth of July, she shielded little Natalie's eardrums from the fireworks when the volume got overwhelming. It was the most maternal Zoe ever felt. She'd been six weeks pregnant—just far enough along to know her suspicions weren't unfounded—and as she cupped Natalie's small ears from the cacophony, Zoe thought: *Maybe I can do this. Maybe I really can.*

Family friends. The term seemed strikingly insufficient, considering all the hours they'd spent together, piled in rental cars, arguing about brands of crackers and best books of the year. Now they sent birthday messages on Facebook, condolences when people died. Natalie, come to think of it, had sent the most beautiful floral arrangement they'd gotten after the car accident—the one that killed Daddy straightaway but took its time curdling all of her mother Sally's insides. Sally would have hated how *basic* her funeral was—small sandwiches, cubes of pale cheese, a single strawberry heaped in a fruit platter. Well, at least, how basic it had sounded. Zoe hadn't managed to come home.

If Natalie was surprised to see her, she was adept at hiding it, or Zoe was the magical combination of jet-lagged, sleepy, and pleasantly buzzed enough not to notice or care. Even though Natalie's arms were full with groceries, she was the one who carried Zoe's discarded shoes by their narrow heels.

"I just got in," Zoe said, realizing that she hadn't spoken in a while and Natalie probably deserved some context. "Straight from Lisbon! I brought you something. Anything. Well, not the bear."

"Let me just put these things away," Natalie said. "You know how cheese can be."

"Oh, God. I would love some cheese. And maybe some grapes?"

Natalie smiled, wiggling the package out from her tote bag. "Seedless, no less. Do you want something to drink? Tea? I have a nice blend with rose and...elderberry?"

"I think I might just rest my eyes for a second," Zoe said, after surveying the space. Natalie had done a good, if predictable, job with her interior decorating: a few vases on the mantel, dried flowers the color of cinnamon. The mirror was too small. Zoe sank into the emerald green velvet sofa. Less comfortable than it looked. They always were.

"Are you okay, though?" Natalie asked. "Maybe you want to take a shower?"

Zoe forced her eyes open. "It was the guy sitting next to me on the plane," she said. "He was drinking so much. He smelled like a distillery. God, I could barely breathe that whole flight, Nat." She might have been overdoing it.

"Oh no," Natalie said, flopping into a plush chair with a floral pattern. "I hate that. On my last trip, to Johannesburg, this terrible baby kept trying to pat my face with her applesauce-y hand. I mean, cute the first time, but not for fourteen hours."

Zoe remembered how Morgan had done that—over and over and over and over and over and over. Tiny fingers, smeared with applesauce, bopping her on the nose. *I'm not your fucking napkin,* she thought, until she said it, and Cheryl whisked the baby away into another room where no one was saying *fucking* or getting so angry at a tiny child that they literally quivered with rage. *Bop. Bop. Bop.*

"Did Bert tell you about the Center for Fiction prize?" Natalie said. It had been a long time since Zoe had heard the old pet name for her staunch, starched brother. He hadn't, because he hadn't told Zoe about anything besides their finances for years. He hated her, which was fair enough. Natalie, apparently, had published a book that was well-loved and nominated for best debut novel of the year. "It's about the intersection of femininity and violence in twenty-first-century politics and society," Natalie said, her voice flattening to elevator music. Zoe fought sleep. She twisted her neck to look at the bar cart, and Natalie took the hint and poured her a vodka soda.

"But the best part," Natalie continued as Zoe took her first, blissful sip, "is my outfit. I really decided to go for it and get something *special*, you know? A real showstopper, as your dad would've said."

At the mention of Daddy, Zoe gulped her drink. It danced down her throat.

"I'll go get it," Natalie said, hoisting out of the chair effortlessly. She was in her twenties, Zoe realized, both marveling at how young that seemed—Zoe, on the precipice of her thirty-fifth birthday—and how old, since in her head Natalie still had her hair in fishtails and couldn't use her chopsticks right, stabbing her avocado rolls right in their mushy centers.

"You're going to die," Natalie called from her bedroom. Swimmily Zoe tried to rest her head on the sofa's arm. It was a beautiful apartment. The wood floors were original, streaked with age. Zoe tried to salvage what remained of her energy. She wanted to unhear Natalie's casual turn of phrase as an omen: *You're going to die.*

Natalie returned with a long, shimmering gown that was too tall to hold comfortably. She jostled the bottom out of its dry-cleaner-bag sheath, smiling widely in anticipation of Zoe's reaction. She strained to focus on Natalie, who had never been much for clothes, just expensive denim, stripes on every top she owned. As Natalie wiggled the dress out into the light, Zoe took in the detailing—the expert draping, the particularly deep shade of azure, the triangle seaming around the bust—and realized it was a design of Gabriella's, Brigid's youngest sister. How many dull seaside holidays they'd gathered around a wide table, Gabriella sketching hemlines and necklines. *Not quite right, I think*, she'd say to no one, continuing to draw. She often used a dark orange thread, rather than black, which caught the light *just so*, Gabriella explained, and here it was, catching the goddamn light.

"I know, I shouldn't have," Natalie said now, stroking the dress as if it were a cat. "Do you recognize the designer?" she asked excitedly. Zoe wondered if she'd bought it partially out of missing Zoe. Once they had been so close. When they did speak, rarely, Natalie always asked after Brigid, showing great interest in her glamorous, vacationing, cheek-kissing family, in a way that twinkled with jealousy. Zoe wrestled the urge to vomit.

"Mmm," Zoe managed. "Of course. Signature stitching."

"Isn't it wonderful?"

Natalie's expression was so open and earnest, it made you feel guilty just looking at her. Zoe waited for an alternate version of herself to sit up, graciously. To sit up and tell Natalie how beautiful she would look, and to ask questions about her novel, about whether she was working on something new, about whether she'd traveled recently or tried cauliflower rice or whatever the fuck people spoke to their loved ones about. Instead, she stayed curled, supine on the sofa, looking at the light wrinkles of paint around the main light fixture, and the whole sad, convoluted story of the past few years came tumbling out of Zoe's mouth, like gymnasts beginning to compete.

Afterward Zoe was exhausted, but she couldn't sleep, so once Natalie slinked into her bedroom and closed the door, Zoe took another shot and promised herself that if she wasn't asleep in twenty minutes, she could have another. Twenty minutes passed and she took another two shots, just to save time, really. She turned her neck and inhaled the scent of the sofa. The tumble of the vodka felt like a blanket. Only now she wanted an actual blanket—it was the only thing she could think about.

Her toes were cold, goddammit.

Her *toes* were cold. Maybe she'd sustain nerve damage. Frostbite, even.

What kind of host was Natalie, anyway? Who had a houseguest and forgot a blanket?

She would find one. She couldn't remember how high up the sofa was, so she crossed her arms in an X and let herself roll right onto the rug covering those hardwood floors. She couldn't remember where the light switch was on the wall, so she groped aimlessly at the dark space in front of her hands. Finally she felt something familiar: Natalie's dress, hanging in the place of honor in front of the decorative fireplace. A multitude of tiny sequins, like shields for the world's smallest swords. They danced against Zoe's fingers, though the slip inside of the dress was soft, almost unbelievably soft. She wanted to rub it against her face. She tried to contort her body to slide inside of it like a sleeping bag, but it was impossible. *It could be a blanket, if it were sliced open down the middle*, Zoe thought. Natalie would understand. She might even think it was funny. Besides, who could say no to the softest fabric in the world against their body? *My toes*, Zoe thought. She found the light switch, the scissors, the seams. The kitchen shears zipped right through it.

Screaming would have been preferable to the low, seismic weeping that came from Natalie the next morning, which awoke Zoe.

"My..." Natalie wailed, not even able to make it to the second word. Loud, was what Zoe thought—she winced at the sound of Natalie's cries, she winced at the feel of Natalie's warm fingers as they ripped the dress from Zoe's body and cried into it, the most expensive tissue that had ever been. A paroxysm shot through Zoe's body: her toes were cold again. She didn't try to explain and Natalie didn't ask for an explanation. *Just be angry at me,* Zoe thought, wanting the reprimand that she knew she deserved, that she deserved a thousand times over. *Yell at me. Let me have it.* It being anger. It being the swell of rage that came with someone fucking up and fucking up and fucking up, on loop, for thirty-five years, across continents, across oceans. Natalie had known her for so long. Suddenly Zoe remembered trying to convince her that rubber cement was a type of cheese you could spread onto crostini, how Natalie's little nose had puckered in confusion as she took a tiny nibble, and Zoe didn't feel bad enough about it. Now Natalie wrenched the dress into her arms but had nowhere to put it. Her shoulders heaved. "My . . . my . . ."

My, my, my, her father used to say, scooping her up and letting Zoe ride on his shoulders. *Look what the cat dragged in.* He only did it when she'd been bad.

Natalie wept into the crook of her elbow. "Why would you do this to me?" she asked. "I don't understand, what did I do?"

"You didn't do anything," Zoe said.

"Okay," Natalie said.

"I . . . I was cold. I don't know. I didn't see a blanket."

"You didn't see a blanket," she repeated. A long silence followed. "I'm going to call Bert to pick you up now," she said. She had never sounded so young and so much like an adult at the same time.

❦

Albert didn't talk to her in the apartment, or walking down the front steps. Albert didn't talk to her when they passed Levain

Bakery, where the line was thick with rhapsodic children in puffy pastel coats. He didn't say a word until he said, "This is my car," and Zoe nearly tripped over a chunk of pockmarked sidewalk.

"Is this new?" she asked.

"Not so new," he said, plucking a child's toy from the seat. He waited for her to sit and reached his keys up to the ignition and then put them back down. She waited for him to reach them up again, holding her breath as if they were children, cruising past a cemetery. *Ashes, ashes, we all fall down.*

He was her brother. He was shouting, his voice rising, behemoth. Did she have any idea what it was like to get a call from Nattie at his *office*, where he *worked*, demanding that he leave to pick up his *delinquent, ghost* of a sister who showed up where *she was neither wanted nor expected* and how many more *fucking times* would he have to do this?

"I didn't even know you were here," he continued, little splatters of spittle falling from his lips. "I didn't even know you were *in this country*. Why would you . . . why would you come to Nattie before me? I'm your only living relative, Zoe. For fuck's sake."

She was still drunk, Zoe realized. She'd have to be careful.

"What are you doing back, anyway?" he asked. "Where's Bridget?"

"Brigid," she corrected automatically, her voice cracking. "Well. I guess it doesn't matter if you don't know her name, now."

"I'm sorry," he said, using his lawyer voice. "That must be difficult for you."

"It is *difficult for me*," she hissed. Her teeth trembled against the meat of her bottom lip. "Thank you for your sympathies. It's almost like there was one person in the world I could count on, and now she hates me and my life has gone to absolute shit."

"Don't do this."

"Don't do what?"

"Don't decide everything is terrible and spiral out. It's exhausting. And, I should mention, very expensive. Thanks for cutting up Natalie's designer gown. Did you know that cost seven thousand dollars? I know our parents would have been *delighted* to see the trust fund cover that extravaganza."

"Well, they're very much dead, so don't worry about it."

"You need to stop spending like money is infinite," Albert said. "I mean it. With this *dress* and my girls' astronomical tuition and taxes on the apartment and the house—it's all adding up."

"What do those *tuition costs* have to do with *me*?" Zoe asked.

He ran his fingers down the longitude of his oval face. "That money is for both of us. It's a *family estate*. I need it for my *family*. You need it for your *habit*. Do you understand? I can't keep neutralizing every disaster that you create, Zoe."

"Where are we going?" she said, twisting to look in the rear-view mirror. "You didn't just pick me up to give me a sweet little lecture about responsibility, did you? Because *you*, Alby, don't have anything to worry about. It's out of my system. I want to go to my hotel and take a nap."

Albert's knuckles blanched on the steering wheel. "Things have to be different this time. I want you to promise."

"Fine," Zoe said. "I won't slit anyone else's evening gown. I mean, I did have plans to knife them up at Barneys, but I suppose that can wait."

Albert didn't smile. "And I want you to promise to leave Julian and . . . to leave them alone."

For a moment Zoe's vision carouseled to black, then returned. How many times now had she called Morgan's number? Did Alby

65

know, somehow? He couldn't. The car still smelled new, and leathery. She wanted to dig her teeth into the headrest.

"Promise me," Albert repeated.

"Fine. Do you want me to sign a little contract? Maybe we can find a notary."

"I don't want to just dump you in the hotel but . . . obviously I can't take you back to the house when you smell like this," he said, putting the car into drive. "Katherine will know. The girls might ask questions."

"Spectacular," she said, resting her head against the cold glass. He didn't need to ask which hotel. They had driven this way before.

7.

*S*trike *when the iron is hot!* advised the Internet. Don't wait too long after your date to establish contact. What exactly was too long? Morgan wondered. It was now three days since the two of them had crowded into the robin's egg blue booth at Donnelly's, slinging their steak fries into aioli. Sadie ate hungrily, with gusto. Morgan was learning that Sadie didn't do anything nonchalantly; she gave it her all, bolting across the moments of her life like it was one long field hockey game and she was only a few inches from stealing the small white ball.

Hey, Morgan typed. Deleted it.

Hi, what are you up to? Deleted. They sounded like somebody's aunt wanting to go out for cupcakes.

In the end Sadie beat them to it. *Fries, redux?* she asked, at the exact moment that Morgan wondered if maybe they should just give up. Outside it was dark, sleeting, and with the windchill it felt like it was thirteen degrees. But Morgan said yes. Of course, it was a yes.

* * *

Raindrops slammed the surface of Morgan's umbrella. Every drop sounded like a miniature bullet. *There's nothing happening*, Morgan reminded themself, but still they felt their fight-or-flight response firing madly. They surveyed each street corner, waiting to see if someone malicious would appear out of nowhere.

Sadie waved from underneath the dome of her umbrella, which glowed an iridescent pink-blue underneath the awning. "Lovely weather, isn't it?" she said in a horrible British accent that made Morgan laugh, and then they couldn't remember what they had been so scared of, after all.

"Nice hat," Morgan said, eyeing Sadie's pom-pom-topped beanie.

"Thanks. I've had it since I was twelve. It ages like a fine wine, you know?"

"I've heard that about pom-poms," Morgan said. The two of them scuttled into the same booth, and Morgan wondered if Sadie also thought of it as *their spot*. She was wearing a necklace with a single milky stone on it that dangled right between her breasts, which Morgan would not stare at. Would not. They pretended to be extremely interested in the daily specials, even though the only thing they could afford was tomato soup. Sadie asked if they wanted to split a grilled cheese and Morgan was doing the math quickly to calculate it with tip—did the grilled cheese come with fries? Was it this hot in here last time? Were they sweating in any visible places?—when Sadie touched their knee with her knee, just for a minute, and looked at them.

"It's on me," she said. "I'm celebrating."

"That's not..." Morgan started. "Thanks. What are you celebrating?"

"I'll tell you, but you can't repeat it to anyone."

Who would I tell? Morgan thought. The waiter arrived, glanced over at Morgan, then at Sadie, then smirked. It was a smirk that lasted only a split second, but it registered somewhere deep in Morgan. They felt that smirk travel down to their toes, like a penny clanking down to the bottom of a well.

"I'm a professional secret keeper," Morgan said. "I'm listening."

Sadie was celebrating because she was famous on the Internet. Nobody from school knew, she emphasized, and she wanted to keep it that way, because people could be petty and weird. (She ordered grilled cheese; fries; two Cokes; extra mayo for the fries, and also ketchup, mustard, and hot sauce.) She ran an ASMR YouTube channel, putting out videos every Thursday and sometimes a second over the weekend if she had time to write and record it then, too. It was two years old, and she never showed her face, only her hair (braided neatly in two plaits with ribbons at the end, like a girl in a fairy tale) and she wore the same white T-shirt, a little see-through but not *so* translucent that it looked intentional. She was called BraidsASMR. She had fifty thousand followers who called themselves *braidsies*. Morgan knew ASMR—knew the torrent of tingles that those videos produced in their own lanky, wayward body—and the sounds that most videos incorporated: bubble wrap, the light snip of scissors during a haircut, the cleaning of earwax and the light touch of a finger against a microphone. Sadie wrote scripts, mostly asking friend-type questions to her listeners: *How was your day? Did you listen to anything you liked today? Did you feel the sun on your face?* and more and more. People tuned in for this one-sided friendship, this public library of affection. Sadie knew she was a good writer, and she saw potential. She set up a

Kickstarter for better sound equipment; she started to pepper her videos with details about her aunt's life in Pensacola, the lizards and the humidity and the thrust of the waves on the beach. She talked about feeling alone and people wrote back, talking about how it made them feel less alone to hear Sadie's voice. *You are an angel*, one subscriber said, and asked if there was anywhere they could donate to Sadie, and she set up a Patreon. Now the braidsies were spoon-feeding Sadie their coffee-and-beer money and she watched it in awe. She created a helmet of sriracha and mayo on the fries and opened her famous mouth wide.

"Some film school guy named Peter is paying me seventy-five dollars a month," Sadie said. "Can you imagine?"

"That's wild," Morgan said, wondering what the fuck they were doing with their life. They were never going to be able to pay $75 to support a YouTuber. All they did was go to school, shuffle to and from their part-time job at the library, and worry themself into a pretzel as they struggled to fall asleep. Rinse, repeat.

"I really want to help out my mom," Sadie said. "She works every single shift she can get at the dialysis center, even Christmas. Don't get me wrong, it's not like I can afford to slack off at school. It probably wouldn't even cover my textbooks if I don't get a full scholarship to MIT." She took a bite of the grilled cheese, pulling its strings into a lavish bite. "It's something, though. I hope it keeps being something. And I know people are creeps, but they think I live in Pensacola. It's not like they'll show up at my house one day, wanting to know why I didn't post at exactly midnight."

"It's awesome," Morgan said, jealousy misting over their snack. "You should be really proud."

"Thanks," Sadie said, brightening. "I've been working on it for so long. It feels surreal to see it finally pay off." She raised a fry to toast, and Morgan raised one, too, even though it meant their fingers were coated in pinkish mayo. "What else should we do to celebrate?" she asked, holding eye contact for a long moment that made Morgan's brain wipe completely clean. What else should we do? Morgan glanced around to see if anyone was within earshot. What did Sadie want them to say? Something flirtatious. They could be flirtatious on command, couldn't they?

"Do you want, um..." Morgan started. "To...go back to your house?"

Sadie tilted her head. "Morgan Flowers," she said in reply, leaning into them a little. Her voice sparkled and drifted over their shoulders, like a shower of confetti.

"Is that a yes?"

"That," Sadie confirmed, reaching for another fry, "is a yes."

The apartment was small, and nobody was in the living room, though Morgan could hear the light rumblings of a brother's voice from behind a closed door. Sadie put a finger to her lips and quickly maneuvered them inside, undetected. Her room was barely wide enough for her bed and a desk, and unlike every depiction Morgan had ever seen of a teenage girl's bedroom, it was meticulously orderly, with only a bulletin board mounted on the walls. Sadie's bed was lofted, a rickety ladder leading up to a twin-sized mattress. She clicked the door shut. Morgan followed her up the steps and lay down next to her. Their bodies were so close to the ceiling that Morgan didn't even need to lift their elbow to reach it. Morgan felt acutely, electrically aware of how close their body was to Sadie's, lying on the sheets where she slept.

Sadie said softly, "I know you must be thinking, essentially, that I live in a coffin. I mean, I'm used to it, but when I see other people's houses . . ." She paused. "I guess I don't usually let people come here."

Morgan nodded. "Yeah," they said. "I know what you mean." They told her about Grandma Cheryl, how she'd bought the shittiest house on their block and never stopped tinkering with all the many things that could go wrong in a fixer-upper: decrepit electrical wiring, saggy floors, windows that let in every gust of cold wind. Sadie tucked her hair behind her ear. They were talking too much about construction.

There was a long moment that unspooled between them. Up close, Morgan could see the faint marks of freckles across her eyelids. She smiled. Gently guiding the neck of Morgan's sweater down, she rested her fingertips on Morgan's collarbones and the feeling of her fingers, grazing their actual skin, made them dissolve. They were just particles now. She reached up to Morgan's jawline and traced the line of it, their jaw, their heart-shaped face, and their body started to tremor a little with how much they wanted Sadie to kiss them, and also how infinitely satisfying it was to know that Sadie Gardner was here, staring right into Morgan's eyes, looking like she wanted nothing else in the world but that kiss. They forgot the tiny room, the distant footsteps and beeps of someone microwaving in the background, the bristling sounds of traffic in the parking lot outside. They forgot everything but the proximity of their bodies, their faces, their lips.

"What are you thinking about?" Sadie asked, returning her fingertips to Morgan's clavicle. Her voice dipped into a new tone, a deeper, softer voice than Morgan had ever heard her use before. It felt like silk, grazing the back of their neck.

"You," Morgan said, and Sadie kissed them then, the warmth of her mouth on theirs. Sadie, touching their arm, the back of their neck with her fingernails. This was what it was like to be kissed. The first kiss grew, and multiplied, and mouths opened and shut, and each kiss became a part of a cotillion of other kisses, twirling through a grand ballroom. They could have kissed Sadie forever.

When there were three long, insistent knocks on the door, Sadie pulled her fingers away from their skin as if she'd been burned. *I'm so sorry*, she mouthed, leaping down the ladder to open her bedroom door. She wiped her lips with the edge of her shirt. Morgan stared, frozen, looking at the texture of the popcorn ceiling, and tried to will themself into invisibility. *Think of unsexual things*, Morgan thought desperately. *Tom Hanks. Sea turtles. Mashed potatoes.*

"Hi, Mom," Sadie said. "What's up?"

"Sadie, Sadie, Sadie. Do we have a rule in this house regarding a closed door and company?"

"We do," Sadie said. "I'm sorry."

"What else?"

"I won't do it again, Mom."

"I'll drop it while you have *company*, but this conversation is merely on pause," Sadie's mom said.

"I know," Sadie said repentantly. "What are you doing home right now?"

What was Morgan supposed to do? Should they turn to look at Sadie's mom, introduce themself? Their current move, playing dead, was probably not right. Every second they stayed, motionless, anxiously burrowed into the twin-sized mattress, their first impression was tanking deeper and deeper.

"Decided to go grocery shopping tomorrow morning instead," Sadie's mom said. "Let me meet your friend. I'll give you a minute to get down that ladder, friend of Sadie's!" she bellowed.

* * *

Sadie's mom (Diana, Morgan learned) moved through the kitchen like it was lucky to have her in it. In her eggplant-purple scrubs and New Balance sneakers, she was dressed like an anonymous health care worker, but her confidence emanated. Morgan sat on a wooden stool at their kitchen table, nibbling on the seedy crackers and canned mandarin orange segments that Diana put out. "Let's get to know each other," she said. "I like to have a sense of who's lurking in bedrooms around here." But her voice sounded amused and chipper, not angry.

"Mom, this is Morgan Flowers," Sadie said. "I wouldn't say Morgan is a bedroom lurker, thank you."

"*The* Morgan Flowers," Diana said. "A pleasure."

Morgan tried to swallow the smile that arose from knowing that Sadie had spoken to her mom about them enough times to be recognized as *the* Morgan Flowers.

There was such an ease between Sadie and her mom—when Diana glanced at the bowl of crackers, Sadie handed it to her mid-sentence, neither one of them missing a beat. Diana asked Morgan about their job, the SATs, whether they liked that fancy school up on the hill as much as Sadie did, all the while ruffling Sadie's hair from the back. They smiled the same way, a little dimple on the right side.

"Sadie, you know what would be good with the—"

"Salsa?"

"You read my mind," Diana said, dropping her hand while Sadie retreated to the refrigerator. "So, what do your parents do, Morgan?"

"My dad works in IT at an educational media company."

Morgan tried to keep their tone even, affable. But they thought of their phone screen: *Unknown. Unknown. Three missed calls.* They watched Sadie slide into the seat next to Diana's and bang the edge of the jar on the table so it would be easier to twist open, and a chasm opened in their chest.

Morgan watched Diana note the omission. "Good salsa," she said. "You want some?"

"No thanks."

"It's actually not good at all," she said. "But it is something else."

"You mean it was on sale," Sadie said. "It tastes like a cumin factory exploded."

There was a brief pause, and Morgan wondered if Diana was feeling that sense of her home being *observed*, watching their eyes glaze over the summit of mail on the dining room table and the faded spots on the chair cushions.

"You gotta pick and choose in this life, kid," Diana said, waving her chip through the air. She gave Morgan a little smile, which they didn't totally understand, but felt the warmth of it anyhow. What would it be like to have a mom like this, who cared about your feelings on salsa, who wanted to know about whether the stranger in your bedroom played a team sport?

Diana invited Morgan to stay for dinner, but they couldn't imagine facing the squad of Sadie's brothers. They said they could hang out for a little while but needed to get back to their dad for dinner, and carefully Sadie led them back to her bedroom, this time with the door conspicuously ajar. Instead of the bed, the two of them sat on the floor, cross-legged on Sadie's spongy carpet. Morgan stared up at the lofted bed for a second, feeling that those kissing moments were already surreal, sliding into the place in their memory that felt reserved for vivid dreams. Sadie reached forward to squeeze their knee.

"Sorry about the questioning," she said. "I know . . . it must be hard, with your mom."

"Yeah," Morgan said, and then, all at once, they were telling Sadie everything from the beginning. How Zoe up and disappeared, getting on a flight to Denmark without a word. Dad and Grandma Cheryl found her car, and credit card receipts, and eventually she called her father—not Morgan's dad—to let everyone know she was alive and in Europe, for a while. *To clear her head.* How that head-clearing time unraveled into most of forever. How little time Morgan had ever spent with Zoe, except for that one, brief summer, when Morgan was nine, when Zoe emerged and wanted to be their mom again. Before she abandoned Morgan in the park, it had been going really well. Suspiciously well. The two of them, side by side on a wrought-iron bench, eating pistachio gelato in Verdi Square on 72nd Street and then going shopping for hats. Zoe talked about how her mother Sally had loved tulips. And skeletons—she'd studied archaeology or something.

It was all so hazy now, the weeks that unfurled carefully before the park incident. Morgan couldn't have even said how long she'd been away before they panicked. Long enough to make friends with a pigeon that couldn't seem to remember how to fly away. Morgan had spent a long time deciding what the right name was for that pigeon, but now couldn't remember what it was. Something Britishly regal. Oliver? George? That sad, purring bird, with its bulgy eyes. It could have explored the whole beautiful city but it stayed there instead, watching Morgan flip out and puke and cry all over their shirt, specially laundered for *a day in the city*, watching Morgan decide it was worth asking a stranger for their cell phone and calling Dad at the office at the number they'd been forced to memorize in case of emergencies. *I didn't mean to be gone so long,* she'd repeated, over and over, when she returned to the picnic blanket.

No wonder she'd left.

"Morgan," Sadie said gently, when they were done. "It wasn't your fault. You're not supposed to dump your kid in a public park and disappear. That's like, the antithesis of parenthood."

Morgan shrugged. "I . . . I just wish I knew where she was now."

Sadie twisted to reach the laptop on her desk. "Let's find out, then. What's her last name?" and Morgan watched in suspended animation as Sadie typed the words that Morgan had thought of so often. *Zoe Willis.* Google spat out search results in an instant, in a fraction of the time it took to cajole the salsa jar into opening. Morgan hadn't considered that it would be quite *so* easy. Or maybe they had, but they were too afraid to deal with the consequences of that ease. And now here it was. Daughter of Harris and Sally Willis, both deceased; survived by one brother, Albert. The family had lived on the Upper West Side, in an apartment that they still owned. Morgan noted the address, repeated it a few times in their head. They would look it up on Google Earth later.

Zoe had her own page on an interior design firm's website; the header of the page was decorated with droopy, fat blossoms in saturated pink and reds. On the bio page, it read: "Zoe Willis, age 34, lives in Lisbon, Portugal, with her partner, entrepreneur Brigid Holm," and went on to list interiors of people's fancy-looking bedrooms and home offices with links.

"Did you know your mom is into ladies?" Sadie asked.

Morgan shook their head. "I don't know anything she's into," they said, their voice sounding far away. They wondered if they should have feelings about this information, but it registered just the same as the other tangle of facts—distant and befuddling. They could picture Brigid's name on the return address of an envelope, pointy and narrow. *A pen pal*, Dad always said vaguely. Morgan relayed this information to Sadie, lines of sweat creeping into their palms.

Sadie tilted her head. "Is your dad the kind of person to be friends with his ex's new partner?" she said quizzically.

"I don't know," Morgan said. "Maybe."

Morgan watched numbly as Sadie typed: *Brigid Holm*. The two of them crowded around the boxy screen, looking through pictures of Zoe and Brigid together at fundraisers, on boats, in group shots clumped with evening gowns in front of country estates. Zoe looked like Morgan, lithe and pale, with the same shape to their faces. They zoomed in on one picture, with Zoe in a crimson gown that showed her shoulder blades, her hair gathered in a twist at the nape of her neck. If I were directing that movie, Morgan thought, I'd have her look over that bare shoulder underneath a streetlamp—classic Hollywood. Morgan wondered what it would be like to dress like that and to have occasions for which there was reason to.

Gotta pick and choose in this life, kid, Diana had said.

"I didn't expect her to be so . . ." Morgan started. *Beautiful*, they thought.

"Rich?" Sadie supplied.

Morgan tried to picture themself on Zoe's arm, waving at a camera. For one brief moment, they allowed themself a fantasy of dressing in one of those luxurious outfits. They pictured silks, leather that gleamed in the light. No worries about filling out soups with bits of tasteless celery or maintaining their GPA for their scholarship, or whether Dad had eaten enough that day, or whether somebody eyeing their androgynous figure in the distance might follow them home. Nothing but champagne flutes and tables dressed in deep black cloth. Nothing but Morgan with their mom: two heart-shaped faces, leaning into a portrait of excess.

"I can't," Morgan blurted, and closed the screen suddenly. "I— It's too much."

Sadie nodded, and they sat in silence for a long time before she spoke. "Listen," Sadie said cautiously. "Do you think . . . I don't mean to overstep or anything, but have you ever talked to a therapist? I don't think there's anything wrong with you, or something, but . . . you know," she said, using air quotes, "abandonment issues? Et cetera?"

Morgan shook their head, their tongue thick. "Therapy is too expensive," they said. "My dad goes. We can't both afford to go, and he needs it more than I do."

Sadie nodded. "I get that," she said. "I'm sorry. This is all so fucked up."

"I just wish I knew if we're going to see each other again," Morgan said.

8.

Time passed—Zoe couldn't say how much. She was out of Xanax and socks. She made it one day, then half of the next. Zoe found herself places, buying things. Another bottle of champagne. Pedicures where tiny fish suctioned the dead skin from Zoe's calluses with their eager guppied mouths.

"Please come get me," she said to Albert over the phone. "I can't do this anymore." He'd wanted to yell at her but he must have heard it, the hardness in her voice that was somewhere beyond depression, beyond burning your skin in a bath so hot in hopes that you might dissolve into a vapor. "And bring Chinese food?" she said.

Albert came to pick Zoe up. When he pushed the passenger door ajar, the syrupy scent of General Tso's chicken greeted her, the Chinese food in precariously closed white containers with metal bars for roofs. Zoe sat and plucked individual lo mein noodles and sucked them down whole.

"I don't want to fight," he said.

"I don't want to either," Zoe said. Suitcases hopped in the trunk as the car switched lanes. She sat on her hands to keep them from shaking. Noodles sank into her stomach, little bits of eraser-like pork. "I haven't been drinking, you know. Not for a while."

Albert nodded. They sat silently until he changed the subject. He talked about horsepower, engines, his hand jolting over the stick shift with confidence. He was a good driver, and good at talking. Zoe wedged her knees to one side of the passenger seat and pretended to fall asleep, and then she did fall asleep.

"How long is she staying here?" Albert's wife, Katherine, asked, when she thought Zoe was out of earshot.

He paused. "She's the only family I have left."

"And for God's sake, why did you buy Chinese food all the way in the city just to bring it back up here? You don't *think*, Albert."

At the dining room table, Katherine convincingly pretended that Zoe's presence was a treat in front of their four-year-old twins, Rosa and Jenny. Katherine drained two glasses of port and Zoe watched the gleam of the burgundy cling to her teeth.

That night, as Zoe tried to sleep, she imagined a hand pulling each of her limbs, jerking her body in opposing directions. She thought of which part of her body would snap first, or whether it would be something inside that would rupture. A spleen, or a stubborn stretch of colon. She was tired of the sound of her own thoughts. She thought: *Maybe if I concentrate hard enough, I can catch the frequency of someone else's thoughts, like a radio scooping snippets of a far-off station.* She concentrated. And she thought of the wine downstairs.

"Sorry we've had to stick you up in the attic," Albert apologized the next morning. "Katherine's in the middle of a guest room renovation and . . . well. She wasn't able to get it ready in time."

"Just call me Bertha," Zoe said. He didn't reply. "That's what the madwoman in the attic is called. From *Jane Eyre.*"

Albert was silent, but she could feel his thoughts twisting with possibilities. Maybe he wanted to tell her not to die in his house since it would traumatize the children.

"I'm concerned about you," Albert said finally.

Zoe laughed. Her head full of tinselly static. "Why?"

"You know I have access to your credit card?" Albert asked. "I can see what you buy."

Albert stood solemnly, solid on his solid legs, and waited for her to respond. He'd always seemed like a bud, waiting to bloom into adulthood with investment portfolios and tuna tartare on little rice crackers. Now he was here, wearing his responsibility like a golden crown.

She thought of the liquor store on 75th, and the liquor store by the Szechuan place, and the liquor store across from the Museum of Natural History with its cute puns written in script on a chalkboard. "Do you care to clarify?"

She noticed Albert inexplicably had goose bumps. So did she. She watched the goose bumps traveling up her arm, the forest of blond hairs raised like quills. He was trying so hard to seem composed. "The fact of the matter is...if you don't get your shit together, we'll have to cut you off financially," he said finally. "Katherine is...very insistent on that point, and it's hard to argue otherwise."

"What does Katherine have anything to do with it?" Zoe said. "Why does *she* get to decide that I need to be *cut off*?"

"It's our future. I want you to be in it, too, okay? It's just hard to make a case for you when you're ordering enough champagne that the hotel staff call to let me know that they have a strict noise policy after eleven. At least you listened to me about...about Morgan, right? You haven't opened up that Pandora's box since you've been back? Because it's a huge goddamn box."

Zoe squeezed her eyes shut. "I called but...it was blocked. Nobody would know it was me."

Anger transformed Alby into a different man—one who was itching with energy. His eyes were bulging discs. "Zoe," he hissed. "What was the *only thing* I have asked you to do? God. Everyone's been so easy on you, your whole life. You just wander around, consequence-free, buying *mink scrunchies* while the rest of us are inundated with *real worries* that—"

"Stop it," Zoe said. "You don't know better than me. Stop shaking. You're not a tambourine. Stop it," she said, grabbing at him by the wrist. His watch shimmied down his wrist. He seemed surprised by her grip.

"I'm not going to do this with you," he said. "You want to make impulsive choices, you want to—what? What's your end game? What if Morgan picks up the phone when it's you? What do you say?"

"I just want to hear what Morgan *sounds* like. That's not a crime, Alby."

He plowed on. "You want Julian to invite you over, you want to play house with your abandoned teenage kid? That's on you. I'm *done*."

Zoe said, "You're too close to my face right now." She pretended to kick him, except she actually kicked him, right in the bad knee. His skin drained grayly.

"Jesus," Albert managed after a moment. "I had *surgery* there."

"I was just kidding around."

"Yes, it was extremely funny. Tell my lack of meniscus that you're hilarious."

"Tell your lack of meniscus that I'm your only sister, and I need you on my fucking side, Alby," Zoe said.

Albert clutched at his knee, teeth gritted. "Well, you're a fucking mess, and if we didn't have a family trust, you'd probably be in jail." He stood then, slowly, as if two invisible hands pushed down on his shoulders. "Tell me why you've never been able to follow through on any individual thing for more than a year. Why you can say you're done drinking, and you've got everything under control, and then steal a bottle of port from my—"

"I didn't *steal* anything. Please. Recovery isn't a toy that you hit with a hammer. I can quit anytime I want," Zoe said, her voice loud and confident, if not entirely making sense. "All you need to do is commit."

"Yes, you seem exceptionally committed."

"Well, maybe Katherine should lay off the alcohol in front of people who are newly sober. Did you think it might be insensitive to gallop her way through a brand-new bottle in front of me? That maybe she wants me to fail? That maybe she'd prefer if I was out of your life altogether?" Her eyes felt suddenly wet, and it took a long moment to realize that she was about to cry. "You know that look she gets when she's saying something nice but her eyes say, *I wish I could knife you."*

If he said he knew the expression, they could be laughing again in a few minutes. Maybe she could buy him an IcyHot stick next time she was at a pharmacy. She really hadn't meant to hurt his knee. He was her brother. He was the only one who had ever remembered she preferred blue Gatorade to red; who remembered their grandfather's laugh and the time they'd accidentally gotten too high at Thanksgiving in their great-aunt's garden shed and tried to eat the cabbage rose centerpieces.

"She doesn't make any sort of face," Albert said. He looked at his phone. "You win. Maybe you can invest in a bobblehead doll that says, 'Anything you like, Zoe,' and that can suit your needs better."

"That's all I've ever wanted from you," she said, stung. "For you to permanently shut the fuck up."

"Nothing I've ever said has stopped you from doing what you wanted," he answered. "It's just... Morgan seems like a good kid, on a... stable path. You'll ruin that if you crash onto the scene."

"How do you know anything about Morgan's *stable path*?" Zoe asked.

"Obviously I've done some... light digging."

"Light digging," Zoe repeated, the words rancid against her tongue.

"You know. They," Albert said carefully, "wrote a little essay about using gender-neutral pronouns in the school literary magazine. That kind of thing, nothing— Why am I trying to justify this to you? I'm not a villain here. I'm only trying to protect us. You have a lot of assets, and if Julian wanted to, he could really take us. We could be financially responsible for all of Morgan's college tuition costs."

"Okay," Zoe said, rising to retrieve her suitcases. "I'm done. God knows Katherine wants me to leave, so I'll stay in the apartment, okay? I'll be fine on my own. Thanks for everything," she said, in the venomous voice she'd learned from her mother, the way to bifurcate your gracious words from your glass-edged tone.

"It's my pleasure," Alby said in the same voice.

She took the Metro-North back to the city. With her buzz starting to dim, she thought of how Alby looked in middle school with his fleecy zip-up and his cheeks doughy, and how he seemed to genuinely love the song "Sweet Caroline" and sang it to himself in his room as he folded laundry and Zoe would watch him from the doorframe. The pain grew until it became enormous. She couldn't remember anything that Alby had said, only the feeling that something bad had happened. Something bad was still happening.

It was in her body. Her body remembered.

Morgan.

For the first year of their little life, each and every day, she'd imagined leaving. From the first few days at the hospital, her body bloated and leaking blood and milk, to arriving back at Cheryl's sad little house tucked in a sad little cul-de-sac, she wanted to get gone. She wanted to tell someone, but who could she tell? While nursing, she played a game with herself: Would you rather be in a cave in Kentucky? Would you rather eat a maggot? Morgan with their guppy mouth and painful grip on the ends of her hair; Morgan who took an hour and forty-five minutes just to close their eyes. Tomorrow will be better, she promised herself, but it never was. Cheryl watched her like she could smell Zoe's failure as a mother coming off her. Cheryl's quiet judgment broke Zoe every day. Julian didn't know she was a terrible mother, and Morgan had no rubric of comparison. But Cheryl knew. She knew to tickle Morgan's toes, or to take them for a drive, or when to wax their little ears. And Zoe hated her for it.

While Zoe was out for a long run, Cheryl baked a cake for Morgan's first birthday, a carrot cake with thick swirls of cream cheese frosting. She made the fucking cake from scratch, shredding those carrots with a box grater for what looked like hours. Cheryl remembered, after Zoe had temporarily forgotten, that Zoe's first craving during pregnancy was for carrot cake with cream cheese frosting. She remembered, and felt sentimental about, this wholly unremarkable detail. Just like a mother was meant to.

But Morgan won't even remember this, Zoe thought. She hadn't planned anything for the birthday. Zoe hung back in the doorway, watching Cheryl piping *Happy Birthday Morgan!* on the cake while Julian sat next to her, worming puzzle pieces together across the wooden table, and Morgan gurgled contentedly in the high chair. They all looked so happy without her. Why was she working so hard, minute by minute, to be present when the three of them were their own perfect unit?

"I'm going to take a shower," Zoe said, sweat pooling underneath her breasts. Julian didn't hear her underneath his noise-canceling headphones, and Cheryl ignored her, and in the moment, that was all she needed for confirmation. She packed a duffel bag and tossed it onto the lawn from the guest room window. She didn't look at any of them when she left through the back door.

She hadn't meant for it to be so long. She thought she would leave for a few months, six at the most. She knew Julian wanted her to marry him, but Zoe knew she could never marry anyone. The restlessness of being so close—of having someone know what time you went to the bathroom, what song lyrics made you cry—

woke her up at night. Even as she got on the flight to Copenhagen to visit her cousin Ingrid during her study abroad semester, Zoe hoped she'd feel the pull in her heart that other mothers felt, the animal intuition that peeked up from dormancy when your baby cried in day care across town. Nothing pulled at her heart besides her own shame.

And then Brigid had found her at a crowded party and offered to cook her a hamburger. She kissed Zoe like she was a delicate treasure to be savored, and she could slice a pineapple and give a massage that loosened every muscle in Zoe's neck, and she wanted to help, and listen. Brigid didn't know that she was rotten inside. So Zoe moved in with her the next week, and the next month they'd moved on from Copenhagen to Paris, and how could she explain a year? How would she explain a year and a half? Time lunged. She was never alone. She made new friends easily and could spend hours talking about nothing. The more people she knew that didn't know about Morgan, the less real Morgan seemed.

❧

In New York, you never had to go home. The guy sitting next to her at the bar explained that he was the world's most prominent player of the glass marimba. The glass marimba player invited her to a karaoke bar with his coworkers. She remembered most of the words to "I Will Survive." The group went out for falafel and Zoe drank the hot sauce straight from the bottle. They clapped for her. People were so easy. It was heartbreaking when you realized how easy it was to get people to think that they liked you.

The glass marimba guy told her that there was a museum in

Zagreb devoted to breakups and suddenly Zoe remembered that Brigid hated scallions. She thought of a scallion, stewing in its juices in a tightly wrapped plastic produce bag. "That's the stupidest idea for a museum I've ever heard," she said, and was surprised to find that he was snaking his hand up her leg.

She thought if she fell asleep, sleep might take her back to Morgan, to Brigid, to her mother. So many places she never wanted to be again. So many leaky scallions in bags, twisted so tightly that the plastic seemed impermeable and you had to dig a thumb in and make a hole where once there had not been one.

Then it was both early and late enough to leave, and she expected her voice to recite her address but instead her voice recited Julian's address. "Oh, shit, but first I need to pick something up. Can we make another stop?"

"Hop in," the cabdriver said, and turned his lights off.

9.

Morgan started attending Sadie's field hockey games. They felt too self-conscious to cheer but clapped when it seemed appropriate. They loved watching Sadie—how strong her thighs looked when she ran, how quickly she could cover the entire length of the field. She was vicious, and goggled, and her hair swung in its ponytail like a metronome. The mouth guard held firm in her mouth made her lips protrude and for some reason it was this detail—not the extremely short maroon shorts—that Morgan thought of, alone, as the water in the shower started to dwindle from scalding to warm.

That night it was a home game, and they won. In the last bit (quarter? period?), Sadie made a goal that led them all to envelop each other, a mass of sweaty huggers. Coach Amir offered to take them out for pizza afterward.

"Can Morgan come?" Sadie asked, slinging the field hockey bag over her shoulder. Her face glowed with sweat, and she panted as she spoke. "Can the MVP bring a guest?" she tried again, leaning in a little.

Morgan protested—it was fine, they didn't need to come along, they brought their bike to ride home after—but at the last minute Coach Amir caved, maybe because Morgan looked pathetic, hungry, and out of their league with Sadie, but who could say. Under the table, Sadie texted them *I'm so happy you're here*, and Morgan felt it glow. In the conversation, Morgan was mostly ignored, but in the nice way where you're occasionally smiled at and in on the joke, and they sucked down a pepperoni slice with Sadie's knee ever so slightly closer to theirs than necessary. Sadie had her bike, too, and afterward they went to the strip mall equidistant from their homes to get a salted pretzel with honey mustard dip and a strawberry lemonade slushie, and then they biked back to Morgan's house, their mouths still dusty with salt. There Morgan saw a person kneeling in front of their house, rooting around in the dirt around the spot where Julian used to hide a key underneath the bird feeder.

"Oh my God," Morgan said, trying to get air to filter into their lungs. They couldn't get a sentence to form, could only raise a tremulous finger to point at the woman, light-haired, scrounging at the earth with a small, expensive-looking suitcase next to her feet. She had on very high heels, the kind of shoes that Morgan imagined wearing in their more glamorous dreams. She didn't look like a criminal, her legs twisted at an uncomfortable angle, the posture of a fawn. But she was here, trying to break into their house. A feeling of inevitability came over Morgan; for weeks they'd been carrying around the certainty that something terrible would happen, and here it was. *I knew someone would come for me*, Morgan thought. *I knew it.*

Sadie unclipped her helmet, the sound surprisingly husky and audible in the night. Squinting, Sadie took a long time before she spoke. "I think that's your mom," she said finally.

For the rest of their life, Morgan would remember this: that it was Sadie who'd been able to identify Zoe, not Morgan. In their mind she was endlessly beautiful, a magazine editorial of lushness, holding a gimlet and staring into the Parisian distance. *This is my mother*, Morgan thought, recognizing her in pieces: a slump to her stance, a fervor to her motions. *What is my mother doing?*

Sadie's expression calcified; she was calculating something that Morgan couldn't see yet. "Do you want to call your dad?" Sadie asked. "Do you want to leave? Come over to my house?"

They couldn't speak. They could only watch her, numbly, as if viewing a movie. *If I were directing this*, Morgan thought, but the thought halted there. A low drone blitzed in their ears, dread getting louder, louder.

For all of their prickly, pimply life, Morgan had hoped to be a person of action. Now they were silent, staring at their mother as she found the hidden key. *Is that why the key was hidden there? Had Dad been expecting her?* Morgan thought, feeling the lumps of pretzel from the mall start to centrifuge somewhere deep in their throat.

"What do you want me to do?" Sadie said. "I have my field hockey stick. I could do serious harm."

Serious harm chimed through Morgan's brain. They got off their bike, tacitly leaving Sadie to hold it next to hers, and an old, woozy feeling of trepidation overtook them. *If this were a movie, I'd be about to die.*

Maybe it wasn't her, Morgan thought. It was dark, and what could they see, really, besides a slender woman in suspiciously nice clothes? Because, even though Morgan had wanted to see her so badly—sometimes even trying at prayer, kneeling on the hardwood floor until their knees stung—now that the moment was here, they wanted to run. It wasn't supposed to be like this. Sadie wasn't supposed to be watching, her lips pinched, her hair crimped with old sweat.

The woman dropped the key and struggled to bend in her long, slim-fitting skirt, and watching her wobble and extend one leg behind the other and then fumble with her phone to get the flashlight working, Morgan thought: *Okay, I can do this. I can say something. I will say something. I will take a step forward. Now. Now.*

"Stay here for a minute, okay?" they said finally, and crossed to the front yard. Blades of grass sponged under Morgan's feet. Now that they were in motion, they couldn't wait for it to be over, and started speaking from too far away to hear. They had to say it twice: "What are you doing here?" and she looked up, her mouth slightly agape.

I have nicer clothes, Morgan thought, wanting to disappear. *I can be presentable.*

"Look at you," she said, reaching for them, but Morgan pulled away so her fingers barely grazed their sleeve. She looked flushed, and a little shaky.

Morgan heard Dad's voice in their head: *I can't see myself without a reflective surface.*

"You're like a real person," she said, her voice slow with disbelief.

"You too," Morgan said stupidly. They stood next to her, cataloguing her traits as best they could in the dark. They watched her doing the same thing, scanning Morgan with her eyes wide.

"Same earlobes," she said, dropping her hand suddenly. "Who is that?"

Sadie watched them, one bike in either hand. Guardian angel of rusted bikes, nine-thirty on a school night. Her skin looked splotchy, rouged against her tall white field hockey socks and the navy blue fabric of her winter coat. She waved.

"That's Sadie. My . . . almost-girlfriend."

"Your almost-girlfriend," she repeated, chewing the phrase over. She didn't wave back to Sadie. "Oh, I have something for you!" Zoe exclaimed, dipping down to her suitcase. "I have something— don't move. Don't go anywhere," she said, craning her neck to smile at Morgan. The smile unsettled them, dripped down their legs like a sticky popsicle melting. The suitcase spilled out all at once; a translucent bag filled with soaps, a pair of espadrilles, other boxed objects Morgan couldn't identify in the jaundiced glow coming from the porch light. It didn't seem like an adult's suitcase, which Morgan thought of as neatly rolled T-shirts, socks twinned at their tops.

"Shit," Zoe said. "Here, here it is." She extended a scruffy teddy bear toward Morgan. "He traveled all the way from Portugal. Actually, probably from a depressing factory somewhere first. Where do they make bears?"

The teddy bear smelled like citrus soap and its fur was matted. *I can't keep this*, they thought, a frozen smile embroidered onto the sad toy's face, and it was at that moment when Dad opened the door.

The moment before Dad spoke was cavernous. Morgan watched him tallying up all of the elements that were out of place: Zoe, in metaphorical disarray; the suitcase, in literal disarray; Sadie standing across the street with a protective arm over both bicycles. Then his focus turned solely to Zoe. "This isn't what we agreed," he said, a scrape of his usual voice. "You can't be here."

"Why not here? It's better than meeting at the hotel. It's *home*," Zoe said. "It was our home!"

Better than meeting at the hotel, Morgan thought. Meeting to do what? How many times had they met? Morgan felt like they'd been handed a clue, but couldn't parse out what it led to. They'd never been a terribly good detective. All they knew for sure was that there was something bristly and intimate between their parents; something Dad had hidden, purposely, from Morgan.

"It's not your home," Morgan murmured, but their voice was so quiet they were sure neither Dad or Zoe could hear them.

"You know that's not the rule."

"I brought you something," she said, over Dad's voice. "It's sardines. They're Portuguese. I brought a few different kinds because I couldn't remember if you liked tomatoes. Do you like tomatoes?" She leaned close to Dad, leaned in a way that suggested she had leaned on him—his solar plexus, Morgan thought, their anatomy and physiology textbook ringing loudly in their ears for no reason—many, many times in the past. Morgan had never seen anyone lean on Dad like that before.

"You need to leave right now," Dad said, twisting away from her. "Sadie, can you bring me Morgan's bike please? Or you can put it in the garage." He was yelling across the street, his face pinkening.

Morgan's toes went numb.

"Jules," Zoe said, pressing her hand flat on his chest like a starfish. "Do you like tomatoes?"

"Stop asking me about tomatoes. I don't care where those came from. You need to leave right now. You need to leave right now. You need to leave right now," he said, his voice gathering speed. "You need to leave right now you need to leave right now you need to leave right now," his voice getting louder, frantic, elastic. He was stuck on the phrase and then his expression glazed over, completely blank and far away. *You need to leave right now*—on and on and on, through Sadie slinking toward them and resting the bike carefully against the garage and then raising a hand to wave goodbye, through Zoe taking one shaky step backward before hobbling into a run in the other direction, toward—Morgan saw now—a taxi sitting obediently with its lights off. Her head ducked down, as if she were about to be pelted by a hailstorm.

You need to leave right now, Dad repeated once Morgan rushed him inside. *You need to leave right now*, Dad repeated while Morgan unzipped his coat and untied his shoes and helped him upstairs and gathered the weighted blanket and laid him down on the bed. *You need to leave right now*, Dad whispered when Morgan came back with all of the emergency supplies. *You need to leave right now*, Dad said while Morgan made peanut butter and jelly and sawed off the crusts with a butter knife and heated up peppermint tea and brought up the VHS copy of *The Princess Bride*. In his bedroom, the blinds shut, Dad went silent. Morgan put the salt lamp on so Dad could see where the tea was, scooted the old VHS into its player.

"I'm sorry," Dad said finally. He looked pale, anemic under the blanket pile.

"Don't be sorry," Morgan said automatically. "It's not your fault, Dad."

"I never thought she'd come back," Dad murmured, and then he was gone.

10.

Julian wanted to talk to Brigid, once he could talk. Words felt foamy in Julian's mouth, as if he were trying to suck them out through a straw before speaking. *Your highs will be higher, your lows will be lower,* he heard his mom say. She rattled around his memories during those lows; he could almost feel her creeping around his body to plump a pillow or to refill a water glass. He knew her ghost was still creaking along the steep staircase in the middle of the night, reminding him to stretch his own weary bones. So he stretched. He sipped tepid tea that Morg had left outside his door on the tray that someone had gotten Julian and Zoe as a wedding gift, only they hadn't been married, and all that was left was a glossy black tray that didn't go with anything else in the house.

He couldn't think about Morgan. Better to think about the tray: Was it made in China? In what year? How many other tray twins, right now, were circulating throughout the world? Maybe he could figure it out. Julian tried to get up and found, after several immobilized hours, that he was able to. When the stairs squeaked with his weight, he said, "Hi, Mom," and the sound of his own voice—propelling itself into the world, after all—was a surprise. He stood blankly in the foyer, trying to remember what he was doing. He hadn't had a reason to go downstairs. He went back up. There was an apple on the tray, which he ignored. All of his joints tingled with effort. In bed, he heaped the weighted blanket over his thighs and settled. *Can you talk?* he texted Brigid, who called right away.

"I have nineteen minutes before my next meeting," Brigid said. "You can skip pleasantries. Tell me how you are. Tell me what happened."

He didn't know where to start. Before The Incident, he'd been swishing through all of his routines, slowly eating a peanut butter and jelly sandwich in the dimmed light, puzzle pieces grouped carefully by color, and going through a playlist of favorite David Bowie B-sides. When he got to "Julie," the lyrics strummed through his ears: *Julie, I'm yours till the end, all the days and memories*, and Julian put down the puzzle and danced then. How could he explain these moments to Brigid? It was the purest joy he ever felt, alone, dancing in a room with his noise-canceling headphones on. No one needed him to be anything but who he was.

When Sadie called, he didn't answer right away. The trill of the phone reminding him of the outside world, and he wasn't ready to have the world singe him again. The call continued, insistent, and it was a New York area code, and Morgan should've been home by now, and when Julian answered, the throaty voice of a teenage girl said, "Hi, I know we haven't talked before, but this is Sadie. I'm outside your house."

Julian's mouth felt glued with peanut butter. "Where's Morgan?"

"Morgan's here. But, you should know, um . . . so is their mom?"

* * *

"How strange that she called to tell you," Brigid said. "What does she know?"

"How could I know what she knows?" Julian asked. "I don't have access to that information."

"I meant it as a question posed in general."

"She must know enough," Julian said, and then took a two-second respite in which he bit down on the meat of his thumb and examined the crescents of indentation left by his teeth against skin. "When I opened the door, Morgan was . . ." He struggled for words. He was talking okay, considering, but all of his vocabulary still felt stiff and far away.

"Distraught?" Brigid guessed.

Instead Julian explained the whole, miserable scene. Words chafed at his throat like tiny shards of glass. "I didn't tell you about the worst thing that happened," he said.

"Tell me about the worst thing," Brigid said.

It was such a short clump of sentences, after all.

Why not here? It's better than meeting at the hotel. This was our home.

Julian recounted. He tried to breathe. "I could've done things differently. I never even considered . . . I never dated seriously, I never tried to meet anyone that would've been good for Morg. I thought, Zoe is in a different box than Morg, and it's fine because if it's hurting anyone, it's just hurting me."

Brigid paused. As with so many social interactions, Julian wondered if there was something he was meant to confess in the pause, if the pause itself had instructions. He squinted through the blinds in the kitchen and realized he had no idea what time it was, or whether they'd sailed past the allotted nineteen minutes for the call.

"I don't know how to talk about it," Julian said finally. "This morning there was a tray outside my room, and I heard the door close when they left for school. But eventually..."

"School will be over."

"Eventually school will be over." Julian waited. "This was against our rules. We had strict rules."

"I know you did."

"I'm a terrible father who's lied to his child for a significant portion of their life, and Zoe's who knows where, and I hate that she did this, and I hate that there's still part of me that's worried about where she is, and where she'll be."

"Yes," Brigid said quietly. "I know quite what you mean, about that last bit."

The two of them stayed on the phone in silence for a few beats. Julian felt as if there were some current of emotion that he couldn't reach, some catharsis that would be such a relief, if only he could find the lever to release it.

"Well," Brigid said. "Are you in search of ideas, or is this a listen-and-empathize call?"

"Some combination is optimal."

"This might be a good opportunity to have that visit with Nancy where you bring Morgan along," Brigid said, and even in the depths of his emotional inaccessibility he felt warmed, a little, that she referred to his therapist by first name. "You could have someone steer the conversation a bit, and maybe make it easier, to be honest. Or at least to know what's helpful to share with Morgan, versus causing further harm."

"Where would Morgan sit?" Julian said, starting to sweat. "There's the sofa but it's really not enough space for two people to sit comfortably. It's a surprisingly small office. I'd say it's under a hundred square feet. It's L-shaped, you know? I don't know if Morgan is comfortable in small, L-shaped spaces."

"I would think Nancy might have an additional chair," Brigid said, not unkindly.

"How good of an idea is it?" Julian asked. "If you had to grade it."

"It's an A-plus idea," Brigid said. "I'm very good. Have I ever steered you wrong?"

"You've never steered me anywhere," Julian said, his laugh tinged with a sigh.

There was something he didn't tell Brigid, even though she asked him before they got off the phone whether there was anything else. It was the thing that he would never tell anyone. He made a sandwich and carried it back upstairs, taking care to stand in the squeaky spot. He luxuriated in those squeaks, shifting his weight back and forth a few times. "Hi, Mom," he said, lowering his head toward the floorboards. *My jewel*, she'd say back, fiddling with the buttons of the red cardigan. If she'd been here, he would have told her. He would have said: *Mom, when the door opened, and the first thing I saw was Morgan looking panicked and tearful, for a second I thought it might have been Dad there.* Even though Sadie told me exactly who to expect. Even though he didn't even acknowledge when you died. Why would he? He left because I wasn't the son he wanted, and I'm still not. Still. Still, I thought, just maybe.

And did Julian like tomatoes? He didn't even know. It had been so long since anyone asked.

11.

The house had been silent the next morning. Usually Dad flurried about, a symphony of alarms on his phone to remind him to pack lunch, to check that he had his keys and phone and wallet. Not today: silent. Morgan had felt that silence itching down the back of their neck like an allergic reaction.

Just leave him, then, Morgan had thought. *Does he really deserve your help? Whatever "better than meeting at the hotel" meant, it meant there were lies. Maybe years upon years of lying.* Images of Dad, wrapping his twiggy arms around Mom while they were both swaddled in expensive white robes. Dad got so obsessed with things happening just like in the movies, and here he was, doing the biggest movie cliché of all: sleeping with someone secretly in swanky hotel rooms. Only instead of cheating on a spouse, Morgan was the one left in the perpetual fucking dark. Morgan had even felt *guilty* for those "working late" nights, guilty that Dad had to log so many hours at a company that was always one firing away from going under. Morgan had always tried to be extra nice on those weekends, pitching in on whatever puzzle Dad was absorbed with, or offering to watch movies that Morgan found alternately exquisitely cheesy or repugnantly dated. Morgan thought Dad didn't lie, that it was against his "code," but maybe that was just one big lie underneath which all the other little lies gathered in repose.

She didn't want to see me, Morgan thought. *She only wanted to see him. So maybe it was personal, after all.*

They'd stood in front of the bathroom mirror a long time, examining the places on their jawline where it seemed like there would soon be pimples, examining the places where it seemed like there might soon be stubble, examining the angles of a face that looked like it was emerging from underneath Morgan's face. Maybe the person underneath Morgan would know what the fuck they were supposed to do now.

In the end Morgan couldn't help it, they'd made Dad two peanut butter and jelly sandwiches and more peppermint tea and a stack of napkins in case he spilled the tea (likely) and placed them all on a black tray that Grandma Cheryl called *the helper*, and at the last minute Morgan decided to add one lonely Gala apple. By then the Gala apple was a little dimpled, and Morgan knew that Dad probably wouldn't eat this (skin too slimy, the crunch too abrasive) but still got fixated on digging a knife to carve out one soft, busted spot, and until Morgan saw the blood they didn't understand what had happened but then there was a lot of blood, little pearls of blood on the cutting board and *the helper* and Morgan's uniform sweater. At first it hadn't hurt. They'd made a tourniquet of paper towels and put the tray outside Dad's door with three quiet knocks, then crept back downstairs to find more blood, now drizzling down their arm underneath the sweater, soaking through the paper towel tourniquet. Dad would freak if he saw blood in the house, so Morgan had balled up tourniquet #1 and replaced it with tourniquet #2 and got their bike, which was still in the not-quite-right position against the garage where Sadie had left it.

What did Sadie think? Morgan wondered, their arms suddenly freezing. What did Sadie think about Mom? About how Dad had freaked out? *No time, no time, no time,* Morgan had thought, getting on their bike. Still very much bleeding, it seemed. School sometimes felt so far away, watching the neighborhoods change from places where everybody was already at work at 7:30 a.m. to places where people were booking it with coffee-shop coffees in hand and expensive car doors to slam. But it had to stop bleeding, didn't it? It was just the bike ride, the grip of the handlebars opening the flappy cut so that it couldn't clot its way closed. All the way there, Morgan had felt like they had a song stuck in their head, only they couldn't remember the melody or any of the words. But as they'd pedaled up the big, last hill before the school's front entrance, they realized it was Dad's voice, insisting—pleading—*you need to leave right now, you need to leave right now, you need to leave right now.*

And she did.

Morgan folded tourniquet #2 behind their back. It was surprisingly hard to get situated with one hand out of commission. Morgan felt aglow with *difference*; they were different from yesterday even if everything else looked the same. Yesterday they'd stood here with two intact thumbs, worried about a geometry test and whether Sadie would walk past them after gym at their peak sweatiest, and now those worries felt a million years old. Their mom had come back. Their dad was sick. Their thumb was gashed. Yesterday their life felt, if not predictable, at least on a steady course; now it was all fucked. When

Sadie approached, Morgan—for the first time—didn't even notice her, so enmeshed in their own anxieties that she was practically kissing them when they felt the presence of her nose next to theirs.

"Morgan Flowers," she said.

"Hey," Morgan echoed. "Can I ask you something?"

"Is it about the trail of blood that you're leaving?" Sadie asked. "Like a little snail, only biohazardous?"

"Shit," Morgan said, squeezing tourniquet #2 as tight as they could. "I gashed my thumb open this morning while I was cutting an apple. I don't know why it won't stop," they said, feeling a wave of tears beginning. *Stop it. You will not cry before school has even started. Stop it right now. YOU NEED TO LEAVE RIGHT NOW,* Dad's voice yelled back inside Morgan's head.

"You might need stitches. Let me see," Sadie said, pulling them by the arm toward a trash can. "Hold still. Don't worry. I'm not squeamish and I'm an expert in determining what's worth a visit to Urgent Care." She unwrapped tourniquet #2 swiftly, like she was peeling a banana. "I think you're okay. Let's put pressure on it for a few minutes and it should stop. You need a new bandage, though. Do you mind if it's kinda old? And scuzzy?"

Morgan shook their head. What a relief it was, watching Sadie know just what to do, watching Sadie not hesitate even for a second as she did the things she knew to do. Sadie was probably one of those people who could lift a car to save a baby. She squeezed hard on Morgan's thumb, hard enough that her own nail marks started to pulse against Morgan's skin. Neither one of them spoke. Wind ruffled Sadie's hair into a cyclone and they both laughed at how wild it got, tangles of blond curls in every direction.

"So what happened yesterday?" she asked finally, loosening her grip on Morgan's hand.

Morgan's stomach clenched. "After you left? I guess...my dad started yelling at Mom to leave and she left. But she said...she said something like..." They cleared their throat. "Um, that it was *better than the hotel*. That it was better to meet at home. So I guess they...have met up? I thought they...I never thought that was...a thing."

Sadie listened. She spread a Band-Aid over Morgan's thumb and pressed down both edges. "Does it hurt?" she asked, keeping her grip tight over them. Morgan shook their head slowly, not wanting to give anything away by trying to speak.

"I can't believe he lied to me," Morgan said finally.

Sadie let their thumb go. "Parents lie all the time," she said. "Especially when they're lying about stuff to themselves."

"I thought you'd be on my side," Morgan said. "You don't think it's fucked up?"

"I'm on your side," Sadie said. "It just seemed like...your dad wasn't just freaking out, but...in a lot of pain. I don't know, I've never...seen somebody shut down like that."

Morgan bristled. "He's autistic. That's just how he shuts down." They pressed on the Band-Aid, a single bead of blood starting to shine through. "I don't think I'm supposed to just *tell* people that. I don't know, actually."

Sadie nodded, twisting her hair into a makeshift doughnut at the top of her head. In the long pause before she responded, Morgan thought: *Please don't be secretly horrible, Sadie. So many people were.*

"My mom's favorite patient at the dialysis lab is autistic," she said after a pause. "He loves watching videos of penguins coming up from underwater."

"Penguins are nice," Morgan said.

"Yeah, they're pretty good. They can jump over nine feet. But you don't want to trade penguin facts, right?" Sadie said, slowly threading her arm underneath Morgan's. "Morgan, did you think . . . *better than the hotel*, couldn't that just mean she was living at a hotel and she wanted to come inside to an actual home?" Sadie paused. "Look . . . it's just . . . you know she was really drunk, right?"

"Yeah, I mean . . . I figured that out," they lied.

"So maybe you should ask your dad about it," Sadie said. "Before you decide that this person, who's basically a stranger, is telling you the truth but your dad is a capital-L liar." Sadie looked down at the ground. "She kept that cabdriver waiting, you know? People like that . . . you can't trust them."

"Rich people?"

Sadie shrugged. "People with an emergency exit."

12.

Dr. Nancy Gold's office was three blocks from Julian's office, and a thirty-five-minute train ride from Morgan's school. Morgan approached the front entrance five minutes early, just as Julian did. Though they lived in the same house, they'd been avoiding each other so stealthily that this meeting—four days after Zoe's crash landing—was the first time Julian really got a chance to look at them. Morgan's face looked heavy, moonstone-colored pockets underneath each eye before they looked away. Julian felt the seams of his socks rubbing, even though these were usually his reliably comfortable socks.

He watched Morgan scan the area and wondered whether they, also, were looking for Zoe, knowing they were within a fifteen-minute walk from that gleaming apartment on the Upper West Side where she was probably hiding from life. Where she'd probably stashed all of those sardines, Julian thought nauseously, the ones she'd brought back from Portugal just for him.

"Thanks for coming," Julian said, though it hadn't really been a request, and Morgan knew it.

Morgan shrugged. "Anything's better than Spanish," they said. "Should we go in?"

Julian found himself explaining the layout of the office as the two of them filed through the foyer. The building itself was well maintained, art deco fixtures on the walls, a magnificent chandelier in the lobby. Cheryl had spent the better part of a year searching for a therapist for Julian, queasily watching as licensed practitioners' faces went dark at the word *autistic*. Nancy had been the first one to welcome him. Julian buzzed into the office. Morgan's fingers were curled into a fist. Julian remembered when Morgan used to try to climb his body like a tree. It seemed impossible, how adult they looked, how they had once called every doorknob in their house *Dada*.

Morgan sat next to Julian on the sofa. With the pillows off, it had plenty of space, and Julian felt foolish at how many times over the past week he'd imagined the sofa shrinking—the size of an armchair, in his mind, the more often he tried to measure it, the two of them, sitting there together on this too-small piece of furniture. *Where did she put the pillows?* Julian wondered, the sweat beading underneath his arms.

"Morgan, I'm so glad you came in. I've been hoping we could all meet for some time."

Morgan shrugged. "Anything's better than Spanish," they repeated, and it crushed Julian to imagine Morgan practicing this line because it was too hard to talk about what it felt like to be at your dad's therapist, under these circumstances. *Please be right, Brigid*, Julian thought.

"I understand that your mom showed up last week pretty unexpectedly," Nancy said. "Morgan, do you want to tell your dad how that experience was for you?"

Morgan shifted on the sofa. "Um...I thought I was here so Dad could talk to me? I don't really want to start."

"What feelings come up for you when you're asked about this?" Nancy said. "What's upsetting about 'starting' the conversation?"

"I'm not upset," Morgan said quickly. "Okay. It was weird, and I felt...ambushed. I was having a really good night, like, *unusually* good. I was with Sadie and her field hockey team, and they won, so...it sounds stupid. I was...with the team when they won. We went out for pizza. Everything felt like it was going the way it's supposed to, like, being a teenager. Feeling part of something. When we biked home, I thought maybe...Sadie and I. That maybe something would happen between us. But then," Morgan said, lowering their chin to their chest. They shook. Julian could feel their body shaking on the sofa next to his body, and he thought about touching Morgan but did not. "But then my mom was there, and I hated her for ruining it for me. The one perfect night, and then Sadie saw my whole family being so *fucked*, and I was embarrassed.

"Then when Mom was like...unraveling," Morgan said, starting to cry. "She said this weird thing about how it was better than a hotel. I keep thinking, I don't know...what that means, whether...I know that's why we're here, right? Let's just get to it. I want a tissue, please."

Julian reached for the tissue box and placed it on Morgan's knees.

"Sometimes," Julian said, trying to speak over the frantic drumbeat of his heart. "I...There have been times when I've seen your mom. We've met up at hotels, but never at our house, and I never wanted her to see you when she was...struggling."

"Struggling," Morgan said, their body twitching with the effort to stop crying.

"With drinking, and with...her mental health. It wasn't that she wasn't interested in seeing you, Morg, but...I was trying to protect you from a situation that's really painful for me, and would be for you, too. I didn't want you to know what it's like to be...enmeshed with someone who's...an addict."

Morgan twitched. "Why do you just get to *decide*? I'm *seventeen*." The word *seventeen* broke something in Morgan and their body seemed to deflate altogether, their torso flat against their knees. "She's my *only mom*. You *kept her from me*."

"Morgan, it's completely understandable that you're angry, upon hearing this," Nancy said. "I think we can both appreciate what a difficult position you're in."

"What if I *died*," Morgan said, quaking. "What if that shooting had happened at my school, and I *died*, and I never knew her?"

Julian wasn't expecting Morgan to say this. He was the one who worried about safety; he was the protector. Morgan was supposed to be free of those worries. "What?" he sputtered.

Nancy said placidly, "Do you think about that often, what happened when that boy brought a gun to your school?"

"What does that have to do with your mom?" Julian said. "I thought you were upset because you think I lied to you."

"You did lie to me," Morgan said, almost yelling. "You *did* lie to me, Dad. I'm just saying...You don't *know* I'm safe anywhere. You just deprive me of this...this person that made me. You kept her from me, and then you fall apart, and I have to take care of you. It's *fucked*, Dad. It's not your fault, I know it isn't, but I slashed open my thumb," Morgan said, holding up a thumb wrapped tightly with gauze. "And I couldn't even tell you because you were so...*gone*, you were just *gone*."

"When did that happen?" Julian said, reaching for Morgan's hand.

"On Tuesday. I was trying to slice an apple for you. For the tray."

"I can't eat apples," Julian said. "The texture of the—"

"Morgan," Nancy said. "Let's go back to some of the topics you touched on earlier. Your feelings about safety. Did you feel unsafe when you saw your mom? Why do you think you were remembering that day at school?"

"At first I didn't recognize her," Morgan admitted. "I mean, how was I supposed to know she wasn't, like, a threat? I was just thinking—things can change in a second. You're kind of...helpless. That's just reality, I guess, I'm realizing."

"Julian," Nancy said. "Is there anything else you wanted to say to Morgan?"

Was there? He wanted to say: *There isn't a second that goes by that being your parent doesn't scare me. I want to know if I'm doing the right thing, but no one can tell me. And you can't tell me, either. You won't be able to tell me for years.*

"My friend Brigid," Julian said. "You know, my friend Brigid who writes me those letters? She's your mom's ex-partner. They're very on again, off again...Anyway, Brigid and I became close friends. It seemed too complicated, because you were so young, and then it was hard to explain, and...I didn't mean for that lie to go on so long. I'm sorry."

"You haven't even said you're sorry about lying to me about Mom," Morgan said. "But you apologized about *Brigid.*"

"I'm sorry it hurt you," Julian said. "I'm not sorry I did it." But he was sorry, and would be forever, about the look on Morgan's face after he spoke. About the sound of the door closing, so polite and yet definitive, when Morgan left the session without a glance back in Julian's direction.

* * *

Later, when Morgan was in the shower, Julian put a GPS tracker on their phone. Just so they could look and see the data that proclaimed: *I am right where you think I am, and I am safe as I can be.* They closed the tracker quickly, wiped the screen with their sleeve. *I'm sorry*, Julian thought. Dishonesty made him itch. He scratched. He covered himself in pink zebra-striped scratches—his shoulders, his elbows, the length of his forearms. In his bedroom mirror, he looked transformed.

13.

Morgan wanted to be anything but angry. Anger rotted your teeth like sugar, Grandma Cheryl used to say. Anger turned you into Ethan, slinging a gun in his stupid backpack with his stupid textbooks for everyone to see. Morgan wasn't going to be angry. They asked Sadie if she needed help practicing field hockey, though she definitely didn't. The two of them met at Van Cortlandt that Saturday, Morgan wearing basketball shorts that were so old the Nike swoosh had completely scraped off. Sadie dumped her hockey equipment in the bleachers, tucked under the first row so it was hidden. "First, let's run until you say stop, okay?"

"Okay," Morgan said. The first thirty seconds were agony; then it was just the effort of putting their foot up and down, up and down, the rhythm of it all. *Let's run until you say stop*, but Morgan never wanted to stop.

"I'm so sorry but I have to pee," Sadie apologized. "I had too much iced coffee this morning. I'll be right back."

Morgan kept going. *She'll be right back*, they thought, but as they rounded the small track, they wondered if that was a lie. Who drank iced coffee before going to exercise? Who would go all the way here just to leave them, running gawkily, in a loop? People were capable of anything. They saw it all again, as if a film: a close-up of Mom, bent over the suitcase. Dad's voice sticking as he repeated himself again and again. And the therapist, observing everything from behind her fancy bifocals. Listening to all the worst things that Morgan said, all the worst things that Dad had done in the name of *being a good father.* Morgan always suspected, and now they knew: therapy didn't help anybody. It just trotted out your ugliness so you had to look at it, and then it was harder to go back to your life because your ugliness was shining as bright as the fucking sun.

When Sadie emerged from the path that led to the porta-potty, with her hand raised up in a wave and her cheeks flushed with the cold, she caught up to Morgan's stride and they thought: *She came back, she came back, she came back.*

"Ready?" Sadie asked then, gesturing at the bleachers, the concealed hockey sticks, and Morgan said yes. They desperately wanted to pound at the ground with a stick, to hear the crisp *thwack* of the ball traveling through the air, just like it was meant to.

After field hockey, the two of them turned deeper into the park, hooking into a circle by the lake. In the fall the trees were a postcard of foliage, caramelized browns and buttercupped yellows.

"About the other day," Morgan said.

They told her then—about why they'd missed Spanish earlier in the week, about Dr. Gold sitting in her squishy leather chair. It had taken Morgan hours to walk home, their thumb's gash starting to reopen underneath layers of gauze.

"I don't even want to look at him now," Morgan said. "Just the thought of them having some kind of..." They trailed off. "He can't even explain why he's stayed so...yoked to her, when it sounds like he hates her, or is afraid of her. Afraid of what she might do."

Sadie paused before she told Morgan about her first serious boyfriend. Tyler: tortoiseshell glasses, slick tongue. She was his emotional wastebasket, a place to unload and rid himself of any responsibility. But she'd stayed with him, even though she saw his sneaky way of twisting any conversation back to his hurt feelings. She'd been fifteen when they met, and stupid.

Morgan thought of the total relationships they'd previously had: zero. *Slick tongue*, they thought.

"The point is, I knew he was bad for me but I didn't stop. You just...You get used to things." Sadie paused. "And your dad, maybe...it's easier for him to deal with things he knows, even if they're hard. Right? Isn't routine a big part of autism?" She examined Morgan's expression. "I've been googling."

"I hadn't thought of it like that," Morgan said. They saw a montage of Dad needing to use the same coffee cup each morning, the same knife to spread his peanut butter. How his voice had sounded when he'd said, *These aren't the rules.*

"Thanks," Morgan said eventually. "For googling."

Sadie stopped walking and Morgan stopped, too, a little short, so that a pebble skittered off the path and into the clear water.

"My cousin Chase is an addict," Sadie said, her voice suddenly soft. Morgan thought they must have misheard her at first. *What's happening right now?* they thought. "Outside of Tampa. He's in rehab, but like...it's not really a rehab if drug dealers are right outside on your stoop, selling clean pee in a jar."

"I'm sorry," Morgan said. "I didn't know."

"I don't talk about it. Especially since my brother Robbie deals sometimes." She shrugged. "Just weed, but still. He's an idiot. But...you know, when we were kids, Chase used to draw with me while all my brothers were beating the shit out of each other. He was different. Kept to himself. Things got to him, things that my brothers didn't see. It's hard to be like that." She looked at the ground. "The next time he gets caught, he's probably going to jail for a long time. Has your mom gone to jail?"

"I don't think so."

"You need to be careful," Sadie said. "Chase isn't a bad person, but he stole my aunt Lisa's wedding ring while she was sautéing onions. Just pocketed it and pawned it and got some heroin."

The mix of wanting to kiss Sadie very badly while hearing a story about a heroin addict confused Morgan's body deeply. Her lips were so full.

"I don't have anything worth stealing," Morgan said finally.

"People steal in all kinds of ways. Like...since she showed up, you seem half here, half not here. It's not weird that you're distracted or anything," Sadie added quickly. "I just mean...you should think about what you'll do if she comes back, you know? It's always better to have a plan. I have a plan for everything."

And she did: a plan to get into MIT for college, a plan to get a degree in biomedical engineering, a plan to study artificial internal organs that would help people like her mom's dialysis patients. A plan for finding roommates, for scholarships, for her ASMR channel. Sadie blinked at Morgan like she was watching a baby giraffe wobble up to take its first steps.

For the first time, they resented her, just a little. Sadie's mom painted her toenails and on Friday nights they made chocolate chip pancakes for dinner and they daydreamed about moving out west, where they could look at mountains in their backyard. Sadie's parents only divorced a few years ago. She knew her dad's favorite season and how he liked his oatmeal and what radio station he had on preset. Sadie didn't know shit about missing a parent that was only the outline of a person.

Morgan took a step away from the lake, and then another. "I know she's not coming back," they said. "It's over now. I can feel it."

Gradually things started to settle. After five days of avoiding each other, Morgan sat down for breakfast in their usual spot, and Dad glanced up, beaming. Morgan ate breakfast as Dad talked about the latest cybersecurity precautions at work, bopping a bit as if he were listening to his favorite song. Morgan nodded along.

"Are we good again?" Dad asked abruptly. "Please answer honestly. Dr. Gold says I can't let this incident go unresolved if we're to have a healthy and mutually trusting relationship in the future."

"Um . . . we're recovering," Morgan said, speaking into the cereal bowl. "It's . . ."

"I broke your trust," Dad said. "I understand. I want to do everything I can to earn back that trust, Morg. Just tell me what I need to do. You're right, you're almost a legal adult, heading soon to college, and I guess . . . I'm a little slow to adjust."

Dad looked over at Grandma Cheryl's chair, at the red cardigan still stretched over the back.

"I know," Morgan said.

"How's your thumb?"

Amy Feltman

Morgan held it out. Dad squinted at the gash, the flap of skin that covered it like a hat. "We'll have to keep an eye on that," he said. "Not literally. I'm not planning to place an eyeball on top of your wounded thumb."

Morgan thought there was nothing so depressing as your parent working so, so hard to be loved. They let Dad rebandage the thumb, carefully meeting each end of the Band-Aid into a perfect hug around their finger.

§

Then, during history, a freshman with a pearl barrette traipsed into the classroom and said she needed Morgan Flowers to come with her to the front office. It wasn't over the loudspeaker, which meant someone had died. *My dad's dead*, Morgan thought. *A minute ago I had a dad, and now I'm zipping up my backpack. This is the first time I'm standing up from my chair after my dad died. The first time I'm walking down the hallway after my dad died.* They felt the Band-Aid rubbing against the cut on their thumb and thought of how gently Dad wrapped the Band-Aid arms around each other, taking care to make sure it wasn't too loose or too tight, and felt sick.

And there was Mom, wearing a dark brown fur coat and bright red lipstick, wrapping her arms around Morgan before they knew what was happening.

"Oh, sweetie," Mom said, and they closed their eyes for a long second, prolonging the inevitable question of what had happened to Dad. The scent of Mom's neck, a little acrid. She didn't offer any more information and Morgan didn't want to ask.

"Let's go outside," she said finally. They followed her.

"Tell me what happened," Morgan rushed, starting to clatter

into an audible volume. "Was it... Was there a shooting? At Grand Central? On Metro-North?" Morgan was talking, filling the silence with more and more details of this shooting: the emergence of a gunman, maybe two, three? Morgan could see this all unrolling in their head, a familiar scene. Dad would have been so upset by the noise, all the commotion. His last moments would have been panicked. He might have been too upset to run.

You need to leave right now. You need to leave right now.

"Your dad's fine!" Mom said, gesturing widely around her. "Nobody's dead. I'm here as a fun surprise!"

The moment that followed went on forever. Morgan covered their face to gag behind the shield of their hand. They tried to unsee it: the chaos of the train passengers scrambling to disembark, the long tunnel of Grand Central filled with commuters sprinting for the grand hall. It was fiction. Dad would be there when they got home. Dad would be there tomorrow, ready for oat milk once again.

"You're surprised," Mom said triumphantly. "I told them your grandmother died. It's a classic move. Have you ever seen *Ferris Bueller's Day Off*? It was on TV, and I thought, why not? You know, why not? We can go anywhere!"

"I want to ask you something," Morgan said to change the subject, though they didn't know where to start. Mom blinked a few times in rapid succession, as if trying to communicate in visual Morse code.

"Shoot," she said.

"I just have to get my bike. I can wait until we get to the car."

"I don't have a car," Mom said.

Morgan paused. "You don't have a car," they said softly. "But you came here to get me?"

"Of course I did," she said, reaching her fingers into Morgan's hair. How dare she say *of course*, Morgan thought. They craned their neck, searching the sky for the bright disc of the sun, lazing behind a veil of clouds. She had to say something eventually. She had to have a better reason for being here than a rerun of *Ferris Bueller's Day Off*.

Maybe she remembered that she loved them, Morgan thought. It was possible, wasn't it? Morgan wanted to be the kind of person to walk away, to tell her to fuck off for good, but here they were with such a warm satisfaction in watching her watch them, trying to make this right even though there was no way, ever, to make it right.

"I guess I can keep my bike here overnight," Morgan said reluctantly. "Or we can . . . pick it up later?"

"Anywhere you want to go," she said. "I'll call an Uber."

"We should leave," Morgan said. "Someone could find out you're lying."

"I'm not lying. Your grandmother's as dead as they come," she said, and just like that Morgan could taste the reheated spongy lasagna that Grandma Cheryl had made in the days before she died so that Morgan would have something to eat if no one else came through.

"You don't have to say it like that," Morgan murmured. It was hard to think. Their brain felt full of earthworms, wriggling out of the saturated mud. "Wait," they said, following Mom, who'd started hustling determinedly toward the end of the parking lot. Morgan understood why people followed her—confidence rolled right off her, as strong as the scent of salt near the ocean.

"Tell me why you're really here."

"I wanted to do something special, to surprise you like you've never been surprised," she said. "I owe you. I know we can agree that I owe you." When they hesitated, she reached for their wrist. Her fur coat was so soft. "Tell me you don't deserve some fun, Morg. You look like you follow all the rules."

"What if I can't think of anywhere I want to go?" Morgan said. This was so typical, that an actual daydream would crash-land into their lives and they wouldn't have a clue how to proceed.

"You'll think of something," Mom said, and waited.

"The zoo?" Morgan said, surprising themself. They had always gone with Grandma Cheryl on free Wednesdays, reciting the same facts about puffins and terns. They hadn't gone back since she died and they missed the wobbly flamingos, how their curved necks looked in the pond's reflection. "Flamingos are my favorite but . . . Dad says that keeping animals in captivity is inhumane and we can't support it. Plus, the smell, he says."

"That sounds like him," she said, and then nothing else. She punched information into her phone. Morgan felt flushed with embarrassment at how decidedly uncool their request had been. Let's go anywhere, she offered, and they picked a place for toddlers to sip juice out of cups shaped like trains. *Following all the rules.*

"I could just go back," Morgan said.

"You're not going anywhere but straight to the flamingo's lair," Mom said, a little too loud. "And look, Sebastian is going to pick us up in two minutes at this very spot."

In the car, Morgan couldn't look at her. What would Dad think when he found out? Mom didn't talk, either, just sipped clandestinely at a water bottle. The zoo wasn't far. Blue skies dappled with clouds hung overhead. They got out of Sebastian's car and waited in line at the gate.

"Tell me why you like flamingos," she said, at the same time Morgan spoke.

Morgan said, "I bet you're thinking, when I was in high school, I was at raucous parties with the basketball team and going to diners. I was sneaking into concerts and getting pregnant, not . . . wanting to see flamingos."

"I wasn't thinking that," she said. "I envied people who had interests. Who cared about things besides ski trips and sunglasses. That's what drew me to Jules. He wasn't exactly the raucous party type."

"You don't have interests?" Morgan asked.

Mom's gaze was glassy. She opened her mouth to answer, but then shut it again. Finally, she said, "I used to be interested in interior design. It was the only thing I was really good at. I had my own client list at a firm, even, but . . . well, sometimes I still look at tiles and think, *you'd be a beautiful backsplash*, or feel this urge to rearrange all the furniture in a room. I look at carpet and wonder whether there's hardwood underneath. Not as much anymore."

She sounded profoundly sad. The mood, deflated as a punctured balloon. *You did this*, Morgan thought. They couldn't think of what to say to fix it.

"What else. I played the viola," she said. "When I was in sixth grade. I was terrible but I liked it."

"Sorry," Morgan said, though they didn't know why they were apologizing, exactly.

She stared at the entrance of the zoo, the thick lines of children and strollers and parents hunched with the paraphernalia of their parenthood. Morgan stood an awkward distance away from her even though they wanted to feel the texture of the fur coat again. They thought about objects that might fit in the space between their bodies. Perhaps a loaf of Wonder Bread.

It was Mom's turn to pay. She handed over a black credit card and Morgan's expression wobbled as they squinted out the cost of two adult admission tickets. With tax it came to forty-eight dollars. More than eighteen jars of peanut butter. Sixteen avocados, if they weren't on sale. Morgan kept the loaf of bread distance between them. Mom handed Morgan a ticket.

"I'm sorry," Morgan said again.

"What?" Mom asked. The zoo sparkled with movement, so many unsteady small humans clasping their respective adults' hands. She walked quickly, decisively, toward the children's zoo.

"Just that it's a lot. For a zoo."

"I don't even remember how much it was," Mom said. "Tell me about the flamingos."

"I like their color," Morgan said. That shrimp-y, halfway point between millennial pink and coral was Morgan's favorite color, one they often imagined painting their nails. "A flock of flamingos is called a flamboyance," they continued. "That was one of my favorite animal facts when I was a kid. I just think they're beautiful, I guess. It sounds stupid."

"Cheryl had one of those tacky plastic flamingos outside, didn't she?"

Your grandmother's as dead as they come.

"Yeah," they said. "She called it Warren. We took him down before a blizzard. Never put him back out."

"Warren!" Zoe said fondly. "God, she hated the cold. She dreamed about moving to Florida."

"I didn't know that," Morgan said. They felt wounded that Mom knew something they didn't about Grandma Cheryl. It seemed unjust.

Mom stared silently at the smudgy screen of her phone. They were so boring. She probably regretted ever coming to get them.

By the pond, the flamboyance of adult flamingos' necks bent like pipe cleaners.

"Um . . . can I wear your coat?" Morgan said. It was the only thing they could think of.

"Oh. Sure." She slid the long strap of her purse over her head and shimmied out of the sleeves. "You must be cold," she said, though she was wearing a silk shell and Morgan still had their uniform sweater and ill-fitting button-down on. The fur's lining slinked against the school-issued sweater. They felt like a treasure.

"It was my mom's," she said.

The animals splashed in the pond. Then, suddenly, one of the flamingos started to squawk differently, harried, and the others followed, running in a frenzy. She and Morgan watched the flamingos, not saying anything.

14.

Zoe looked at Morgan, standing there as the flamingos squawked mercilessly. They looked like they were about to swarm Morgan from all sides. Sunshine plodded into Zoe's vision. Klonopin glittered underneath her hangover.

"Mom?" Morgan said. She blinked, at first searching for a different version of herself that heard this word every day until it had no meaning besides *me*. A few wide-eyed, staring-contest babies caught Zoe's gaze. They all seemed to be judging her. *The type of woman who would leave us*, the gooey infants in their warm, perfect swaddles goggled.

She fell through that trapdoor of memories, the darkest of her doors. All the things she couldn't talk about. The things she had said to her mother. The things she had never said to Julian. All those hours in Lisbon that she'd pretended to be at AA when she was really playing beach volleyball with strangers. She knew Brigid worried. She knew the worrying consumed Brigid day after day after day and still she bumped the ball until her forearms glowed with pink.

"You said I could ask you anything?" Morgan prompted. When had she said that? It did sound like her. She could never turn away a confessional as the buzz set in.

"Anything," she repeated. "But first, come on, I'll buy you a drink. Do you have a fake ID? You look really young." Zoe fingered a number of useless objects in her purse: a ball of receipts, a stray gum wrapper. "I totally forgot how pretty your eyelashes are. It's a crime when boys have such pretty eyelashes."

Morgan lowered their head. "Um, I don't have a fake ID," they said finally.

"Did I say the word *pretty* too many times? Are you fragile?" Zoe didn't wait for an answer. "This is going to be fun, I promise. And, look, we saw your bird friends! They were fucking *noisy*. But they do have a nice color, I'll admit."

"What about their eyelashes, though?" Morgan asked, and then they were both smiling matching smiles.

"I didn't know you were funny," Zoe said drowsily, and it pulped her heart to see Morgan beam.

Zoe escorted her beers to a picnic table, where the two of them sat across from each other. She was careful not to knock knees. The combination of Klonopin and alcohol was a slow exhale. Pleasure diffused inside of her like a scented candle.

Morgan asked her rapid-fire questions. They drank their beers, Zoe taking great, almost unbearable care to drink hers slowly, while Morgan regarded every sip with caution. Who was this person? she wondered, but it caused her some pride to watch how not-addicted they seemed. Her favorite food was octopus. Her favorite city was Lisbon, but she didn't want to explain about Brigid, so she said Paris. Her favorite color was peach. "Why are you asking me all this?" she finally asked. Beer made her feel like a teenager, clandestine, clinking green bottles on a fire escape. She toasted their plastic cups.

"Honestly?" Morgan said. "Because I don't know if I'll get another chance to ask you."

"But don't you want to have it out? Tell me to go fuck myself? I mean, it's the zoo. It's a prime spot for familial tension. Plus, isn't it satisfying that nothing you could say to me would be undeserved? It's a free pass," she said, placing both hands on the table in front of her. "I want the whole shipwreck."

"I don't want the shipwreck," Morgan said. "I want it to go well."

"Why?"

"Why don't I want to have a huge fight with you in public?"

"That's exactly what I'm asking. Yes."

"I don't fight. I don't really know how to."

"But you must be mad at me," Zoe said, and let herself take a long drain from the cup.

Morgan kept their gaze focused solely on the picnic table. Little cracks of algae lit up the wood.

"Yeah," they said. "Yeah, I am mad at you, but . . . I don't know how to talk about it. So, it would be better if you could just like me."

It was so tender, and so plainly said, that it took her aback. Morgan drank. She drank. Sunshine drawled over their arms. She realized she hadn't said anything back to Morgan and looked up in surprise, after what felt like a long time. She felt bubble-wrapped in their vulnerability.

"I'd rather get into a car accident than talk about my feelings," Zoe said.

"How bad a car accident?" they asked. "Bruised or broken?"

"Depends on the bone."

"What about an arm?"

"Right or left?"

"You're a lefty, too," Morgan said, watching Zoe drink her beer. "So . . . left."

"I'd rather break my right arm or sprain my left wrist," Zoe said, after a minute.

"I wonder what else I got from you," Morgan said.

"Do you have acid reflux?" Zoe asked. "Do you hate the smell of chicken stock?"

"Yeah," Morgan said. "Both. I have both of those things."

"Are you queer at all?" Zoe said, a fraction of a moment before she realized she should not have asked this. Morgan turned a furious pink. They focused on the table, etching all the cracks with their finger. "I just mean, it runs in my family," she said.

"Um . . . you met my girlfriend," Morgan said quietly, after a pause.

"I remember her," Zoe said. "But that doesn't mean anything. Anyway, it's not important. Or you don't want to talk about it. Either way." But she couldn't let it go. She loved watching things escalate. When she'd been a girl, she would never let a scab heal. She loved to watch that new blood drip over the slope of her knee.

"It runs in our family?" Morgan asked.

"All the way up. Great-Great-Great-Aunt Bobbie and beyond. Well, she went by Bobbie. I think her name was Carol. My mother wanted to kill herself when she found out about me. Maybe we should get something to eat? What do people eat at the zoo?" Morgan avoided looking at her.

"Dippin' Dots," they said. "There's a stand."

"I can go get it," Zoe said. *Run*, she thought.

"I don't mind."

"I don't mind, either," Zoe said, leaping to her feet.

Morgan watched her, a little wary, or maybe afraid. "Okay," they said.

She bought two more beers for them to share. Then she threw up in a bush next to the bathroom. She couldn't remember why she'd ever thought this was a good idea, or what she'd said to make Morgan upset. They should be anywhere but here, at the zoo. *At the zoo, oh oh oh*, she hummed to herself. She would bring back ice cream. Mint chocolate chip, banana split. She imagined hacking a banana with an axe. Morgan was in exactly the same spot where Zoe had left them, memorizing the texture of the wooden picnic table.

"I thought teenagers were glued to their phones," Zoe said. "Mint or banana split?"

Morgan paused. "What kind do you like better?"

"I'm rarely charitable, so you should take advantage of this opportunity," Zoe said.

"Mint," Morgan said. She nodded in approval, then passed it over.

"You're different than I thought you'd be."

Morgan chewed slowly. "How did you think I'd be?" they asked tentatively.

"Shorter. And less interested in . . . pleasing people." She put her own ice cream down on the table. "Unemotional, I guess."

"You think I'm emotional?"

"Not in a bad way."

"You said you'd rather get into a car accident than talk about your feelings."

"I didn't say I'd rather get into a car accident than talk about *your* feelings," Zoe said. "Someone else's emotional baggage doesn't touch me. Nothing really touches me."

"What's that like?" Morgan asked.

Zoe thought about it for a second. "Here," she said, unspooling her earbuds from her pocket. "I'll play a song for you. This is what it's like. Close your eyes."

With Morgan's eyes squeezed shut, Zoe hit play—the song that was her soul, "Fast as You Can" by Fiona Apple. Their expression when listening looked just like Julian's, the way their lips curled together and their head moved, just slightly, to the rhythm. She and Julian had spent hours and hours listening to music together, lying on his twin-size bed with the little packets from the CD case to read the lyrics. Debating which musician you'd revive from the dead if you could revive anyone—Zoe's choice was Kurt Cobain, obviously—and ranking favorite albums. *When the Pawn* was always Zoe's number one. How slowly—painfully—Fiona Apple sang the words "fast . . . as . . . you . . . can," the struggle in getting anywhere even though it was your only option.

When Morgan's eyes were closed, she took another pill, just in case. Tiny beer bubbles rushed down her throat. She couldn't stop remembering those early nights with Julian. Watching him pull up his basketball shorts and then his socks, scuttling to the bathroom to wash his hands with Dial soap after he made her come. He thought she should try to be in a band, even if it was just a wild rumor. Julian loved when she sang along to the Smiths, how easily she could reach the high notes. He bought cherry Pop-Tarts for her to eat at his house when she said her mother refused to buy them, and it wasn't until she saw the barren cabinets that she realized what a declaration of love this really was.

Morgan returned the earbuds.

Her Dippin' Dots were melting. She watched them pool in the bottom of the cup. "It's my song," she said dumbly.

Morgan sucked their plastic spoon. "I get it," they said. "I realized when you left... that you're pretty fucked up right now, right? It's embarrassing that it took me so long to see it." They drained the last frothy wisps of beer from their cup. "Maybe you won't even remember this."

She looked at the table. "Maybe. My memory is like... a kaleidoscope."

"Okay," Morgan said. "Let's finish these and go for a walk."

"I love walks," Zoe said. Around her, the world became hazy, out of focus.

They walked. "Do you know how to say *flamingo* in Spanish?" Zoe asked. "It's *el flamenco*. Like the dance." She and Morgan split around a group of backpack-clad children and returned to each other. So simple, to just be walking next to this person who was also her.

"I hate how words in other languages have a gender," Morgan said. "Every single thing is gendered. Boats, birds, candy." Their face was flushed, and their voice a little loud, all of those inhibitions, tucked away. "In English, even. You can be a child, or a parent, or a sibling. But you have to choose to be an aunt or an uncle."

"You'll never be either," Zoe said, poking their elbow.

Morgan paused. She thought they might stop walking, but instead they sped up, a pace that was uncomfortably brisk for Zoe's stacked heels. "How do you know that?" they said, throaty.

"How do I know what?"

"That I'm not either."

"You're an only child," Zoe said dizzily. She had the old pounding in her chest, the one she remembered from high school. Your cells could feel the conversation shift into dangerous territory. "So you'll never be an aunt or an uncle. I mean, biologically."

"Oh," they said. Morgan's hands shook visibly and they crossed their arms into an X over the fur coat, lowering their chin toward the ground. It was as close as you could come to fetal position while standing up. "I thought because . . . I'm nonbinary?" Their voice hinged, as if it were a question. "So I'm, you know, a *they*."

"Yeah," Zoe said. "I know. I found your essay in that school magazine online." Albert had found it, but this sounded better. Her voice was light, breezy, and it contrasted sharply with Morgan's hunched, nervy posture. "That's fine," she said, unsure what she was saying, or supposed to say. Nobody told you what to say.

Morgan blinked in her direction. "I didn't know you were like . . . researching me." They cleared their throat. "I didn't know you . . . thought about me."

She knew it was a serious moment. But instead of responding to what was in front of her, Zoe laughed, a wheezy sputter. "I'm never not thinking about you. To quote Virginia Woolf. Who was queer, too! It's you, and me, and Virginia Woolf." She desperately wanted the conversation to return to normal. She would've let those flamingos eat her hair if it meant this would stop.

"I just didn't know if you'd care about it," Morgan said. "Or if you were one of those people that thinks pronouns are stupid. Maybe you wouldn't want such a complicated . . . offspring."

"You're a fine offspring," Zoe said, her feelings sloshing like water in a pail. She was wreathed in impatience and nerves.

"Do you like me?" Morgan asked, staring intensely at her for the first time.

"I like you," she confirmed.

"Tell me again," they said, looking nauseous. Maybe she should take back the fur. Her mother would be *pissed* if she gave the fur to Morgan and then they used it as a toilet.

No. Her mother was dead. That's right.

Morgan didn't speak for a long time. "My heart is like . . . "

Zoe waited. "Manic?" she said.

"Yeah."

"Here's the secret. Don't talk about it. Just throw some other topics on top," Zoe said. "You'll feel better."

Morgan smiled. "You don't seem like the best emotional counselor."

"That's entirely true," Zoe said. "But I've survived this long. Kind of." She poked Morgan's elbow again, in something that had become her go-to move. They still had an expression gridded with panic. "Tell me some more things," she said. "I want to hear it all."

15.

For days, then weeks, and then a month, Morgan thought of Zoe saying *I want to hear it all.* They'd believed her. As soon as the Uber dropped Morgan back off at school, Zoe blew them a theatrical kiss, and then—nothing. No reply to Morgan's texts or calls. Morgan felt like they might have imagined the whole thing. They felt hoodwinked, and also idiotic for thinking it would be different this time. They were sure if they told Sadie, she would think *I told you so,* and then there would be an additional layer of shame added. So Morgan stayed silent, the sting of Zoe's disappearance shadowing their days. Sometimes Morgan woke up to find their face slick with tears. Where had she gone to? Maybe back to Lisbon, to her beautiful apartment with beautiful Brigid and beautiful clothes—all the ingredients of her life that didn't include Morgan. She was just gone, like usual. Like always.

Morgan pedaled to Sadie's apartment on a Saturday morning. Every car that edged near their bike felt like it might swipe them right off the road; their shoulders twinged with vigilance. They hid around the back of the parking lot before meeting Sadie down-stairs, trying to get their wheezy breathing to return to normal. *I'm okay, I'm okay*, they said quietly into the heel of their hand, before Sadie bounced down to retrieve them.

How did anyone look so good in sweatpants? She kissed Morgan in the elevator until their head went light and dizzy. Morgan wanted to ask when Sadie's mom was coming back, whether it was safe for them to just be here in the doorway. Sadie broke off the kiss, pulling Morgan into her room.

"Guess what," Sadie said, cross-legging on the floor. She scooted her laptop toward Morgan—it was so old that it couldn't be unplugged without shutting off completely. "See how many views that ASMR video got? Almost a *thousand* in two hours."

"That's amazing," Morgan said, trying not to gawk at the body underneath those clothes. Sadie smelled like citrus, and Morgan's whole body sizzled as she reached and brushed a piece of hair behind Morgan's ear. "What can I do to help?"

Morgan set up the Twitter account for BraidsASMRfans and took a picture of Sadie's braids and the bottom half of her face—just lips and blond hair. Right away followers trickled in. *I wish you were my girlfriend xx, so glad you joined the Twitterverse you goddess!!!!*

"These people kind of freak me out," Sadie said, watching her DMs climbing. "Can you make the notifications go to you?"

Morgan nodded, flushing. Their earlobes felt hot. They'd had the opposite reaction: envy. How many of these messagers would've wanted to talk to Morgan? Would've been compelled to declare their enthusiasm about Morgan's presence in the Twitterverse? They nodded eagerly, stuffing that jealousy down deep.

"Just make sure nobody's *too* creepy," she said.

"This is the cuddly Internet," Morgan offered. "People just want to feel less alone and fall asleep at night to your voice."

"There's no such thing as the cuddly Internet," Sadie said, and before Morgan could reply, she'd calculated how many more people on her Patreon would pay for car insurance per month. She couldn't wait to have her own car, preferably red, Sadie told Morgan.

"Let's try some whispering."

"What are you going to whisper?"

Sadie shrugged, but her face looked happy. "Girlfriend stuff," she said, crawling closer to Morgan.

"I missed you," Sadie whispered, once the recorder was on. "All day I wanted to hold your face in my hands and tell you: you can tell me anything. Did you know that? You can tell me anything and I'll still be right here, waiting for you to come home."

The longer Sadie talked, the more Morgan thought they might die from a combination of wanting to have sex with her and wanting to run to the bathroom to cry in private. When she was done, she clicked the recorder off. She put coconut oil on her lips straight from the jar.

"That was good," Morgan managed.

"I meant it, you know," she said. "We can make out now but you have to tell me what's going on sometime."

Morgan blinked. They were still getting used to the idea of making out in reference to their life after so many kissless years. "Okay," they agreed. "But . . . not yet."

Sadie wrapped Morgan in a hug. They loved the feel of her. *Anything could happen*, they thought, but mixed in with the potential came a twinge of fear. What was wrong with them? Why couldn't they pull Sadie close to them, rest a hand on the inside of her thigh, the way they did in dreams? The moment was here but they were doing nothing about it. Nothing was happening besides the hamster wheel of worry, circling faster and faster.

"Are you holding your breath?" Sadie asked, her voice a buzz in Morgan's ear.

Morgan's exhale felt like it was made of corn syrup instead of air. "Sorry. Sometimes I feel far away from my body. Like I'm watching myself on a screen. Do you get that?"

Sadie shook her head. "Are you okay?"

"It just happens now if... I'm scared or... happy. They register the same, like... adrenaline." Morgan tried to clear their throat but no sound came out. "I... I guess I'm nervous."

"You don't have to be nervous around me," Sadie said, resting her hand on Morgan's collarbone. "We can just lie down." She curled around Morgan's body on the mattress. With all that field hockey practice, Sadie seemed like she could crack Morgan in half.

Maybe there's something really wrong with me, Morgan thought, pedaling home. Maybe I'm going to fuck up every opportunity to be with Sadie like this. Instead of making the most of having the apartment to themselves when it actually happened, what had Morgan done? Shivered next to her as if they'd been rescued from a boating accident. They didn't know what incited their weird fucking behavior—Sadie was the most beautiful person they'd ever seen. They wanted to know every single inch of her. But when it was real, and possible, their brain wouldn't stop firing. *Don't get too attached because anything could go wrong. Don't get too attached because she'll leave you, just like everyone else has.*

Stop it, Morgan had thought in that awful moment. *Stop ruining this for me.* They massaged the base of Sadie's neck, feeling all the tiny tense spots around her shoulder blades. But the doomful voice-over hadn't gone away. *Morgan couldn't have known then, as they rubbed Sadie's shoulders, that they would both be dead soon. If only Morgan could've seen into the future to know what the next day would bring. If only Morgan knew*—

Morgan couldn't get that leaden, faraway narrator that dusted everything with dread to stop. Not when they took off their shoes, or talked to Dad about construction on the parkway, or reheated turkey chili and ate it in a chipped bowl in front of the TV. Not when they brushed their teeth or changed their socks. Morgan lay down. In bed, they thumbed down the feed of every social media platform but nothing worked to soothe their nerves. Finally they logged onto the BraidsASMR Twitter. There was an inbox full of direct messages. Most recently:

> *Hi Braids. I never send DMs like this, but I just wanted to tell you how much your videos help me. I'm a pretty anxious guy and I could finally relax when I listened to your spa day video the other day. Anyway I just wanted to say thank you, the Internet is pretty much a hellhole and I'm trying to do my part to go against the grain. Yours, Peter.*

Before they knew it, Morgan was clicking through to Peter's Twitter profile (BicycleThief2293). It wasn't hard to sculpt a picture of Peter—a student at NYU and looked it, a black beanie and wool coat the color of caramel. Small eyes accentuated by his wire-rimmed, round glasses. Peter, Morgan learned, was studying film. He would be an actual director, instead of telegraphing every scene in their own head. For a second Morgan saw it all: thick books of criticism, a folding chair with their name on it. *Let's try it again, but with more yearning,* Morgan would say. In their daydreams, they gesticulated grandly, with assurance that everyone nearby wanted to hear what they thought.

Morgan started to imagine Peter beyond his major, sitting next to Morgan on a bus. No—Peter was the kind of person who would always walk, even if it took twice as long. Morgan flopped onto their stomach, scrolling through pictures of Peter's culinary adventures and shadows on crisp golden leaves. *If Peter were here,* Morgan thought, *I could tell him.* I could say, *Hey, can I talk to you about something?* and Peter would say, *Of course,* his expression shifting slightly to anticipate Morgan's mood. And then Morgan could tell Peter about the blurriness that existed between being excited and being afraid. How every moment of hesitation felt like it snipped another tender string that drew Sadie to Morgan; how they worried about touching her because it seemed too good, too undeserved, and how much harder it would hurt later when it all disappeared.

You're doing it right now, the voice-over whispered. *You're making that bad dream come true every time you wander into this dark corridor, Grasshopper.* And then Morgan would realize they'd been thinking of Grandma Cheryl, missing how easy it was to confide in her with their faces blocked by fanned cards over the kitchen table. But maybe they'd be able to talk to Peter. To find that rare, easy honesty, and capture it, like a firefly trapped in a mason jar. A few pinpricks, letting the air in.

As long as she never finds out, Morgan thought. What harm would it do if she never found out? Their fingers hung in suspended animation. They knew it wasn't fair to Sadie to reply. She'd specifically said she found these messages creepy. But wasn't it mean to ignore *all* of them? Weren't these people just eager to express their appreciation? Morgan didn't see how it was necessary to hurt their feelings. And if Morgan should find a friend, a confidant, in the process, that was just an added benefit.

Hi Peter, Morgan typed, and with a rush, they hit send.

16.

Zoe woke up in a bed that was not her bed. She was in West New York, near an exotic bird store. That was what her phone revealed under *Current Location*. Someone was making bacon. She could hear it sizzling. Zoe, upon examination, was covered in small fingerprint-sized bruises up and down her arms. This person was playing Nina Simone's "Feeling Good" over poor-quality speakers in some nearby room, not this room. Was the bacon intended for Zoe? Her mother's fur coat lay discarded on the floor. Zoe held it up above her head, inspecting for stains. It was clean enough. She found her silk shell, her wide-leg trousers, her clunky heels. The coat was last, then lipstick. Blot. She tumbled out of the room, scooping two slices of bacon from the pan as she left. "Um, bye?" called the woman who'd made the bacon and, ostensibly, created the bruises along Zoe's limbs. Her brain held no thoughts, just a low squeal of static. She'd taken all of her Klonopin. She'd eaten all the bacon. Zoe sucked the grease from her fingers and called an Uber.

* * *

At her parents' apartment, she ordered liquor to be delivered—all types, so it looked like a party. Then she thought, why *not* have a party? Spending money felt like popping a row of blood blisters. Garden roses in dainty peach, her favorite; imported cheeses cut into cubes. Every time she clicked *order*, it was a relief. Ordering wasn't about disappointing Albert or Julian or Brigid; ordering stuffed grape leaves with creamy mint sauce and hummus and pita chips wasn't about remembering how last night she'd stayed until last call and gone home with someone in an un-ironic bowler hat. *I dare you to squeeze as hard as you can*, Zoe remembered saying now. Now she was having a party! She needed an outfit.

At Barneys she flipped through stacks of shapeless black shift dresses. She called Natalie. It rang and rang, a slow realization that Natalie may not answer her calls anymore, or for a long time. She let it go to voice mail and tried again. This time Natalie picked up, and over her hesitant greeting, Zoe shouted: "I'm having a party! Do you want to come over? Will you bring friends? I feel like I don't *know* anybody anymore."

For a minute she saw it all: Morgan in front of the flamingos— a *flamboyance*, she remembered, only to have her spirit deflate instantly. It had not been a good idea. The minute Morgan hurried out of school, spouting hypothetical scenarios about shooters in Grand Central, she realized it. But once you make a mistake, all you can do is ride it out, right? Zoe could tell they were crying in the car as they left the zoo, but she pretended not to notice. Fuzzy images of Morgan's tearful expression floated into her thoughts, but she clenched her phone in her hand and waited for Natalie's answer.

Natalie said, "I'm not sure . . . that's a good idea."

"I just want to make it up to you," Zoe said. "I know I owe you and I want to do better, okay? I love you." She loved the sound of the dresses on the rack, the hangers clacking. She loved the music in the store and the sour-faced cashier. She loved hearing Natalie lose her resolve.

"I mean . . . maybe," she said. "I was planning to go out tonight with a few friends, maybe we could stop by for a bit. I actually have some good news. We're celebrating."

"I can't wait to celebrate you," Zoe said, almost shouting.

"I don't know, Zo," Natalie said. "Last time . . ."

"I'm just so sorry, Nattie. You're like a sister to me. I guess I felt like I could take my anger out on you because we were always so *close*, you know? I know that's not fair. I love you. Please come over."

"Okay," Natalie said. "Okay."

After they got off the phone, Zoe felt a kick of adrenaline, like she could've run a race right then. "What do you think of this? Too purple?" she asked the woman next to her at Barneys.

"Too purple," she said. "I like the black, though."

"Do you want to come to a party? It's casual. Bruschetta, you know."

"Oh my gosh, are you Sydney's mom? I'm Henry's mom! So sorry, I didn't recognize you with the sunglasses!" the stranger said.

"I am Sydney's mom!" Zoe beamed. "And I would love for you to come over tonight. You deserve an evening out," she said, extending a hand to this woman's arm. "You really do."

Natalie came with a gaggle of identical friends—leggy, Chelsea booted, high-waisted denim, and they each brought a significant other who grouchily parked themselves by the hummus platter. Henry's mom put on Bruce Springsteen and stole all the pomegranate seeds. Bubbles zoomed down Zoe's throat. "To Natalie!" Zoe said, instantly realizing this was the right choice. Humility looked so good on her.

"Natalie, what are we toasting to, babe?" Henry's mom asked. She was the kind of straight woman who flirted with women easily.

"Six-figure book deal," one of Natalie's clones replied. She had on a red beret and a white-and-navy striped shirt. It looked just costumey enough that it might've been a joke, but also not. She raised a flute. "To Natalie's latest book! *The Sliced Dress!*"

"*The Sliced Dress!*" everyone around Zoe said, clinking.

Across the room, Natalie watched Zoe hawkishly. Their gazes aligned, suddenly magnetic. *The Sliced Dress*, Zoe thought. She excused herself to go to the restroom and googled it.

"From the acclaimed novelist of *The Moon Shines Bright* comes the story of a self-destructive New York socialite in a downward spiral. Sold in a major deal, at auction, with film rights and international rights..."

Zoe looked at herself in the mirror for a long time. It was loud and she hadn't gotten one pomegranate seed before Henry's mom got to them. She plucked at the thin skin of one eyelid, and then the other.

"Don't do this," she said to herself.

If only Natalie had waited right outside the bathroom for the inevitable confrontation; if only Zoe had never decided to have a party that night. Natalie was next to the hummus, flanked by the significant others, and she was radiant. The next thing Zoe knew, her voice was hoarse with screaming and the girl with the beret was saying she could call the police. "Laurel, I can handle this, thank you," Natalie said, the icy voice that sounded just like Zoe's mother had when she was *exhausted* by a situation and the situation was, as always, Zoe. *You should've been Sally's daughter, not me,* Zoe thought, and the next thing she knew, she was chasing Natalie down four flights of stairs and

Zoe woke up in a bed that was not her bed. Her body felt cold, but a cold that radiated from the inside, like a fever. Maybe if she closed her eyes and never opened them again, she reasoned, she wouldn't have to deal with whatever followed. She breathed deeply and the breath impaled her; she breathed deeply again and felt the impale return. She thought about slitting open that evening dress and how Natalie was going to be an international bestseller and everyone was going to know just how many occasions she'd set fire to her stupid little world and then emerged with her lungs full of smoke. Sober, alone in a hospital bed with a ponytailed woman in pink scrubs taking her vitals, she knew this.

"Look who's awake," the ponytail said. "You took a nasty fall. I'll go get your friend."

Zoe found herself unable to form a sentence besides "Okay," which was just as feeble and fragile as she felt. Somebody in another room was weeping loudly, the hiccupy weep of somebody who's taking a stroll in the valley of the shadow of death. Hospital time was a different modicum of time and here at 4:00 a.m. the nurses were all smiles, checking things off on a clipboard.

The friend was Natalie, who had a long, feline scratch across her cheek with a lightning bolt of blood in the center. In the wispy neutrals of hospital gowns and sheets and machinery, her one-shouldered lilac lace dress looked particularly out of place.

Anxiety hives, which Natalie always had as a little girl, splattered across her exposed shoulder.

Zoe looked down at her arm, at the IV spritzing saline solution right into her veins, and then at a cast that was around her wrist and fingers. A *cast*. Why didn't she feel anything? Her feet were cold. Natalie screeched a chair next to Zoe's bedside. Tension skittered through Zoe's mind but not her body. She closed her eyes, imagining a world in which she could unhinge her jaw like a snake, swallow a bottle of vodka whole, then opened her eyes again at the sound of Natalie starting to cry.

"You broke two ribs," Natalie said finally. "And your wrist." She touched her cheek as if to say, *And you broke me, too.* "Do you remember any of it?"

Zoe curled her bottom lip over the tops of her teeth. "I remember leaving the bathroom," she said foggily. "I remember Laurel . . . and the top of the stairs. You were writing a book about me. That horrible woman ate all my pomegranate seeds."

"You chased me out of the apartment," Natalie said. "You said you were going to torch that fucking dress. Do you remember that part? We had all been drinking but you were so *fast* and when you fell, the sound that it made . . . I thought you were dead."

Again she thought of Morgan. If she prayed, she would pray for Morgan. If there was a God, she would've hit her fucking head the right way at the bottom of those stairs and it would be over now. Maybe that's what she'd been thinking—not chasing Natalie. Chasing her own messy ending, turning herself into a pile of blood and bones. She couldn't even kill herself right.

"I fell, too," Natalie said. "You should see the bruise, it's black. I can hardly sit. They gave me painkillers, but . . . I don't want to take them, I don't know." She fidgeted with the strap of her purse.

Zoe very much knew why she didn't want to take the painkillers.

"I tried to grab you," Zoe said, cratered memories slowly coming back to her. "That's when I fell. I tried to grab you by the throat."

Natalie leaned forward to show Zoe the thick makeup pancaked over those bruises, the ones that swept around her neck like a row of diamonds. "You grabbed me; then you lost your balance. The paramedics said it's a miracle you came away as well as you did.

"I want you in rehab," Natalie continued. "I talked to Alby, and he . . . agreed. That's why I'm not pressing charges."

The ellipsis held every doubt her brother had ever housed, plus a price tag. They both knew it. There was a reason that Alby wasn't here.

"Okay," she said. "I want to get help, too. I do."

"I wish I could believe you," Natalie said. "But I—"

"No, I know," Zoe said. "I know." She tried to inhale, then winced. "So, what do you do for cracked ribs?"

Natalie reached her hand over the bed to touch Zoe's wrist. "Nothing," she said. "You wait for it to heal."

17.

Julian checked the GPS tracker records on Morgan's phone and saw that Morgan had been to the Bronx Zoo in the middle of the afternoon four weeks ago Tuesday. *The zoo*, Julian thought. All of those animals behind bars, living in captivity for greedy capitalists to enjoy touristing through nature. Julian triple-checked it. He called the school to ask if there had been a field trip even though he loathed speaking to strangers on the phone, unscripted.

"Did Morgan sign out early on Tuesday the ninth?" Julian asked then, and in the moments before the answer came, he knew it already.

"His mother signed him out," the school administrator said. "We're so sorry for your loss, Mr. Flowers. Your wife seemed...distraught."

"She's not my wife," Julian said. He wanted to scream it. She laughed when he proposed one night in the backyard, with a little ring he'd fashioned out of twine until he could afford something real. *I'd rather live on the moon than get married*, she'd said, but now people were almost ready to live on the moon, and they were both alone. For better or for worse. For better, and for worse.

Julian left early. He sent his boss an email about a migraine and shielded his eyes with sunglasses. He ate his sandwich in the park. *Stay for the vitamin D,* Julian thought, the sun's warmth heavy on his scalp.

Nearby, two teenagers were plunking baby carrots into a vat of baba ghanoush. Julian marveled at the ease with which they swung in and out of each other's sentences. Maybe they would know what to say to Morgan, Julian thought. Maybe any person in this park would be more competent at handling delicate situations than he was. Julian closed his eyes, thinking there was no way he could stand the next few hours. He needed to go; the anxiety was starting to solidify, roping him inside of his own body. *I need to find Morgan,* Julian thought as he boarded the train. *I'll know what to say when the opportunity is there. I'll say: Listen.*

Listen, Julian said to imaginary Morgan. Listen: when you were about a year old, I woke up in the middle of the night, and I stopped in your bedroom and saw you standing on your little legs. You had pajamas that my mom picked out—blue planets hugged by iridescent rings, boisterous red spaceships—and you were lowering yourself onto the mattress and then reaching over to the bars of the crib and pulling yourself back up. I wondered if you were afraid you'd forget how to do this new trick, or whether you were afraid of something that had reached you in your sleep. Nobody knows what babies dream about. Maybe the dreams are horrible, a ricochet of nightmares beyond what adults can imagine. There was something sinister about such a small person exuding what seemed like too much effort for a little body in determined, painstaking silence.

Why didn't you help me? Julian imagined the imaginary Morgan asking, but Julian wouldn't have been able to answer. In his own bedroom, he checked the baby monitor to make sure it was working. *I didn't want to interrupt,* Julian told the imaginary Morgan. *It seemed like you were busy. You were focused.* Maybe it was truer to say he'd been afraid of this baby who seemed to see something that Julian didn't. *I was afraid that we would never understand each other,* Julian could admit, only to himself. He thought of this memory often. Morgan's pale, resolute face in the darkness. *I should have reached out and touched you,* Julian thought, but he'd kept his hands in his pockets.

18.

That same day, Morgan rode their bike home from Sadie's apartment, soaring with the sheer amazement of an orgasm assisted by someone else's hand. Sadie's voice buzzed in their ear. Her lips were so soft. The moon looked like a generous slice of apple pie. Inside the lights were off, though Morgan didn't remember Dad saying that he was working late. Maybe they'd eat something that hadn't been in the slow cooker all day, Morgan thought. Maybe they'd make something an actual adult who had orgasms with other people would make. Maybe they'd zest a lemon.

Only: there was Dad, sitting in the dark. He was sitting completely still, staring at the blank wall opposite the dining room table. No headphones on. No music playing. Nothing on his face at all. He didn't look in Morgan's direction when he asked, flatly, "Why were you at the zoo on Tuesday the ninth?"

How did he know that? Morgan wondered. Had they left the ticket somewhere? There had to be something they could say to make it better, some explanation that Dad would believe.

"Why were you at the zoo on Tuesday the ninth?" he repeated, but this time he didn't leave space for Morgan to answer. Morgan felt a heaviness, expanding, as Dad talked about Sadie—how aloof Morgan had become, lying when they'd never lied to Julian before, *skipping class* when Morgan knew, didn't they, what a *catastrophic* situation it would be to lose their scholarship? To receive anything less than a full scholarship to college? Did Morgan want to risk everything for a girl they'd just met?

Before they could curb the impulse, Morgan defended Sadie. "Sadie would never do that. She gets up at five a.m. to study in case there's a pop quiz. She's literally the valedictorian; she's not going to throw that away."

"That doesn't compute," Dad said. "You paint a picture of her as erudite and mature, but then...that's inconsistent. So I have to extrapolate that you're lying," he said, his disposition turning from stoic to frazzled. "Either you're lying to me about Sadie, or you're lying to me about something else?"

Morgan stood in between two dining room chairs, unable to move.

"Someone else," they said finally.

Morgan lowered their gaze to the table, to the splotch of nail polish remover left by Grandma Cheryl, which had eaten right through the wood. They couldn't look at Dad as they admitted the truth. After they finished talking, Dad was silent for a long time. The clock in the kitchen ticked and tocked.

"Why would you go with her?" he asked, after a pause so long it felt infinite.

Because I couldn't figure out how to say no to her, Morgan thought. And then they had another thought. "How did you know I was at the zoo?"

"I called the school," Dad said. "I spoke to a receptionist named Pamela."

"Mom just signed me out for the afternoon. She didn't tell anyone at school where I was going...She didn't even know where we were going when we left."

Morgan laid their tongue between their rows of teeth.

"So how did you...so how did you know that?" Morgan managed.

Then it was Dad's turn to lower his face. "Morgan," he said. "It's my responsibility to know where you are. What if something happened to you?" He exhaled nervously. "I installed a GPS tracker on your phone. I don't look at it much. I just...need to know that you're safe."

"Dad, that is a total violation of my privacy," Morgan said, heaving through the sentence.

"Yes. That's accurate." Dad's eyes went vacant, dark. Morgan watched him go to that other place. "I need to know that you're safe," he repeated. "You can't do anything like this again, Morgan."

It doesn't matter anymore, Morgan thought. *She's gone. She's never coming back.*

"I understand why you're upset," Dad said, filling the silence.

Morgan felt tears dribbling down their cheeks at an embarrassing velocity. "I understand why you're upset, too," they said, their voice quaking with anger as they left the room. "Good thing we both understand why the other one is upset," Morgan called over their shoulder from the bottom of the stairs. "Otherwise we'd have a real problem where we can't trust each other anymore."

Even in a flurry of anger, they couldn't bring themself to slam their bedroom door closed. They wanted desperately to stop the fight with Dad from looping through their thoughts, growing as loud as a clanging drum. He'd been tracking Morgan like they were a fucking *criminal*. They'd followed every little rule for the first seventeen years of their life, and it hadn't mattered one bit. No one trusted them. Not even Dad.

They thought of Mom, how easily she'd breezed through the world. Morgan felt restless. Was this how it would be forever? They didn't want to obsess about her, minute by minute, day after day, for one moment longer. They wanted, desperately, to be swept into something hugely engrossing, a different drama as destructive as a tornado. They wanted to be in the eye of the tornado.

They opened Twitter, staring down the message that they hadn't replied to. Even just seeing the message made Morgan sweaty with possibility. *I met my best friend on Twitter, actually*, they imagined saying. *I know! I know. But it's true. We can tell each other anything. Some people are just meant to be in each other's lives.*

Okay, Cornball, Peter would say. Peter wasn't sentimental. Peter loved walks and caramel-colored coats.

You're both such cornballs, Sadie would say, squeezing Morgan's hand.

Hey, Peter'd written. *I can't believe you replied. What are you up to? Want to see a short film I directed? It's called "The Story of a Hat."*

Sure, Morgan typed back. *I'd love to. xoxo.*

BicycleThief2293 has sent you a direct message!

Peter's film looked like it had been plucked right from Morgan's brain: Easter candy–colored sets, those Wes Anderson shots perfectly symmetrical and dreamlike. Peter even used the same fonts in his credits and slow-motion technique the same way Wes Anderson did. Morgan watched in awe at what Peter created, how *real* it all was. Peter didn't just ruminate over his dreams; he got out his camera and told his actors to twist in a pause that lasted three full minutes.

It's great, Morgan typed. *I loved the shot of Tatiana's scalp at the end.*

That's my favorite shot of the film, Peter said. *I was going for a Royal Tenenbaums look. I love how he does close-ups.*

Me too, Morgan typed. *After Sofia Coppola, he's my favorite.*

AFTER Sofia Coppola?!?! Peter typed.

They talked about film for a long time—Morgan ranked *The Darjeeling Limited* after *Bottle Rocket,* controversially—but then the questions broadened. Peter asked: Where would you go, if you could go anywhere? Would you rather be invisible or be able to teleport? Sprite or Mountain Dew? Peter asked question after question and the attention warmed Morgan like a hand over a radiator. He seemed to genuinely care about their answers, even the soda preferences. Things that wouldn't matter, Morgan thought, unless you were really close with someone. Morgan asked Peter questions about studying film, and even told him their secret dream to be a director. Peter said he thought Morgan (well, Sadie, Morgan thought with a pang, and then worked to reforget this slippery detail) would be great at it.

How do you even function sounding so perfect? Peter typed. *Haha. I bet you're so pretty you would never even look at a guy like me.*

Morgan scrolled to a picture of Peter and zoomed in. Peter was good-looking, arty and serious even in repose. His jawline was sharp and defined; his hair was a soft auburn. He had a five-o'clock shadow in almost every picture.

What are you talking about? haha. You're totally good-looking.

You think so?

If you were on a commercial I bet people would buy whatever you told them to.

What if it was something really awkward? Like hemorrhoid cream?

Even that haha. Tho maybe we don't talk about hemorrhoid cream again.

Yeah deal. haha. Well thanks, that means a lot.

Then suddenly they were telling Peter about things. How Morgan had been bullied for being such a gawky, little child. How none of their crushes had ever been reciprocated for the first sixteen miserable years of their life. They always felt like their loneliness created a force field around them that other people could feel, like a tiny earthquake. Then, at the beginning of high school, the pressure to reinvent themself and then the cataclysmic realization that they'd failed to reinvent anything at all, that they were the same gawky little mouse, only now they were tall.

I am deathly afraid of mice, Peter typed, and then was quiet.

Being vulnerable with someone reminded Morgan of when Grandma Cheryl had taken them ice skating, and very slowly they let their hand drift from the outer edge of the rink. Their first step, tentative; the second, a slow thrill starting to mount with each glide of the blade against the ice. It was almost enough of a rush to forget their own life existed; everything shrunk down to the width of their laptop screen, to Peter typing a reply.

Peter said: *Thanks for sharing all of that with me.*

It wasn't the response that Morgan expected, or hoped for—so tepid, given how itchy and exposed they felt. A dull emptiness and disappointment settled at the base of their throat. Was it always going to feel this way after they confided in someone? But then Peter typed:

I feel really close to you now.

I feel really close to you now too, Morgan wrote, their heart whizzing in their chest like a mechanical toy.

19.

For thirty days, Zoe had her vitals taken and said her name in a circle when it was her turn and nodded sympathetically when it was not. Every wall was painted beige or pale blue, such heavy-handed attempts at tranquility it made her want to throw a chair through the windows. She shook, she vomited. She went to therapy and ate organic broccoli. What does anybody do with their fucking lives? Zoe wondered. With all the time?

Albert and Natalie picked her up at the end of the term. Natalie in the back seat, as it had always been. Zoe felt self-conscious of the weight that she'd put on, the change in the shape of her face and her arms. Albert had grown a beard and it was sprigged with gray.

"Thanks for coming to pick me up," Zoe said. When she inhaled sharply, she could feel the spots where her ribs had cracked. Her body seemed to be knitted together so precariously. In the rearview mirror, she checked Natalie's face. Everything healed.

It would be different this time. She would let the people

that she'd loved move on. She wouldn't arrange any other hotel rendezvous with Julian; she wouldn't call Brigid with anecdotes and promises. They deserved to eat spaghetti with someone who loved them in the right way. They deserved someone who'd care for their plants.

I swear I won't contact you, she thought, picturing Morgan's face. She drew an outline of a flamingo on the inside of her wrist with her fingernail. She tracked two dates in her phone: her sober-versary and the last time she'd contacted Morgan.

Albert had a plan. The plan was: Zoe would return to the family apartment on the Upper West Side. Katherine's sister's design firm needed an assistant. Besides avoiding herself, this had been all that Zoe was good at. She'd practically run the interior design firm in Lisbon for years. Even drunk, she knew what textures and colors worked together, draping ceilings with baroque wallpaper and layering tasseled area rugs. Now she would be back to coffee runs. Zoe huffed, every gulp of air like trying to break an ice cube with a bendy straw. *God grant me the serenity*, she thought.

She did not drink on the train, though it was so fucking easy to drink on the train that it shocked her when people didn't take advantage of it. She was not drinking on this, day one of her new job. Her hair was recently dyed many gradients of spritzy blond. Heels made the outfit: burgundy leather, three inches and change.

The building was in the grim part of Soho where every stump was occupied by a homeless person, but all the brick still looked majestic. It was a shared workspace with a number of start-ups; most people in the elevators wore amorphous black clothes and oversized glasses.

Zoe's supervisor, Ophelia, introduced herself. "I put everything you need to do in that folder. Can I get you anything from the kitchen? Coffee? Beer?"

Zoe rubbed her tongue against the roof of her mouth. "No thanks," she said.

For the first few days, Zoe worked out of her folder, fumbling through Google Docs. Zoe refused to enter the kitchen. No need to hydrate. No need to eat anything that needed refrigeration. Her hunger tickled. She brought in a pile of kiwis and ate them one after the other. It was 10:36, it was 2:14, it was 4:32. It was time to go home.

Sometimes she would try to speak to Ophelia—questions about file folders, protocol, the weather—and be met with stony, impossible silence. Fine, Zoe thought; she didn't need friends. Tuesday was almost Wednesday was almost Friday.

The next week, Ophelia switched desks so that her chair was almost touching Zoe's chair; if either of them rolled an inch out of their usual trajectory, they would collide. Zoe watched the shadows of Ophelia in her desktop screen. If she could just catalogue every single motion of Ophelia's—every word she said, every rectangle of her gum chewed—then Zoe could erase herself altogether.

"Why don't you eat lunch?" Ophelia asked her later that week. She didn't take her eyes from her Excel sheet. Zoe wasn't sure whether she should pivot.

With her eyes down, Zoe said, "I'm more of a grazer."

She could always, always hear the keg in the kitchen. That slight sigh of carbonation.

"You should come out with us Friday after work," Ophelia said.

"It'll be fun. Just me, my friend Sylvie, her roommate Casey, and some girl Casey's dating who thinks she's the next Bob Dylan."

"I can't Friday," Zoe said, after a long pause turned her body to cement. She would drink. She had to say no. She had to.

"A rain check, then," Ophelia said kindly. Zoe preferred her tone when she was curt, professional. This dulcet voice sounded like a stranger who might bring her a gift basket. All she wanted was to have someone push her against a wall and kiss her until her lips went numb.

Ophelia invited her to play shuffleboard and Zoe said okay, despite herself. She took a cab to Brooklyn, where the garages wore their graffiti tags proudly. Outside the cab window, smells wafted from the Gowanus Canal and industrial buildings still labeled with their original uses poked into the sky. *Coffin Factory*, one such building boasted in thick red letters. Everyone seemed to be wearing wide-legged pants and gold hoops. Zoe walked into the shuffleboard court, her nails gleaming poppy red. Inside, people carried fries in checkered paper cups. Ophelia waved Zoe over to the court with a boozy smile. "You came!" she said, clenching Zoe into a hug.

Zoe ordered an iced tea. She waited for something horrible to happen.

"So, how exactly does one shuffle on this board?" Zoe asked, and Ophelia laughed a little too hard.

"Let me show you," Ophelia said, letting her hand brush Zoe's.

It was a split second. It was nothing to report, but it was also the beginning. Zoe knew the beginning.

What was Brigid doing right now? She probably had a new, beautiful girlfriend who cooked risotto and didn't have any issues.

Zoe swallowed. She let Ophelia stand behind her and push her arms like a doll's.

"Place the puck as far down the board as you can," Ophelia said, a murmur. "And ideally you want to use both hands. Okay?"

If you're going to do this, at least enjoy it, Zoe thought. She could see it all laid out in front of her: the tap of Ophelia's fingers on her elbow. The moment when the eye contact went on for too long. The rush: the adrenaline of being unable to wait one more second to discover every place on the other's body. She wiggled her fingers underneath Ophelia's grasp. Ophelia smelled like raspberry and gin. Zoe took a long inhale of that smell.

It started the way it always did: with a promise. *Just this one. You've been doing so well, you can have just this one.* Gin buzzed in her throat. Giddiness made her light-headed at first; then it settled right back into the space in her body where it used to live. *Why did I ever think this was a problem?* the other part of her brain said. *What are you going to do now? What next?*

Here's what was next: another.

A different kind of promise. *I'll get another drink and it will be quiet. I can erase it and just be.*

Zoe said, "Maybe we should get out of here." Ophelia walked fast, talking about a time when she'd had her aura read by an old Polish woman, and Zoe was already thinking about how far gone she was, about to return to the cave where the whole world was dark but for now she fizzed and fumbled and firecracked.

"I want to know everything about you," Zoe said, so she wouldn't have to think anymore. "I want to know what color your aura was."

"Pink," she said. Then Ophelia pulled her by the wrist against the brick wall of a Connecticut Muffin. Zoe pressed her hand tight on the back of Ophelia's neck. She had a great neck. "I've wanted to do that for a long time," Zoe heard herself say.

First zipper unzipped, first shirt untucked. First egg scrambled. First login from a new network. First glass of wine, red. First sharing of childhood trauma. First kiss in the office bathroom. First bottle of wine, hidden—red. First spontaneous singalong. First excuse made about seeming distracted, far away. First time they laughed until they cried. First time they fought until they cried. First time not touching before sleep. First time Zoe skipped work but Ophelia went in without her. First time Zoe left without saying goodbye. First time Ophelia didn't look up from texting when Zoe came into the room. First time they fucked without looking at each other. First time they ate dinner in silence. First time Ophelia found the bottles hidden underneath the cabinet. First time she told Zoe to get out, please. First time she told Zoe that she hoped they could remain professional at work and Zoe told her to go to hell, she didn't need this job, or any job, or anyone.

And that night, she heard from Brigid. *I'll be in New York next week*, she emailed. *I would like to see you, if you are sober. Would you like to see each other? x*

20.

Brigid's sister Gabriella, her favorite, emailed the family: her work would be honored at a gala in New York. Gabriella, the youngest of the four sisters, had recently shifted her identity from *the sister who works in fashion* to *the sister with three divorces underneath her belt before forty*, and Brigid could feel her insecurity peppered throughout the message. *I quite hope some of you will be able to make it?* she'd written; none of Gabriella's usual flair. It was Gabriella who'd coordinated little Christmas plays for the family at the country house as a girl, everyone done up with plastic-bag hats and clownish rouged cheeks.

Beatrice and Isobel were obsessed with their adolescent children's woodwind recitals and football matches; her parents were hopeless about transcontinental flights. All Gabriella's life, she'd loved attention, and Brigid could picture the empty semicircle of chairs around the guest of honor's table. But: New York. *New York.* She'd never planned to return after Zoe left. She preferred to think of Zoe dissolving into the atmosphere like a greenhouse gas. Brigid knew she would spend the entire trip searching for her, scanning the body language and gait of every blond woman in nice shoes.

Then again, Brigid thought, stirring a glob of honey into her chamomile tea, maybe this timing was... She hesitated, even in her own thoughts, to use the phrase *meant to be*. All these years, nearly sixteen of them, she and Julian had never met in real life. Their friendship always came mediated through a screen or sheets of creased paper. She had pondered suggesting a trip to meet him—and, moreover, the possibility of meeting Morgan—but she wondered if it might seem too eager, and showy about how little financial constraints factored into her life. Before, she'd visited New York with Zoe, which meant meeting was out of the question. Maybe seeing Julian would make this breakup different. Final.

Brigid clanked her spoon around her porcelain cup. She allowed herself, just for a moment, to picture Morgan receiving her warmly: *I've heard so much about you*, they might say, and reach their lanky arms around Brigid's body in a hug. *I remember when you were so small*, Brigid would think, although what she remembered was a series of photos as attachments; what she remembered was Julian recounting how long Morgan could spend with their hands pressed against the glass of the back window, trying to see the neighbors' black cat with its glowing yellow eyes luxuriating on the roof of their shed. She remembered how Julian described Morgan's halting, staccato attempts at ice skating with Cheryl, how they would never let go of the edge of the rink. She thought of the three of them, together. Maybe she could have that now, if only for a few hours.

Can't wait to be there for you xx, Brigid replied.

* * *

The weeks trickled by, and each day Brigid felt a fist at the base of her throat starting to tighten. Could she really go to New York and *not* see Zoe? Was she capable of it? Brigid started to wake up in the middle of the night, in her silent apartment, imagining Zoe slumped in an orange seat on the subway. That bit of vomit on her cheek. That time she'd tripped over the sidewalk and nearly broken her wrist. That time she'd burned the skin on her forearm trying to make bacon, the skin bubbling furiously while Zoe flipped each curly slice in its pool of grease. *I just need to see that she's okay*, Brigid convinced herself.

But there was another part of her, the part that remembered Zoe's cartoonish expression when she was pretending to be shocked by salacious behavior that always made Brigid laugh. How good she was with Brigid's family, undeterred by their complex webs and stuffy traditions. When Zoe wasn't drinking too much, she seemed to emanate a comfort and ease that wrapped around everyone like a warm blanket. She missed Zoe's laugh. She missed dancing with Zoe, even though they always danced in place. Never moving forward or back.

I just need to make sure she's okay, Brigid thought again, and opened a new window. *Dear Zoe*, she typed.

At the coffee shop in New York, Brigid was too queasy with nerves to take a sip of her drink. She watched the flurry of motions that accompanied Zoe's entrance—jacket off, swerving to drape the scarf across the back of her wooden chair. "Did you get the macadamia milk?" Zoe said cheerfully. She skipped right past hello.

"It's nice," Brigid confirmed, though Zoe should've known that she hadn't been able to try it yet with her nerves. She'd been here for an hour; the latte would be practically undrinkable. *Better to be alone than with the wrong person. Remember what it felt like to find her hiding vodka in the olive oil you didn't like. Remember what it felt like to get phone calls in the middle of the night and wonder whether she'd died.*

"If I get a black and white cookie," Zoe said, leaning over the table so that her hair nearly brushed Brigid's latte, "will you share it with me? For old times' sake."

With her skin dewy and a glossy berry lipstick over her lips, Zoe looked radiant. Could she look radiant if she were still drinking the way that she had been? Maybe she'd taken it seriously this time, Brigid thought. Maybe she'd stopped, after the thing with the zoo. Maybe seeing a teenaged Morgan gave her sobriety a weight, a purpose, that Brigid never could.

"Fine," Brigid agreed.

"I'll get you a new drink," Zoe said, already standing. "That looks...lukewarm?"

Brigid watched Zoe stand in line, the way that she tilted her chin upward just slightly. Just enough to make you feel like, perhaps, she saw something beautiful in the world that you didn't. There was a dour, twisting voice in her head, probably her mother, that said: *You're too old to let someone else make you feel this way.*

She watched Zoe sprinkle cinnamon over her latte and it made her ache.

Would she remember that if she were still drinking? Brigid thought. *Would she?*

Zoe returned with two cups frothing with macadamia milk and a black and white cookie. "I know what you're thinking," Zoe said breezily, "and I have kept up my side of your deal. Honestly, I'm *exemplary* these days."

"That's wonderful to hear."

"Being sober is incredibly boring. Do you like your coffee?" Zoe asked.

Brigid put her coffee down. "It's lovely. I'm very glad to hear that you're doing so well."

Zoe crimped her lips together. "So, how's Julian? How's Morgan?"

Brigid could feel Zoe squelching the intensity of the question by making her smile as wide and toothy as possible. She looked off-kilter.

"I think things have calmed down a bit."

"Well," Zoe said. "I've kept my distance, you know. You do what you can for the people you care about."

Since when? Brigid thought, and then was ashamed. She touched Zoe's hand.

"On my way here," Zoe said, staring at the hand, "I saw some of your serums in a boutique. The orchid-jasmine one? I remember when you were first working on it. It's so strange to walk past a store and see it there."

"It's one of our best sellers now," Brigid said. She was staring at their hands, too. The longer they kept their hands sandwiched together, the longer that it seemed impossible to move them. "Some Australian pop star said it was an 'invaluable resource' in her skincare routine."

Zoe slid her hand out of their hand-pile for another opportunity to break a piece of the cookie. "I brought you something," she said abruptly, pawing into her purse. It was a small envelope, wrapped in mint-green paper. *Please don't let this be an engagement ring,* she thought.

It was a package of seeds. "I know I ruined your garden," Zoe said softly. "I'm sure you've probably replanted everything, but . . . the man who sold them to me said high humidity, low light would be best. I wrote it down on the back."

Brigid clenched her toes tight against the bottoms of her shoes. "Thank you," she said. "I'll have my half of the cookie now, please," she said, and held out her hand.

In the washroom, Brigid splashed water on her face. No one proposes with an envelope; she knew. And it wasn't what she wanted; at least, that's what she thought right up until the moment that she opened it. *I don't even want to get back together*, Brigid thought. *I don't even know what I want.* Though it might have meant something to her if Zoe knew, at least, what she wanted and that wanting to be with Brigid was permanent. *When you turn this tap off*, Brigid thought, *you will have pulled yourself together.*

A gentle knock. "If you're hiding from me, I'm here to tell you it's not necessary," Zoe said.

Brigid turned off the tap. "I'm not hiding from you," she said. "Just washing up."

"I know all your moves, Bridge," Zoe said. Which was true.

Zoe asked whether she wanted to go to Riverside Park. As they walked, Brigid filled Zoe in on Gabriella's divorce. "I'm surprised that human saltine lasted as long as he did," Zoe said, and soon they were both laughing, imagining Tom with saltines in his blazer pocket. "Salt only, please," Zoe imitated, a perfect deadpan of that bland, showboat tone. "And the way he'd lean all the way back. Like he couldn't bear to *sit up*."

"He'd scoot forward so Gabriella would fluff his pillow," Brigid said. "His *tailbone pillow.*"

"And *they* couldn't make it work?"

"Apparently not." Brigid stepped on a crispy brown leaf and felt it crunch underfoot. "Have you been seeing anyone?" she found herself asking.

"No," she said. "They say you shouldn't date anyone for a year."

"I know," Brigid said. *We've been through this before*, she didn't say. *I know what you sound like when you lie*, she didn't say.

"What about you?" Zoe said. "Anyone special?"

Brigid could feel Zoe's eyes on her, but she kept her gaze straight ahead. "Plenty of not special, I'd say," she answered, and Zoe laughed. "So many nice, boring people who've stared into my eyes with their unfettered hopes and soft sweaters. A bounty of shared fruit plates."

"I miss Lisbon," Zoe said. "Maybe I'll come back, in a bit."

"Where will you stay?" she asked, trying to swallow.

Zoe paused. "Bridge," she said, her voice dipping low. "Come on."

Fuck, Brigid thought, but what was she expecting? Couples huddled together on the park benches, overlooking the river. She felt the old energy between them, fizzing.

"You know we're meant to be together," Zoe said, low. "It seems silly to circle it, like this."

"I'm not circling," Brigid said. "What about waiting a year? What about your *recovery*?" She hadn't meant to say it in that tone, closer to mocking than questioning.

Zoe's expression shifted. "This wouldn't be like starting something new. It would be . . . coming home."

Brigid shook her head. "I'm not your home."

"Then what are you doing here?" Zoe said, her voice bleary. "Why did you agree to meet me? I did every fucking thing you asked."

"It's not a *checklist*. I want you to do it for *you*." Her body always knew when a fight was getting too serious to brush away, when it would stay lodged in her brain weeks later. She glanced at the sunset, twinkling along the choppy texture of gray water. "You need to be clean," Brigid said. "Permanently."

"What if that never happens?" Zoe asked.

Brigid paused. "I don't know."

"You never know what you want," Zoe said. "That's your problem, Bridge."

"Is it?" she asked. "Funny, I didn't think we were discussing *my* issues."

"That's why you never had a baby," Zoe said, as nonchalantly as if they were discussing double coupon day. "And you've watched your sisters get pregnant and living the life you wished for and then pretended like it's never even crossed your mind. You know, you barely pay attention to yourself. That's why you can't commit to anything. You don't trust your own intuition."

"I'll trust my intuition now, then. Goodbye. This was a mistake." She turned to leave and Zoe followed close behind, her voice frenetic.

"That's why you're friends with Julian," Zoe said. "That's why you're so obsessed with protecting Morgan. You wish you had the life that I had when I was nineteen. Don't you think that's strange, Bridge? A little pathetic? You look down on *me* like I'm the only one who's a mess. But you hide behind your business, your hobbies, your perfect clothes, as if it's a full life."

"You know how to hurt me," Brigid said. "I get it. Mission accomplished." She walked away faster. Then she said over her shoulder, "If you want to self-destruct, that is fine. I will not stop you."

* * *

Too indecisive to even commit to my own child, Brigid thought. Couldn't it be a bit right? Couldn't she have started trying earlier, instead of staring at the names of sperm banks online and spending a decade gathering the courage to go? Couldn't she have been more proactive with doctors, waded into other options like IVF? And then: Morgan. The family that she'd expected, just out of reach. She treasured Julian's divulgences of Morgan's life. And maybe she did, perversely, enjoy the drama that Zoe created, the opportunity to manage the fallout. To be important and helpful.

With every new baby, she'd reassured Beatrice and Isobel: *You're doing a wonderful job.* She wondered whether they heard her saying *I could never do what you do, day in and day out.* Days trembled into months into years. *If I had a baby at forty, that baby would be in kindergarten. If I had a Morgan, that Morgan would be twenty-eight.* She measured time with her hypothetical children at their hypothetical ages. Drinkers of juice. Dunkers of cookies. But there was no one, dunking nothing.

On the night of the gala, Gabriella wore a dress that flared into a mermaid's tail. Brigid let her sister dress her in a purple tuxedo so dark it was almost black; a cross between 1980s glam and a little drummer boy. "Thank you for being here," Gabriella said, nervously applying her lipstick.

"Of course," Brigid said, trying to put Zoe out of mind. They took a car to a venue that had once been a church. Brigid drank a blackberry cocktail in a small glass with an edible flower—the flavor of the night. "So nice to meet you," she said. People gushed about Gabriella's innovation, her altruism and vision. A mirthful, bedazzled evening.

Brigid nodded along but found herself drifting. "Don't you look dashing," a journalist admired Brigid. Pass the bread and butter. Yes, it is awfully loud in here. "I've lived all over," Brigid said to the inoffensive couple to her right. "Cooked just right," Brigid said to the inoffensive couple to her left.

"Can you grab me another cocktail?" Gabriella asked. "Before."

"Of course," Brigid said. At the bar, there was a melodious laugh that echoed, and two figures standing by the row of empty stools. One of them, slightly taller, in thick, red suede heels; the other leaned over the counter. "We'll have the cocktail of the evening," the voice announced, and Brigid craned her whole, panic-ridden body to see who the other figure was. Then she bolted back to her chair.

She didn't need to see.

She needed to leave, but it was time for Gabriella to go up to the stage. Triumphantly Gabriella held a glass award plaque up, her earrings gleaming under the spotlight. Brigid hoped Gabriella's acceptance speech would never end. Applause spread, diffuse as mist, and fleeted.

It was such a typical Zoe move; if Brigid had been thinking more clearly, she might have predicted it. She'd been obsessing about Zoe nonstop since their coffee, but now that she was near, Brigid wanted to dissolve. She wanted to be a magician's assistant. Or maybe the rabbit, lurking in the ether before emerging out of a transcendent black hat.

Gabriella returned to her seat. Brigid whispered into her ear. "Zoe's here."

Gabriella took a sip of her wine. "Of course she is. Zoe made it, but barely any of my own family." She glanced at Brigid's face and cleared her throat. "Sorry. Would you like to . . . escape gracefully?"

Yes. My God, yes.

"No, that's all right. I'm here for you. I'll go get that blackberry elixir. Chat with all of these well-dressed people. They're here for you, too."

Gabriella pinched a grateful smile. "Thanks, B."

She was just here, Brigid thought. She thought of probabilities, a single dice rolled across a blackjack table. What would Zoe have wanted? Just to remind Brigid that she could appear whenever she pleased? The bar was empty, save for a few bird-boned women with coiffed hair. Brigid ordered two drinks and crumpled a napkin into an angry ball. She could be poised. She could feel nothing but the smooth generosity of a supportive sister.

"Look who the cat dragged into the event space," Zoe said cheerfully behind her, swinging an arm around her young companion. They were wearing one of Gabriella's designs that she'd gifted to Zoe; black, beaded overalls with luxe orange stitching. A curtain of brown hair obscured their face.

"Two drinks?" Zoe observed. "Tough night, Bridge?"

"One's for Gabriella," Brigid said. *Cool as a fucking cucumber,* she thought. "Won't you introduce me to your date, Zoe?"

"This is my cousin," Zoe said. "Um…Rolf." Zoe laughed, a noise that Brigid felt dislodge something deep in her chest. She took one of the drinks out of Brigid's hand and smiled.

A chill spread across Brigid's body. She knew that she needed to sound gentle, approachable. This was the moment.

"Morgan?" Brigid said.

21.

Three months after Dad found out about the zoo and Mom scuttled off without a goodbye, Morgan found themself standing in front of Zoe's building. Not doing anything weird, they promised themself; just seeing what would happen. It wasn't as though they'd pretended to be sick to get out of their shift at the library and taken the subway down to the Upper West Side and stood across the street to monitor Zoe's building. Not anything weird like that.

Morgan had been having nightmares. They lay in bed, night after interminable night, deciding whether to brave a sleep aid or just let the minutes thickly drag by. Sometimes they'd tweet from Sadie's account and read the comments, let the sweetness of those ASMR devotees worshipping her voice trickle in, as if it were for them, too. Peter was always one of the first to reply.

Dad had started late-night cleaning. First it was the night after the fight, and Morgan could hear the clamoring efforts of his scrubbing the grout with a toothbrush. Morgan knew it was their fault that he couldn't sleep, either. Their insomnias ran parallel, Morgan lying in bed with their knees up, trying to think of something serene, a green field full of docile sheep, while Dad scrubbed every speck of dirt away from those stubborn tiles.

In the mornings, they sat side by side, pretending things were normal. Biting into toast. Rinsing plates in the sink. Wishing each other good days.

BraidsASMR: I had the weirdest dream last night

BicycleThief 2293: What happened in it?

BraidsASMR: I was dressed like this Italian heiress, in one of those Renaissance-era gowns with the big skirts. I was holding this leafy branch in my hand and trying to hide behind it. I was super sure that no one would recognize me if I ducked behind the branch

BraidsASMR: But then my mom was there, and we were dressed in the same outfit, and she came up to me and said: "no one will ever find me but you." And then she plucked one of the leaves off the branch and told me to hold it under my tongue until it dissolved, but it kept growing until it took over my whole head

BicycleThief 2293: Man. Can I use that in a movie? That's symbolic as hell

BraidsASMR: What do you think it means?

BicycleThief 2293: Um, that you're afraid of becoming your mom and it'll kill you?

BicycleThief 2293: You can trust me. I took Psych 101 last year. ;-)

BraidsASMR: Nice winky face at my deepest fears of decline & mortality!!!

BicycleThief 2293: Those are the only things to wink at in this life.

BraidsASMR: I keep thinking... that I need to see her

BraidsASMR: That we left things unfinished last time and that's why I keep having these weird dreams

BicycleThief 2293: After the zoo, you mean?

BraidsASMR: Yeah. Do you think that dreams mean anything? Like your subconscious can be dropping hints?

BicycleThief 2293: I'll tell you what I think.

BicycleThief 2293: In my screenwriting class we talk a lot about inciting action. Like, the first thing that happens to send the hero on their quest. There are no stories that build on somebody doing nothing. Inaction is the opposite of a story. What kind of movie would you want your life to be?

BicycleThief 2293: Besides, if it gets weird, I'm here if you need me.

BicycleThief 2293: What's the worst that could happen?

Peter was right; nothing came from nothing. They signed out of school early, leaving their bike locked up in the lot, and slipped onto the subway. They got off at 72nd Street and sat in a cluster of benches next to a waffle truck. Sunshine warmed their neck; children on scooters narrowly avoided running over Morgan's ankles. *You can still leave,* Morgan thought, their anxiety squeezing into a fist. *Wasted $5.50 and a few hours. Home before dark. No one has to know that you followed this impulse all the way to the Upper West Side.* They stood, desperately needing to pee before returning home. Inside the large grocery store, they flitted upstairs to the restroom. After, they stopped to admire the selection of imported jams: quince, passionfruit, mango.

"Morgan?" Mom asked.

They took in her appearance—her skin splotched with red, and her eyes looked a little bloodshot, though her hair looked freshly dyed. Maybe she has trouble sleeping, too, Morgan thought. Mom laughed nervously, hugged Morgan tight. She was wearing cashmere sweatpants, and she smelled sharp. A new perfume,

Morgan thought; it reminded them of something they couldn't quite place. Or maybe they could place it, and they just didn't want to be right.

She started to talk quickly: it was so funny to run into each other, and it was such a beautiful day, she'd just stopped in for some olives, no one could attend a gala on an empty stomach.

Don't you want to know why I'm here? Morgan thought. But she didn't.

"Do you want to come? Oh, this is going to be perfect, Morg. I can dress you up! Those eyelashes." She clenched their shoulders for a second. "Morgan, I'm so sorry I...I missed you. Your dad told me to stay away, but I...I missed you so much. Please believe me. Do you believe me?"

She must think I'm so gullible, Morgan thought, but when they saw her wavering smile, they said: "I believe you. I missed you, too." And of course they would go with her to the gala. They would go with her to anything. They'd always wanted to get dressed up, to slip into a Marie Antoinette fantasy. *Dad's going to kill me*, they thought, but if they called it a sleepover with somebody, wouldn't it be fine? They pictured the dress of their dream, the long, floral silk sleeves. Twirling on a pedestal like a tiny ballerina in a music box.

"Follow me," Mom said, grabbing a wheel of Brie. "This is going to be so much fun, Morg," she said, flashing her teeth.

Mom walked three or four paces ahead of Morgan and they wondered if it was because she regretted inviting them over. They remembered how boring they'd felt at the zoo, asking whether she liked cold weather. Was it Dad's word that had kept her away, or was it Morgan's far from ravishing personality? This was going to be a big risk, Morgan thought queasily, and how could they know it would be worth denting Dad's trust yet again?

Nothing comes from nothing, Morgan thought. Isn't this what Peter meant?

Their phone was off. The GPS tracker knew nothing.

"Follow me, Morg. I take the elevator now," she said, pressing the button hard until it lit up orange. "After I fell down the stairs recently and cracked some ribs."

"After you what?" *So that's where you've been*, they thought, wanting to cry. They made themself cough to counteract their watery eyes.

"Oh, don't worry about me. It'll take a lot more than a staircase to slow me down."

Morgan swallowed. "I do," they said softly. "Worry about you."

"I'm so glad you came to see me," she said, pressing the button again. She didn't look at Morgan.

"Are your ribs okay?"

"They're healing up," she said, looking at them at last. They knew from the way she made eye contact that she was also talking about something else. Maybe she was fine now, Morgan thought, searching into her eyes for something tangible. She wasn't drinking beers at the zoo anymore; she'd made it to the other side, and now things were going to be different. Then the elevator doors opened, and Morgan followed her inside.

Mom bounded into the apartment while Morgan hung back, unsure whether to take off their shoes. "Sit, sit!" she said. Gingerly Morgan carried their backpack and shoes inside. Besides the mess, it was an almost painfully beautiful apartment. They gazed at the exposed brick, the fireplace mantel crowded with novels.

Light suffused the room. Tall French doors reminded Morgan of their favorite shot in *Marie Antoinette*, and they imagined filming something meaty and dramatic in here, something cutting and claustrophobic.

"Let's put some music on," she said. "Do you know Mitski? I love Mitski."

"I love Mitski, too," Morgan said.

"You do?" Mom sounded awed. Speakers perked up with the first organ notes before Mitski sang: *You're my number one, you're the one I want.* The music was louder than Morgan would've listened to it. She unloaded the Brie and olives from the grocery bag. "I don't know where the plates are," she said apologetically. "But I definitely have a knife."

They cupped their hands underneath a wedge of Brie and tried to be dignified.

"This one's my favorite," Morgan said when "A Pearl" started. They closed their eyes to hear Mitski's voice, clear and solemn: *You're growing tired of me / and all the things I don't talk about.* Mom started to sing along, too, her voice carrying. *There's a hole that you fill, you fill, you fill.*

They knew that they would never be able to listen to this song again without evoking this night, whatever this night was going to be.

Mom came out with her hands full of makeup tubes. "Go pick out something to wear," she said, "and then I'm going to do a makeover. It's going to be tremendous. Are you ready to be tremendous?"

"I can't just *wear* . . . your clothes. People will . . . *notice.*"

"We can go shopping if you want," she said. "Just look in there first. You must be starved for clothes with that dopey uniform."

Dopey reverberated through Morgan. They wormed through the bedroom to see that it wasn't a bathroom but a walk-in closet. Inside held more clothes than Morgan had ever owned. Every item looked special: sumptuous silks in marigold yellow or midnight blue, plush velvets and vintage furs.

They ran their fingers across the cloth. Didn't they deserve this? To feel beautiful, and expensive, for one night? In an alternate reality, this could've been Morgan's life—their own walk-in closet of silken fabrics and heels in every color of the rainbow. Morgan touched the sleeve of the fur that they'd worn at the zoo and imagined showing up at Sadie's doorstep, looking old Hollywood. *Come with me*, they imagined saying to Sadie, before whisking her off to somewhere impressive and elegant. *I didn't know you could look so good*, she'd say, admiring them from head to toe.

They just had to reach out and pick something from the closet. They could be anyone, Morgan tried to convince themself, but they were a million decisions away from being able to wear a dress outside. They were a million small steps away from being a person who didn't spend every day trying to hide in plain sight.

"What's going on in there?" Mom called.

"I'm just...trying to scrounge up some courage. Or...self-esteem."

She walked to Morgan. They felt their body tense at the presence of another person. *It's just Mom, it's just Mom*, they repeated inside, but their fight-or-flight had been cranked up so high they could hardly think.

"I know something that'll help with that," she said.

❦

"It'll take the edge off," Mom said, handing them a small white pill as she started pulling out makeup palettes. And she was right. With the pill came complete erasure of self-consciousness. By the time they arrived at the event, Morgan was unconstrained. Morgan, in Mom's red heels, in the sleek fabric of designer overalls, makeup swept just right over their cheekbones, danced. Morgan danced and even though they saw all the small, distant faces of people who seemed greatly at ease—in their conversations, in their calla-lilies-and-mini-crab-caked world, in their gender presentations—it didn't touch them.

Mom looked beautiful, in a yellow dress arrayed with voluptuous pink flowers; she looked like the only person you would notice in any room. Morgan thought of Sadie; of how she would think Morgan looked. Matching lipstick on their face and Mom's. Maybe one day Morgan could take her to something like this—another luminous party for Morgan to look the way they wanted to look always. Maybe they could all dance together. Their limbs felt loose, gliding. "Let's go dancing after this," Mom said, and Morgan expected to feel the old jolt of anxiety above their sternum. There was Dad to consider, and how hurt he would be; and Sadie, who would hate this story and think Morgan spineless and short-sighted.

But all of that felt far away now; Morgan's happiness was impenetrable. And they allowed themself to imagine a new kind of life. One where they had a mom who took them places, and beamed at them in wonder. A mom who wanted to make plans with Morgan and keep them.

22.

Z oe, is this— Are you joking?" Brigid reached toward Morgan, who flinched. "Are you drunk?"

"You've heard of Brigid, haven't you, Morg?" Zoe asked. "She's a notorious buzzkill. Bridge, we are having *so much fun* tonight."

"We're having so much fun tonight," Morgan repeated meekly.

"Does your dad know where you are?" Brigid asked. A scroll of Julian's frenzied emails filled her brain. How deeply he worried about Morgan's every move. Then she remembered what Zoe had said, about Brigid being desperate to usurp Zoe's nineteen-year-old life, and it made her stomach twist into her throat all over again.

Morgan lifted their hair away from their face. Now that she knew, Brigid could see they were so *young*. "Not . . . exactly. Are you going to tell him?"

"I am," Brigid said. "And I'm taking you home right now."

"I don't even know you," Morgan said. "Why should I go with—"

"We're all going," Brigid said. "Right now. Come on, Zoe."

* * *

She'd thought about meeting Morgan so many times, but never like this, Zoe sprawled across the back seat smelling absolutely pickled, Morgan so shivery that their body seemed to be condensing into a smaller form. Brigid yanked on her suit jacket to remind herself that she was the one in control. "It'll be three stops, please," she said, reciting Zoe's mother's address. From the center seat, Morgan stared at her blankly.

"What are you going to tell my dad?" Morgan slurred. "Because I've already disappointed him a lot this year and I don't know that either of us can take any more. It's like...I can't seem to get back in...line with who he thought I was or something. And now I do things even though I know it'll hurt him. Like this."

"Explain to me how this situation arose," Brigid said to Zoe.

"I left to get olives," Zoe said, "and Morg was standing right there, by the jams, looking totally lost in the world. So, naturally I brought them to the event. I wasn't going to banish them! Would you have asked me to banish them?" Zoe reached into Morgan's hair with a long, drowsy hand.

"I was doing really well," Zoe said. "Before we had that awful fight." Her mood was leaden, dour, and she met Brigid's gaze. "I don't know how it happened. It felt so...inevitable, I guess. Like the floodgates had burst."

"It wasn't inevitable," Brigid said coolly. "You did it. You made it happen."

"Don't you think I want a different life?" Zoe asked raspily. "Don't you think I want to escape this...compulsion just circling and circling in my head? Don't you think I want to be able to hang out with my only child without being forcibly removed and have them sent home?" She bit her lip. "Unsupervised," Zoe said, though she seemed to be talking to herself now.

"It's okay, Mom," Morgan said, clamping her shoulder with tenderness, or maybe fear. "Why are you talking like that to her?" they asked, leaning past Zoe to look Brigid in the face. "Why are you so . . . closed off?"

Brigid stared into her lap. Only a few more blocks until they reached Zoe's apartment, and it would be over. She didn't want to say *You're so naive, you have no idea.* She didn't want Morgan to hate her, but she also didn't want them to feel the truth of what she and Zoe had been through together.

"I don't know how to answer that," Brigid said, curt. "I . . . I'm sorry if it comes across as cold to either of you. I know you struggle, Zoe. I do."

Zoe looked at Brigid then. "I'd give everything up to be like you," she said. "I really would."

Traffic turtled along miserably all along Broadway. No one said anything. Eventually Zoe reached across Morgan's lap to touch Brigid's hand. "I'm sorry," she said. "I know I haven't said that enough."

"You've said it plenty," Brigid muttered. "It doesn't change anything."

"Right side or left side?" the cabdriver asked.

"I ruined it," Zoe said. "Didn't I? This whole thing, it was supposed to be . . . romantic. It was supposed to be that moment when our eyes locked across the room."

Morgan cringed. "But I ruined it," they said. "It was supposed to be romantic, but I invited myself along. That's what you mean."

"Left," Zoe said in response to the driver. "By the flower bed. Thanks."

"Of course not," Brigid said to Morgan. She didn't sound reassuring. She cleared her throat to try again. "It was never going to be like that. Nothing you could've done would change our situation. For fuck's sake," she said, pulling Zoe's hand out of her purse as she rummaged for her credit card. "I'll pay for it. Just go."

"You found me," Zoe said to Morgan as she struggled with the fabric of her dress against the back seat. "If it comes up with your dad, you have to tell him. I stayed away just like I was supposed to."

"Okay," Morgan said, deflated. "I'll tell him."

Zoe reached to touch Morgan's cheek. "Makeup looks great on you," she said, and closed the car door.

❧

In the cab, Brigid thought of herself, sitting on the edge of the bathtub while Zoe was God knows where, examining the photos of Morgan that Julian sent every year for Christmas. Morgan in a crayon-red turtleneck, playing with a wooden train set. How dutifully she'd watched them grow up from across the ocean.

Now it was happening, and everything was wrong.

After dropping Zoe off, Morgan's leg quaked against the seat. "I feel really weird to be like, in this cab, going home with somebody who just dumped my mom. Why would you care about what happens to me if you don't care about what happens to her?"

"I care about what happens to her," she said. She reminded herself, they had no idea how hard she'd tried to make it work with Zoe. "You must know it's not appropriate to take you to an event and let you drink cocktails until your skin turns green. She should be taking care of you."

"You never broke any rules when you were seventeen?"

"Of course I did. But I didn't follow anyone with a substance abuse problem when they were going on a bender, either."

"We were fine before she saw you."

"Morgan," Brigid said. "That's just not true at all."

She felt the difference immediately. It surged like an electric storm.

"Don't tell me what's true," Morgan hissed. "You're a stranger."

Brigid didn't say anything for a long time. They left the city; streetlamps few and far between burned pinpricks of light. She looked over at Morgan, pressed so far away from Brigid that their body practically became part of the window. The cab slowed toward their exit off the parkway and Brigid felt the echo of Morgan's sigh travel.

"What are you going to say to my dad?" Morgan asked quietly.

When the cab pulled up to the house, Brigid paid the driver; then she and Morgan sat in the car, motionless. "We should go inside," Brigid said, though she also wasn't moving. This wasn't how she was supposed to meet Julian either; they were meant to go to the Cloisters tomorrow, admire medieval art and Julian's favorite unicorn tapestry. Everything was off course.

Brigid peered at Julian through the blinds. He wore a pair of headphones that wrapped around his ears, dancing. Morgan said quietly, "He's going to be wrecked about this," and Brigid thought of a wrecking ball, how it flashed through the air before demolition.

"The longer you wait, the worse it gets," she said.

Morgan opened the door. "Fine," they said, the sullen voice of someone who never wanted to see Brigid again. "Thanks for the advice."

* * *

What the two of them didn't see through the blinds was Sadie.

Morgan stood, wavering in the embroidered overalls and Zoe's pristine suede booties, then teetered forward. "Sadie, what—" they said, upon seeing Sadie on the sofa. Her mouth was curved into a thin, clenched line, her body stiff. She looked ready to cannonball into an imaginary pool, knowing that cannonball might kill her.

"I couldn't get in touch with you," she said. "I figured I knew the reason that your phone was turned off. I thought maybe I was being paranoid. Whose *clothes* are those?"

Morgan flushed. "My mom's. I...I mean...we were going to go dancing—"

Sadie shook her head. "I don't want to hear your flimsy excuses. What makes you think I would spend my Tuesday wondering where the fuck you are? God...it's like you're cheating on me or something. This double life. It's simultaneously so stressful and really boring."

Sadie followed Morgan's line of vision to Julian, who was still dancing and piecing his puzzle together with his back to them. "Mr. Flowers," she shouted. "Look who's back."

When Julian saw Morgan, and then Brigid, his demeanor changed instantly. "I'm missing information," Julian said, his gaze darting from Brigid to Morgan and back. Morgan cradled those red suede shoes. "Tell me the information I'm missing," he said, shakily. "Hello, Brigid."

Brigid smiled wanly. "Hello," she said.

"Mom said I couldn't see her because *you* said I couldn't. I didn't mean to..." Morgan looked at Sadie, then back at Julian. "I just found myself...there on her corner."

"Sure, you *found yourself there*," Sadie said.

Morgan plowed ahead. "And I thought, okay, if I see her, then I'll know I was supposed to see her. And I did, and she said . . . that the timing was perfect because she was going to this—"

"The gala," Brigid interjected. "For Gabriella."

"But then things got weird," Morgan said, and Brigid felt nervous watching them try to explain. "And it wasn't supposed to be like . . . I guess Mom didn't really want me there after all; she just wanted to be . . . " Morgan said, starting to cry, long tears dribbling down into their hair. "In the car she said she'd just wanted to see Brigid, and it was supposed to be romantic. I was just a . . . plus-one."

"Morgan," Brigid said. "That's not all you are."

"Yes, it is," Morgan said. "To her, it is. All she said was that I looked nice in makeup and that I had to tell you that it wasn't her fault. So I guess it was mine. I waited for her at the grocery store, I drank whatever she handed me, I was ready to do whatever she wanted."

A long silence followed. Brigid felt so obtrusively mismatched with the house—a pyramid of soup cans in an open cabinet, sharp against her tuxedo. *Jealous of the life that I had when I was nineteen*, she heard Zoe say again. What kind of parent would she have been? Morgan's pitiful expression, the deep shame with which they clutched the shoes—she thought she would feel more sympathy but it annoyed her, actually. *Take responsibility for yourself. You're not a planchette on a Ouija board.*

Julian's face was completely stoic. "Sadie, why don't you go home?" he said. "Is it too late for you to ride your bike?"

Sadie shook her head. "No, I'm good. Thanks."

"Sadie," Morgan said. "Can I—"

She held up a hand. "No. You can't. Thanks for the sandwich, Mr. Flowers."

Sadie clicked the front door shut and the three of them stared at each other.

"We can talk about this tomorrow," Julian said finally. "Take some aspirin and drink a glass of water."

"I should go," Brigid said. "I just wanted to make sure Morgan got home safely." Now she wanted to cry, too. Maybe she hadn't done the right thing. Brigid had given so much time and advice, and for what? For someone who wanted her to disappear into thin air.

Julian said, "Bridge...I'm sorry. I just can't...handle this and...meet you right now. I just don't have it in me."

"It's okay," Brigid said. "Another time."

"Please," Morgan said simply. It was such a tired, beleaguered request. Brigid heard herself in that one word, the culmination of all those long nights with Zoe where they were fighting about nothing and everything. She knew that it was easier to blame her. Morgan could blame Brigid for all of the events of the evening, and then she'd be gone.

"Morgan?" Brigid said. "I...just want you to know..." The voice that had emerged from her was the voice of a younger, crushed Brigid, one that she hadn't heard aloud in many years. She knew the timing was terribly wrong, but there was nothing she could do to turn back now. "I want you to know that if you ever find yourself...you should come stay with me for a bit, in Lisbon. In Portugal," Brigid continued. "Where your mom and I live. Lived."

The change of tense hung among them like a chandelier.

Morgan looked at her. "I'm not going to *find myself* in Europe, like . . . poof."

"All right," she said. "I just wanted to . . ." She dug into her purse for the key and handed it to Julian, the brass keyring like a baton. Julian stared at it.

He handed it back to her. "I don't think . . . we need this," he said.

Her cheeks burned. *But I'm trying to tell you I love you, the both of you. My family. Almost.*

"Well. I'll let you head off to bed, then," Brigid said to Morgan. She wished she were wearing anything but a fucking tuxedo. She watched them leave the room.

"Stay," Julian said quietly. "Please."

Brigid nodded. Upstairs, Morgan was vomiting behind a closed door, the strained retching barely muffled by the tap running. Julian opened the door next to the bathroom and gestured at a twin-sized bed with little floral sheets.

Julian said, "I have to go to bed. My brain feels soupy."

"I'm sorry," Brigid said. "I'm just so sorry, Jul."

It was the guest room where Zoe had slept, those first months after Morgan was born, because she said she could never sleep with those sporadic grunts that emerged from her small squealy baby. In Zoe's bed, Brigid peeled back the comforter and lay down. *So this is where you were*, she thought, picturing the Zoe she'd met all those years ago. Barely nineteen, with her long legs in knitted gray leg warmers and black cutoffs. Brigid could still feel the weight of their first kiss as she fell asleep.

In the morning, she folded the sheets into perfect rectangles in a perfect pile and put the key on top.

23.

The next day, when Zoe woke up in her yellow velvet dress, her pillowcase streaked with mascara and foundation, she thought there would be a flurry of texts. The feeling of knowing she'd made mistakes, but having no recollection of those mistakes, was one with which she was well acquainted. But there was something even eerier about being completely left in the dark—a void of communication from anyone involved. Her dining room table was cluttered with makeup from getting ready with Morgan. The Brie oozed onto the counter, having changed texture to a solidified rubber cement. Everything was silent. She was alone. When she finally gathered enough energy to take a shower, her Spanx had indented a clear line across her belly button, like a surgeon's sharp cut.

24.

Julian listened to the tap running, the splashy water barely concealing the sound of Morgan retching on the other side of the wall. In Julian's bedroom, it was dark, and he couldn't summon the energy to lift up his socks where the top had begun to droop down toward his ankle on the right side.

The sock needed to be adjusted. *But I can't move*, Julian thought, pleadingly, to the mom that lived inside his head now. She would've told him gently: *You can, Jules. Of course you can.* If he could have cried, he would have cried. The blankness filled him like an impossible weight. *If I can't fix my sock*, Julian thought, panic congealing into a fist at the base of his throat, *what can I possibly do about Morgan?*

How many nights had he spent, listening to the water run, wondering whether Mom would want company or privacy. The Internet couldn't definitively tell him the protocol for supporting a parent who was dying of cancer while they vomited every sad scrap of food they'd tried to keep down. In the end, most nights, he would sit in the bathtub, holding her foot so she knew he was right there. He had to apply peppermint oil underneath his nose, which burned the skin a bit. *You don't have to stay*, Mom would say, dabbing her mouth with a handkerchief patterned with little white daisies. But he was already calculating the time they might have left.

If the chemo didn't work, the doctors had said, she had about a year left. If she died in a year, that would be 8,760 hours. If you slept eight hours a night, 2,920 hours of that remaining year would be spent asleep. Only the average amount of sleep a night would probably differ for a cancer patient. Where could he find the average amount of sleep a cancer patient would need? He needed to calculate. He needed data. Mom flexed her foot into his hand sometimes if it started to get really bad but she couldn't talk. Sometimes he fell asleep in the bathtub, waiting for her to feel better, and she'd be the one to wake Morgan up for school and Julian up for work the next day. *Good thing you're already getting ready for your shower*, she'd joke weakly.

The tap turned off. Julian heard Morgan fumble down the hallway.

How had they gotten here? Hadn't Morgan promised this wouldn't happen again? Their phone wasn't on, the GPS dot was gray with its lack of information. Sadie said, *I think I know where they are*, and Julian didn't want to think she could be right even for a minute. Julian was just starting to trust Morgan again, that this was in the past. Maybe Morgan had reconnected with their old friends, he suggested, or they were working on a group project. Sadie looked at Julian like he was so gullible, and maybe he was. *Just pretend I'm not here*, Sadie said, busting out a textbook and a yellow highlighter. So he did. Julian dove right back into his puzzle, turned up the music on his noise-canceling headphones. They really did cancel the noise.

Julian thought how strange it was, to have a third person sleeping in their house that wasn't Mom or Zoe. He imagined a different, alternate world, one where he and Brigid had gotten to meet at the Cloisters tomorrow like they'd planned. He'd been nervous— the worry of what your face looked like, how your voice sounded, whether you were what the other person had constructed as a representation of you.

Julian slowly scavenged the energy to turn on his nightside lamp and get out his phone. He turned on his speech-to-text app and scuttled underneath the covers with only the dim light from his phone screen.

"Brigid," he whispered. "I'm sorry about tonight. It all went wrong. Send text."

We'll try again. It'll be all right.

"What about Morgan? Will Morgan be all right? Send text."

Brigid took some time to reply. *Most teenagers do things like this. I know that doesn't make it easier on you. But Morgan will be all right,* she said. *I think you need some sleep. Tomorrow you'll come up with a plan. I'll help if you want. OK?*

"OK." Julian's hands shook. "Thank you for bringing them back."

Of course. Good night, Jul.

Brigid was right; he needed a new plan.

Julian thought: What if every time Morgan broke the rules, they owed Julian money? A different cost for every infraction. Morgan didn't make enough at the library to stray very far. Everything could have a place on a list. Everything could be planned out and regimented.

Julian started to make a list on his phone. *Drinking to excess*, he typed, his fingers clumsy. *$200*. He started to reel through scenarios he'd seen on sitcoms and it felt like a balm. *Gilmore Girls* had been Zoe's favorite show during high school; she'd joked that she was *pulling a Lorelai* when she found out she was pregnant with Morgan. So, the time Jess destroyed the best snowman so Rory and Lorelai could win? $100, for lying and destruction of property. The time Rory fell asleep in Miss Patty's dance hall and never came home after the dance? $500, for breaking curfew to an extreme. Julian spent an hour outlining different circumstances and felt a light, dizzy peace return to him. They were not going to circle infinitely while Morgan followed the same thorny, miserable path that Zoe pummeled. This was a new plan. This could work.

25.

Morgan had to take the train to school the next day. According to Dad's thorough and terrible new system, Morgan owed $372 for the entire gala incident. After taxes, it was three entire paychecks. So many hours, just to have it all disappear. They wanted to tell Sadie, but they had a woozy memory of her being there last night. They paused, staring at the texts from this morning that Sadie hadn't responded to. Maybe she hadn't checked her phone yet. Or maybe she hated Morgan, and they didn't even remember why.

They thought about how beautiful they'd felt, in luxurious clothes that lay just right somehow. Standardized test scores, FAFSA, the weekly grocery budget—it all disappeared at the gala. Inside, they glittered along with everybody else, holding an identical goblet. Inside, it had been so easy to pretend they belonged.

Down the street from school, there was a pizza place Sadie liked. Morgan stood in front of the door knocking frantically. The guy working inside was a sucker for romance, he told Morgan, after hearing a simplified version of the story. The pizza guy handed Morgan one slice of pepperoni on a white paper plate and wished them good luck.

"Yeah, I'll need it," Morgan said casually, which got a huge laugh. They couldn't afford this pizza. They couldn't afford to lose Sadie, either.

Morgan lurked by Sadie's locker, feeling stupider by the second. It would be cold if she didn't arrive soon. Their thoughts whirlpooled around the moment when Mom said to Brigid how desperately she wanted to be her. Looking at Brigid, her manner so impervious and cold, it made Morgan want to push her out of the car. *This* was the person who'd kept Mom from coming home? What was so great about Brigid? She didn't even stop to consider Morgan, just shepherded everybody out of the gala. Maybe it would've been the best night of their life.

When Sadie finally emerged, Morgan was so lost in thought they didn't see her right away. "Oh hi!" they blurted out, like a child. The look that Sadie shot them further cemented that sticky feeling of realizing something was critically misaligned but not how to move it back into place. Sadie seemed tired, a bluish hue underneath her eyes that Morgan hadn't seen before, and her hair was pulled into a doughnut at the top of her head. She eyed the pizza, then stared at Morgan for a second before she spoke.

"Is this your big gesture to get me to forgive you?" she asked.

"It's the inaugural gesture. Soliciting forgiveness: episode one."

Sadie swiped the plate, barely touching Morgan at all. "It's going to take a lot more than this," she said, taking the first bite. Long strands of cheese followed the bite, and instead of smiling at

Morgan as she tried to slurp the cheese strands into her mouth, she cinched the cheese with a fingernail and piled it atop the slice. Morgan felt this. Morgan knew this was Sadie's way of saying *I'm done now.*

"Can we talk later?" Morgan asked pitifully.

"No," Sadie said. "I'll tell you when."

She moved so easily through space, Morgan thought, watching the light bounce off her bun as she bounded toward the Spanish wing. She made everything look easy. Including giving Morgan up.

Later Morgan would clean the bathroom, beating Dad to it. It was nine, late enough that Morgan had finished the top-tier homework but not late enough to slither into bed with their thoughts circling like a centrifuge. When they looked up from pushing the wet Swiffer across the tiles, Dad was watching them.

"Why are you doing that?"

"I'm helping you," Morgan said.

Dad's eyes looked glassy. "I need to clean. It's what I've been doing to try to calm my nerves before bed. Dr. Gold said this was a good outlet, and I—"

But I was trying to help you, Morgan thought. It was going wrong, which shouldn't have been a fucking surprise at this point.

"I'm sorry," Morgan said finally. "I didn't know."

Dad looked at Morgan then for a long beat. "I can feel this...broiling. Underneath. I can feel that I feel something. It's like...feeling a fire from the other side of a door. Do you understand what I mean?"

Morgan nodded. "I could spill something. Then you could clean it up."

"Maybe just a glob of toothpaste," Dad said, turning to leave. "Or hairs in the sink."

"Okay, Dad," Morgan said. Then they were alone again.

Morgan's tongue felt heavy in their mouth. They remembered how it felt at the gala, their body seemingly incapable of feeling anxiety under those dim lights by the bar. Morgan could picture Zoe smiling hugely, swathed in velvet, promising they were going to have so much fun together.

Morgan put Mitski on, loud enough that it hurt their eardrums. *You're growing tired of me*, she sang, *and all the things I don't talk about.*

Every day there were notebooks open, pen smudging, clock staring. The second hand sludging around the perimeter of the clock. Sadie's hair, all of those golden hairs frizzing above her scalp like a halo. Sadie twisting to pass a worksheet behind her to Cassandra Baker. So Cassandra Baker gets to look at Sadie, Morgan thought.

Under their desk they messaged Peter. *My Spanish teacher wears clogs with socks every single day.* Peter was right there, feverishly typing back: *Maybe she owns a stake in the clog factory.* There were a million exchanges like this. It felt like sticking their head in front of the air conditioner on a miserable July day. A week passed that felt like a month.

That Tuesday, Sadie texted: *Let's meet up after school to talk.* Morgan stared at the message with awe. *Okay*, they said, knowing the rest of the day was completely shot. They couldn't even take a bite of their waxy cheese and turkey sandwich at lunch. Peter asked about their day, but Morgan couldn't think of anything besides the period Sadie had used after *talk*. She probably wanted to break up, which would be like this past week of torturous, roiling silence, but forever.

The bleachers by the baseball field were hot from the sunshine. Sadie sat in the third row, smoothing the pleats of her skirt down. Morgan didn't know how close they should sit to her. They kept their gaze focused on the field. Neither one of them spoke.

"I miss you. I tried not to, but I do. So, I'm ready to hear an exquisite, once-in-a-lifetime apology whenever you're ready," Sadie said lackadaisically. "No pressure."

"I am so fucking sorry," Morgan said. They tried to remember everything they'd done wrong, but it was like trying to sift out one grain of sand. They were sorry for getting so drunk and losing control and being a person they weren't proud of. Sorry for turning Sadie into a girl she wasn't proud of, either.

"No more of your mom," she said. "Okay?"

"I can't just..." Morgan said, trying to get their voice to work. "She's my mom, Sadie. What if I asked you not to talk to your mom?"

"Our moms are not the same species," Sadie said.

"You can't ask me to do that," Morgan murmured. "It's not fair. I waited my whole life for her to come back. What would you feel like, if you were me?"

"I'd feel shitty," Sadie said. "And probably really alone."

Morgan pinched their lips together. "Yeah."

Sadie considered this. "I get that it's not...okay for me to ask for that, I guess. So...what about this? No more Mom drama, okay?" she said. "No more drinking in zoos, or floundering your way through formal events."

Morgan nodded. "Okay. I promise."

"There's something else," Sadie said. "Last week, the guidance counselor asked me if I wanted to be a counselor at this gifted student summer camp in Portland. It'll look good for college, and it comes with a stipend, and I've always wanted to see the West Coast, so . . ." Sadie smoothed the pleats of her skirt. "I leave right after school ends in a month. For four weeks."

"That's . . . that's really great, Sadie." *Portland. Oregon.*

"It's okay, you don't have to pretend to be jazzed. I know the timing sucks, and a month is a long time." She leaned against Morgan's shoulder, her cheek against their collarbone. "I think we can figure this out, though, right?"

Morgan pressed their hand to the back of her neck. The weight of her was such a relief, that physical not-aloneness that they'd missed. "We can figure it out," they repeated, and kissed the part of her hair. They were getting sunburned, but wouldn't move until Sadie moved first.

On the way back home, Sadie asked about the rest of the gala. The two of them rode their bikes next to each other, various automobile sounds filling pauses in the conversation. Morgan focused on Brigid—how weird it was to meet someone who'd followed their life from afar, how weird it was that she and Dad were friends.

"My dad made me write an *apology note* to her," Morgan said. "I guess I was an asshole. The whole thing was so awkward. I can't imagine going to *stay* with her."

Sadie cast them a look. "What do you mean?"

"She asked me to come visit her. In *Portugal,* like I might just happen to *find myself* in Europe. It's nuts."

"Would she pay for you to go?" Sadie asked. For once she

looked envious. It satisfied Morgan, like they'd just flipped the perfect pancake.

"It sounded like it, I think," they said.

"So you're mad at someone who's been a good friend to your dad and offered to give you a free trip to Europe?" Sadie said. "Man. I always hate when a fairy godmother swoops in and says, 'Hey, Sadie, want a better life?' I'm kind of busy, you know?"

"Okay, okay," Morgan said.

"Maybe you're jealous of her," Sadie said. "Since your mom kind of chose to be with her over you. Maybe that's why it feels weird."

Sadie had hit the most sensitive point in their life with a fucking sledgehammer. There it was. "Yeah," Morgan said finally. "You're not wrong. Feels kind of bad to hear it, though."

At the next red light, Sadie reached over to squeeze their hand. She said, "Maybe you should hold on to this feeling, you know? If you're mad at your mom, and you don't want to talk to her anymore, that's like, your survival instinct finally rising to the top. Congratulations, survival instinct!" Sadie said. "You made it."

"I made it," Morgan repeated, staring at the light, waiting for it to change to green.

School ended and they filled their days without Sadie. Shifts at the library, babysitting gigs at night from families who wanted a non-female to watch their unruly little boys. Soon they'd paid back Dad for their $372 transgression. If they kept their brain busy during the day with tiny goals—do ten jumping jacks, learn ten new vocabulary words—the time slogged on by.

At night they felt the loneliness, rolling in like a tide. What was Sadie doing right now? They scrolled through Instagram, seeing her wearing identical cobalt-blue T-shirts in front of an aquarium with a group of geeky tweens. When Sadie returned, she'd return with a whole array of memories and names and references that Morgan wouldn't get, and what if she didn't want to tell them everything? What if she met a better, shinier person who wasn't on relationship probation?

This was when they'd talk to Peter, anxiety rushing loudly as if they'd pressed a seashell to their ears. It was summer, so classes were out and Peter worked part-time as a barista. He got yelled at for making his latte art *too elaborate*. Was it his fault that he was an artist in the cutting-edge medium of *foam*? Morgan shared Peter's plight. Morgan shared everything with Peter, actually: the Merriam-Webster word of the day (*chapfallen*: 1. having the lower jaw hanging loosely; 2. cast down in spirit, depressed); the sale on gelato at Stop & Shop. Morgan shoveled every tedious detail into the Peter fire and Peter swept it away, into embers.

They barely even saw Dad. He placed a dish in the sink and Morgan washed it. He laughed in another room, and Morgan heard it. Their debt was settled. Sometimes Morgan told him about the library, or something funny that one of the kids did while babysitting, and Dad laughed and then waited to see if Morgan would say anything else, and Morgan went upstairs. Peter was waiting for them.

Peter was always there, waiting.

Soon they were telling Peter about how they wanted to have sex when S. returned from their summer "internship," but that being vulnerable with someone freaked them out to their core. That they loved S. but it was like drinking four cups of coffee in a row, they couldn't cross the line of actually being *with* someone, did Peter get it? *It's scary*, he said. *You have to feel comfortable. That's normal.*

But what if they never felt normal? Had they always been so scared of things that other teenagers couldn't wait to do? Had it started recently, when things were actually possible rather than abstract ideas? Had it started after Ethan brought the gun to school?

Morgan changed the subject. It was fine. Maybe lots of people were so afraid of what they wanted that it kept them up at night, a woodpecker drilling into their neck.

26.

At a certain point Zoe found herself parked outside of Julian's house. She had, apparently, acquired a car. It was a Mazda, and she could imagine that she'd picked it because there was a Z wedged in there, for Zoe. It was a brassy color her mother would've said "screamed harlot."

She decapitated a Teddy Graham and washed him down with vodka from her water bottle. *So long, little bear*, Zoe thought, her head lolling. If she closed her eyes, nobody would notice her here. She wasn't *really* doing anything wrong, was she? It wasn't illegal to park on a street and watch Julian's house, was it?

Sunlight warmed her skin through the glass. She remembered, suddenly, when Zoe and Julian had been in high school, one of those long, buzzy conversations on the phone led to Zoe asking about the happiest day of Julian's life. Julian said his mom had set up a tent in the backyard and baked his favorite cookies. Snickerdoodles. In the tent he read a series of books about an alien prince who falls in love with a robot. That was it, the whole story: quiet, reading, full of cinnamon and sugar, on a beautiful June day. Zoe thought she had never been content, not even when she'd gotten things she really wanted.

The water bottle. Here it was, asking her: *Don't you want to feel a little less? Right now? Right now?*

When Morgan popped up next to the car, gently tapping the glass of her car window, she felt like a zoo animal disturbed from its slumber. Vodka turned her body ropy, bungling. Some old instinct took hold, one that knew how to beam a bright smile and sandwich sentences together. Some old instinct took over that knew: *I can't be the one with my foot on the gas.* She guessed that Julian hadn't taught Morgan to drive and, from their perky posture, she guessed right. Now she had something she could give, and it felt good.

"I have to turn this off," Morgan said, staring down at their phone screen as it flushed black. "Dad has a GPS tracker."

Zoe knew something bad had happened between them, but she couldn't reach it. Finding memories felt like groping in the dark for the light switch. Maybe it didn't matter. She took another sip. She told Morgan they were a natural, even though she had never seen a less comfortable driver.

"Buckle up," Morgan said, and Zoe swelled with fondness. They didn't want her to die. They wanted her safe and sound, even now. Morgan wiggled the keys into the ignition and spent a long time checking the angles of various mirrors Zoe had never thought about.

Driving, Zoe imparted to Morgan, is about confidence. Not where you keep your hands or checking your mirror. Morgan stared at the different gears for a long time before extending a hand and switching the car from park to reverse.

"Everything is fixable except killing somebody," Zoe said sagely. "Now turn the wheel as far to the right as you can and we'll get out of this spot. Are you hungry?"

Morgan was quiet as they wormed out of the parking spot. "Yeah," they said. "I could eat."

The pizza was a tactical error, because it was 10:00 a.m. and fucking sweltering. Sweat dribbled underneath the underwire of her bra. Chirpy noises trilled from the register; the radio played hackneyed pop songs about true love. A man with a grease-splotched apron handed them slices: Zoe's decked out with medallions of ham and chunks of pineapple, Morgan's piled with pepperoni hugging oil pools.

"The gala with Brigid," Zoe said suddenly, resting her fingertips on the metal napkin dispenser. "That's the last time we saw each other. That whole thing."

Morgan's expression froze, as if it were buffering. "Yeah," they said. "That *whole thing*." They looked down at their pizza, then back at Zoe. Pity, she thought; or maybe just misunderstanding. After a pause, Morgan filled in the scene that followed her departure, which ended—puzzlingly—with Brigid asking them to come visit her in Lisbon. She'd left a key.

"That's my key," Zoe said, struggling not to yell. "That's my *home*."

"I didn't mean to take it from you," they said softly. "I can try to get it back, if you want, but it might be hard...with Dad." Morgan met her gaze for the first time. "It's nice to think there's somewhere else to go. Everything feels..."

Zoe waited for the rest of the sentence. "Overwhelming?" she guessed finally.

And then Morgan started to talk—really talk, more than she had ever heard them talk before. Sentences that rolled into each other, gaining momentum. Talking about their girlfriend Sadie; about the ASMR channel the two of them ran together; and finally, about somebody named Peter. An Internet friend? An Internet friend who thought Morgan was... Sadie? Zoe had trouble following the thread. She decorated her pineapple slice with so many red peppers that she could smell the heat. *Just pay attention*, Zoe thought, a low wooziness taking hold of her body, rendering her limbs heavy. Sooner or later, Morgan would stop talking, and she'd have to reply. Her pizza was appallingly spicy. Her fault. Of course.

"So... what are you going to do?" Zoe asked evasively, when Morgan paused.

"What do you mean?" Morgan asked, panicked. "Why do I have to *do* something? Can't I just keep... lying? I mean, does the truth really help anybody?"

Zoe felt a gust of confidence. Lying was a topic she could speak to. "Let me tell you something important. Just tell the fucking truth because it's hard to lie. It's hard to plot out your lies and always have to memorize that diagram and see where you are in the midst of it." Zoe reached across the table to pull Morgan's hand into hers. "Sooner or later you'll slip, and you'll lose everything because you weren't the one to get the story going in the first place."

"Yeah?" Morgan asked scratchily.

"Yes," Zoe said.

Morgan paused. "So you think I should come clean?"

"Come clean, and then everything will be better," Zoe said. "I promise."

* * *

Morgan drove themself home, parking a few houses down, just in case. Zoe squirreled into the driver's seat. Now what she needed was a massage. What she needed was for someone to dig their professionally trained fingers deep into her muscles. Zoe swerved close to a beat-up car with its bumper duct-taped to the back. HONK IF YOU LOVE JESUS, the car implored, and for a second Zoe thought about honking. Maybe she'd be better off if she followed every direction that came her way. "Oh, thank God, a massage parlor," she thought, turning the wheel until

Later the doctor called Zoe *lucky*. Lucky she'd been wearing her seat belt. ("Buckle up," she'd heard Morgan echo in her head, and she must have listened.) Lucky she'd only clipped the side of the sedan. Lucky, though no one realized this but Zoe, that she'd eaten that pizza, since it kept her just a hair below the legal limit. Her arms scratched with prickles of glass from the impact. The doctor sutured Zoe back together with a distracted sense of care. "Very lucky," he repeated. "What if somebody had been in the car with you?"

Morgan had driven back to the house from the pizza parlor, and Zoe had waved them off, saying she was fine to get back to the city, she was *fine*. Morgan held up a hand in goodbye like an aged parent, cringing to see their reckless teen peeling off. She was the reckless teen to everyone. Even to an actual seventeen-year-old.

They could've been sitting in that crunched metal knot.

She could've called any number of old sponsors. Natalie, too, would've been sympathetic. Brigid had never turned her away in a capital-E Emergency. Instead, she called Albert. She wanted to be yelled at, really yelled at. She was frivolous and pathologically self-centered and she wanted to hear about it. She wanted to hear the thunderous rage of somebody who'd held back for nearly four decades and was ready to let the floodgates open.

"I'm done," Albert said. "Whatever you have to say, I'm finished, Zoe." And he hung up before she had a chance to even say good-bye. When she called Julian, it went straight to voice mail.

27.

Mom's advice seemed right, didn't it? It was so much effort to keep lying, to mix together all of the different lies like ingredients in a cake. They would tell Peter who they were. It would be fine, Morgan thought, sitting queasily in front of their laptop.

Do you ever lie about who you are? Maybe not the way that I have. But I bet you do—I bet you have an uncle who thinks that you loved basketball, that you ate and slept and lived basketball when really you wanted to have a camera in tow. Peter—it didn't start out as a lie. I AM the person behind the ASMR videos you love, I'm just not the head that's attached to those braids. Is it that important? You're my friend. We got to be friends, suddenly, and it was like I had been lying to you this whole time but I never meant it to be this way. It was just too hard to stop it once it started. I'm sorry. That's where I should have started: I'm sorry. The girl with the braids is my girlfriend. I guess maybe I wondered what it would be like to

be her, and you assumed I was her, and I went with it. The
other stuff—the confessional stuff—that was all real. I hope
you can forgive me.

BicycleThief 2293: what the fuck. what the FUCK.

BicycleThief 2293: who are you even?

BicycleThief 2293: i told you actual shit about my
life. i told you things in fucking confidence and what,
you're a stranger who wants to be his girlfriend?

BraidsASMR: It wasn't like that.

BicycleThief 2293: that's so fucked up to do to someone how could you do this, how many other fucking
people are you lying to? and for what. do you get off
on this? on knowing that i'm picturing you and thinking about you and you're some fucking guy?

BraidsASMR: It wasn't like that. Like I said, everything else I told you was true, it was just too hard to
turn back to tell you that I'm not the person you're
picturing. Does it spoil everything? Each and every
thing?

BicycleThief 2293: of course it does. do you know
how much time i wasted with you? do you think i
would've talked to you even for one minute if i knew
who you were? i had a plan and at the end of it there

was a beautiful girl on my goddamn arm. not a decep-
tive Twitter-hopper trying to soak up attention
wherever he goes. you know what, no wonder your
mom left you. she could probably tell you were
damaged goods.

BraidsASMR: I thought we could still be friends. I
thought you cared about me.

BicycleThief2293: i don't even know who you are
besides a person who's going to be very fucking sorry.

Then Peter was gone and a new Peter-shaped person was telling
Morgan all about the ways in which they'd be *very fucking sorry.*
He'd already captured Morgan's IP address, and did Morgan know
how easy it was to swoop in and steal their passwords, to back-
track through the IP address and find them? To empty out their
bank account with a few swift security questions? (*I know everything about you, and everything I don't know, I can find out.*) To start,
Peter promised, he would track down the girlfriend and send her
the transcripts. Every word. Morgan thought there was no way
that Peter could find out who Sadie was. Could he? What if he
just put them out on Reddit, let the rest of the work happen
through angry peers with schadenfreude for days? Peter wouldn't
need to find Sadie, they realized; they would just need to find
someone who recognized Morgan from school and put things in
the right hands.

It was all over and it was just beginning.

Morgan threw up in the sink.

* * *

Very fucking sorry. The words clenched around Morgan's throat. There were other words, words that Morgan could barely repeat inside the privacy of their own head, words that Peter typed after the conversation was over, after he wasn't himself anymore but a stranger who hated Morgan, who hated people like Morgan. Morgan watched the back door as if it might break off its hinges with the gust of Peter's rage.

Morgan wasn't hungry but found their hands crunching tortilla chips in half. A block of cheese rubbing furiously along the concave holes of the grater. Commas of cheddar cheese stacking up into a mountain. Nothing was enough motion, enough friction. They thought about what angry people did every day: plotted their revenge, stormed locations with their legally procured guns and their tirades about snowflakes. They put the plate in the microwave and leaned their forehead against the warm door.

28.

At home, Julian put his shoes in their spot by the door and then there was Morgan, dancing with their arms extended wide like wings. For a moment Julian felt guilty, being there in the house, interrupting their joyful solitude. He knew, better than anyone, what it was like to need to dredge up some extra energy to interact with a person when all you wanted in this world was a book and a neatly configured snack.

All at once Julian realized that Morgan wasn't dancing, they were flailing; that they weren't joyful but in despair. Morgan's little face, crumpled, splotched with pink from crying. The earbuds fell from their ears and the music buzzed audibly. Morgan wiped their eyes with their wrist. "Dad, I didn't know you were home," they said, quickly averting their gaze. The microwave trilled.

Say something, Julian thought. *Say something comforting.*

"I took the six-seventeen train from Grand Central, so I got in at six forty-four, and it took me eight minutes to walk to the house."

Morgan whimpered like an animal who'd accidentally ingested poison and just realized what's to come.

"Dad," Morgan said. "I ruined everything," and later Julian would see this was It, the capital-I moment for him to initiate a hug. In the moment Julian peered around Morgan's head, the slope of their neck into shoulders, to squint into the microwave and determine whether the nachos were burnt beyond repair.

It was a time for tenderness. It was a time for sensitivity. It was not the time to tell Morgan there was no probable way that a person on earth could ruin *everything*, not unless that person instigated an international nuclear war. Removing the nachos from the microwave, Julian laid the plate on the table and sat next to his only child, who wept volcanically.

"I'll explain," Morgan said. "But please don't be mad at me."

Julian recognized a certain tone in Morgan's voice, which usually accompanied Zoe. "Is this about your mom?"

Morgan shook their head. "It's about me."

Julian wished that he'd been given a synopsis of whatever Morgan was trying to tell him. Every detail sparked an array of questions: When did they start talking to this person online? What did it have to do with Sadie? What was ASMR and how many people, approximately, experienced the tingling sensation with the tiny sounds? *But why are you crying so much?* Julian wondered. *When is the part coming that explains the crying?*

They said, "I never should've pretended to be Sadie but once I started..." And then the explanation that followed—the reveal of the information, Peter's subsequent anger—fell into a narrative Julian understood. Betrayal, he understood.

"He said he would hack into our network. That he could see

everything I'd ever looked at, every credit card we'd ever used. He said he could find out where we lived so easily. He said he didn't know who I was besides a person who'd be very fucking sorry." Morgan kept their eyes fixed determinedly on the table in front of them.

Julian pictured their ceiling fan, suddenly detaching from the ceiling, a dramatic crash against the ground. All of the things that needed to be done—the credit cards, the passwords, the security on the network. The painstaking work he'd done on his credit score after Mom's death; those unending medical bills.

"Does Peter have pictures?" Julian asked. "Anything that could identify you?"

Morgan shook their head. "No pictures."

"What about Sadie?"

"Just the bottom of her hair," Morgan said, their voice a whisper. "Not her face."

"Does Peter know where you go to school? Does he know we live here?"

Morgan paused. The pause made Julian want to fit his whole fist in his mouth.

"I don't think so," they said finally.

"Go upstairs and put masking tape over your computer's camera," he said. "I'll call the bank and have them alert us for any suspicious activity."

There were innumerable details to tackle, and with what energy could he tackle them? So many people to speak to, and to explain— what? My child made a huge error in judgment and now all of my private information could be available to the highest bidder? And who knew what kind of person this Peter was; did he just want to see how far he could push it? The two of them had so little.

The *two* of them had so little, but of course: Zoe.

"Morg," Julian called hoarsely, twitching at the base of the stairs. "Peter, does he know about your mom?"

Leaning down from the banister, Morgan said, "Yeah, he knows about Mom, too."

"After we talk to the bank and change all of your passwords, we have to call her," Julian said. Just when she'd finally listened, finally respected the boundaries that Julian had worked so hard to erect, there it was.

"I don't want to talk to her," Morgan said. "Please."

The doorbell rang, and it was a lanky kid carrying a dozen pizzas. The lanky kid stared and Julian explained that they hadn't ordered any pizza and the lanky kid read out the receipt and Julian wanted to scream, and then Julian did scream. It had been a long time since he'd lost his temper, using all of those techniques—rip a piece of paper into shreds, punch a pillow until you tire yourself out—but then he was yelling, he would never order pizzas *plural* when there were just two of them here, haven't you ever heard of harassment? Did he, the pizza kid, have any idea what it was like to feel monitored in his own home?—Julian sputtered, and the lanky kid took off then with the pizzas piled in the back of his Chevrolet.

Julian looked up at Morgan. "Let's go," he said.

29.

*G*o *where?* Morgan thought. Dad was the opposite of impulsive. *It's so bad I can't even look at you,* Morgan imagined Dad thinking, a speech bubble bobbing over his head. *It's so bad we need to evacuate.*

Part of Morgan thought Dad must have been overreacting—all those podcasts about identity theft rendering him paranoid. But Peter had threatened them, hadn't he? *Very fucking sorry.* Then the pizzas arrived, their usually delicious scent wafting into the house with malice. They weren't pizzas at all; they were an exclamation point after Peter's threat.

"Okay," Dad said. "We're going to spend the night at the Super 8. I don't want to use our Wi-Fi network to make any of these changes, just in case. Did you use the VPN? It seems like you ignore me when I remind you to use it."

"I did ignore you," Morgan murmured.

"How technologically savvy did this Peter seem?"

"He studies film. He likes Wes Anderson."

"He's probably just trying to scare you."

"Well, it's working," Morgan said.

Dad bit down on his lower lip, and Morgan wondered what he was thinking. Morgan's heart thwacked against their chest.

Inside the car, Dad craned his neck, one long arm snaked over the back of Morgan's seat as they backed out. He mentioned network security and Morgan knew that once Dad started, it would be a long time talking about Internet networks and spyware.

"There are things we can do," Dad said as they entered the motel's lot. *Dim-dim, dim-dim,* the blinker chirped. It felt like a year ago that Morgan had relished that sound, driving on their own for the first time. A girl was in the pool on a unicorn float, staring at her phone. "If things get worse, Morg, there's a procedure for what to do when you're doxxed. I hope it doesn't come to that but I want you to know, there are steps to follow."

The word *doxx* made their mouth go dry. "But . . . that won't happen, will it? I thought that was just for feminists who talk to Nazis on Twitter."

"You lied about who you were for a long time," Dad said. "Isn't that what you said? Did I misunderstand the story?"

"No, you didn't misunderstand the story," Morgan said quietly. "I lied for a long time."

Dad parked, turned the key in the ignition. The two of them sat in their Toyota, looking at the entrance of the Super 8 in the distance as if it were Bigfoot spotted in a forest.

"What I don't understand is why you pretended to be Sadie to begin with," Dad said. "Is it . . . Do you think it's because I'm autistic? Is that why it doesn't make sense?"

"No," Morgan said, but their voice was a wrinkle. "I don't think anybody would think it makes much sense." As long as they kept their neck bent, kept their gaze fixed on the stitching of their jeans, then maybe it would be okay. "It's . . . I was lonely, I think, and when it started, I thought it would just boost my confidence, not become a real friendship. It isn't." Morgan's voice cracked. "Obviously I know that now. I haven't had friends since the thing with Tiana and Aiden and it was . . . nice. I didn't want to wreck anything with the truth when the truth didn't seem to matter."

"The truth always matters."

"I know, Dad." Morgan's neck started to twinge.

"If Grandma Cheryl were here, she would . . . know what to say. We were a good team . . ." His voice trailed. "You made a big lapse in judgment and put yourself in danger. You should know better than to—"

"I do know better. I just didn't do the better thing."

Dad turned his head then. "Why not?" he asked.

"Because I . . . I wanted to know what it would feel like to be a girl," Morgan said. "Not because I'm a girl, but because . . . I'm not . . ." A goopy tear spilled from their eyes. "People always assume I'm this thing that I'm not. I feel like I'm never doing *gender* right, the way I walk or the way I talk or feel. It's like I was cast in a play but everybody else just gets to live the way they do, by default, but I'm always . . . calculating."

Dad was quiet for a minute. "Did you know a few years ago, they discovered a zebra finch that's body was split in half with male characteristics and female characteristics? On one side it had the typical male plumage, scarlet feathers, and on the other side the typical female gray. It's called a *bilateral gynandromorph*." Dad cleared his throat. "Sorry, my point is . . . in nature gender can be quite complex, and human consciousness is much more complex than other animals."

Morgan's tongue felt tangled in their mouth. "Okay," they said. "Yeah. Finches. But I...I don't feel both male *and* female. My feathers aren't red or gray. They're...green?"

"You don't have feathers."

"It's a metaphor," Morgan reminded him.

"Right," Dad said, nodding. "Morg, I...I know what it's like to try very hard at something that doesn't come naturally, and I...I guess I hoped it would be easier for you."

"Me too," Morgan said. The girl in the pool climbed from her float. She looked so at ease in her black bikini, walking from the pool to the room as if she were anywhere, wearing anything. Morgan looked at the thin black bow tied behind her neck, the middle of her back. Her life was simple. She was a girl in a bathing suit.

"I don't care what color your feathers are," Dad said. "To use your metaphor," and he reached to open the door. "Come on, there are passwords to change, customer service hotlines to call." Morgan followed, heaving the backpack over a shoulder. "It's not just finches," Dad continued as the two of them crossed the parking lot. "It's also been seen in crustaceans."

Morgan scuttled closer to Dad. "Like what kind of crustaceans?" they asked, and looked at him. "Lobsters?"

Dad's face softened. "That's right," he said. "Exactly like lobsters."

Dad procured lukewarm coffee and individual creamers, and the two of them worked silently, thoroughly, changing every password, every security question. Two-factor authentication. "Thank God you didn't give Peter your phone number," Dad said, though the only reason they hadn't was that Sadie might see. Somewhere in all the fixing, Morgan forgot about Peter, then re-remembered.

Friendless, and soon girlfriendless, because why would Sadie put up with this when she didn't have to? Outside, somebody was fighting with their husband, telling him if he was going to go, then just *fucking go already*. Her voice was rampant with tears.

Just fucking go already, she repeated, and Morgan thought of Mom. This was all her fault. She'd given terrible advice. Then, a slow reckoning: she'd been drunk. Slurry voiced, unable to focus, unable to do much of anything but mumble and prod her pizza. She'd polished off the remains of that water bottle with such aplomb, but Morgan thought she was just thirsty, or maybe diabetic.

So naive.

It was obvious: they needed to delete Twitter. *You're being so stupid*, Morgan thought, but how could they just walk away from this other person they got to be? They thought of Sadie and how many hours they spent on each video crafting a script, recording the *pop-pop-pop* of bubble wrap with their phone. The tingle test, Sadie called it, leaning over Morgan and whispering in their ear. Morgan remembered seeing Peter's name. Clicking through. Remembering the first time Peter had confided in Morgan about his grandmother slapping him at Christmas so hard it nearly knocked a baby tooth down his gullet. *Delete profile*, Morgan clicked, and then it was done. *I don't exist*, Morgan thought, flopping back onto the twin-size bed. *I don't exist anywhere anymore.*

"Want to see the zebra finch I was describing earlier?" Dad asked. It was a beautiful bird, split down the center: red feathers on one side, a tired, dirty-laundry gray on the other. This was love, in its own way, Morgan knew.

"In Pennsylvania," he said, "there was another bilateral gynandromorph studied, and that bird attracted a male partner with typical plumage, and they were recorded singing to each other. Since all northern cardinals sing."

Morgan clamped their lips together. "Thanks, Dad."

Dad went into the bathroom to change into his embarrassing pajamas with their neat white trim. He said through the ajar door, "It doesn't look like anything's been tampered with. No fraudulent charges or suspicious activity that I saw. Did you?"

"No, I didn't see anything either."

"That's good. Unless it's part of a larger strategy to lull us into a false sense of security."

"Peter's impatient," Morgan said. "He can't even roll down the plastic on a cucumber." Now they heard how it sounded, if not sexual, then at least full of innuendo. At the time Morgan had wondered who paid extra for the seedless kind that came in plastic? Their face warmed. Sadie always said Morgan was gullible, too sweet for someone their age.

Dad came out of the bathroom. "That's good," he said. "People like that don't often follow through. Morg...maybe you'd like to talk?"

Morgan shook their head. "I'm so tired," they said, which was partially true. Their brain was tired. Their body hummed with caffeine. They wanted desperately to nullify the hum, to absorb *content*—shiny pictures of pets and wide-eyed girls taking selfies against decorative walls. But they couldn't do that anymore.

"I should call your mom," Dad said. "Before we go to bed."

The moment when Morgan could've said *Dad, I have to tell you something. I saw her this morning. She was parked in front of the house. She'd been drinking and she kept drinking and she told me to do this* passed unceremoniously. Dad called her from the bathroom, but the walls in the hotel were thin.

"Zoe," Morgan heard him say. "I don't think that's a good idea. It's been an arduous ordeal and I don't think showing up will help Morg relax, okay?" A pause. "I know you're trying. I know.

"Well, what could you possibly do to help besides that?" Dad asked. *Besides what?* Morgan wondered. "No. That doesn't solve anything. That doesn't— Okay. Tomorrow, then. I will." Then, softer: "You know I do, Zoe."

Dad unlocked the bathroom door and flipped the lights off. "Time to sleep," he said, though Morgan knew that he knew that neither of them would fall asleep for a long time.

30.

Julian's brain felt impossibly busy. How many people had slept in this hotel, cumulatively? Had there ever been a bedbug infestation? Once the bedbugs found you, Julian knew, it was almost impossible to get them out. The more he thought about bedbugs, the calmer he felt. Julian read on his phone: when bedbugs feed, they inject the person's skin with an anesthetic. That way, the host never even knows the bug is feeding. They aren't attracted to dirt or clutter. They're attracted to blood, to warmth. The information felt like aloe over a sunburn. *I'm not a bad father, I'm not a bad father*, he repeated to himself—first internally, and then in an urgent whisper. *I'm doing the best I can.* On the adjacent bed, Morgan twitched to the side closest to Julian and then there the two of them were, looking at each other in the dark.

"Morg," Julian said, but there was too much to say. *Morg, tonight I talked to your mom. She was drunk and tired and crying and she wanted to come over right then to try to help, and I made her stay away like I always try to, but she'll be back, and you should understand that her help isn't help. You should understand that trying only matters to a point. Morg, I've always known there was something different about you, just like there's something different about me, and I haven't cared what its name is, or whether it has a name at all. Would you have been happier somewhere else? Would you have been so lonely that you'd pretend to be someone else? Are you lonely because of me, because I don't ask the right questions, because I don't need the same things you do?*

"I think the coffee kept me up," Morgan whispered, after a long pause.

"I have so much I want to tell you but I can't," Julian said at the same time. "I can't figure out how."

"Do you want any almonds?" Morgan said after another long while. "I have some."

"Thanks," Julian said. "Yeah, I could use a little something."

🌿

In the morning, Julian took a hot shower. Energy seemed a distant, weak memory. Energy to move into a new day when he was again the parent, again the person who needed to monitor any deviations from the norm in Morgan's behavior, again the person to scribble a signature on a receipt for something he couldn't afford.

He didn't hear the knock, but he did hear Zoe's voice. For a second he thought: *I'll just stay in this shower forever.* But then Julian thought of Morgan and jerked the shower nozzle off, imagining all of the many ways Zoe could fuck up this scene even further.

But the scene he saw was different. Morgan sat on the edge of the bed, their elbows balanced on their knees. Effortfully Morgan tried to breathe—Julian could see right away, the strain of a panic attack glowing across their temples—and Zoe sat at their side, rubbing circles across their back.

"I didn't tell Sadie about any of this...and now...I don't know what's going to happen. What if something happens to Sadie? What if Peter can't find me, so...he finds...Sadie..." Morgan shook.

"It's okay, it's okay," Zoe said, in her voice, but also the voice of a stranger. She looked wildly out of place in her high heels and tight black sheath dress. Julian could see the plunge of the neckline revealing a tiny bit of cleavage. Her arms were deeply scratched, whiskered with blood and stitches. She looked up at him with an expression that he couldn't place. Julian's damp hair dribbled down the back of his neck.

Julian slid next to Morgan and placed his hand on their back, too. "It's okay," Julian said, not against Zoe but with her. Two quiet voices, melding in reassurance. And they were, weren't they? Soldered together forever through Morgan, through this poorly rested, tightly coiled person, just starting to realize what it meant to make mistakes that might have consequences.

An alternate life. A life that didn't include the dry kiss she'd left on his mouth, saying, *I'm going out for a run, okay?* and him falling back asleep and in the morning there was a note on the kitchen table that said *I'm sorry* and nothing else. Without her, the baby didn't seem especially upset. Maybe the baby knew all along; they'd grown inside her, they knew her better than anyone else.

So Cheryl bobbed Morgan on her knee and sang "Yellow Submarine" but Julian couldn't stop thinking about the internal logic of the song—we *don't* live in a yellow submarine—and then he went outside and lay facedown in the grass and screamed with his mouth full of soil. He could hear Cheryl doing a kazoo noise over the baby and he gripped the ground until he felt a worm wriggling in his grasp and he let it struggle until he thought it might die. But it didn't die.

That was the moral of the story.

Julian's hands met Zoe's hands. *It's okay. It's okay.*

31.

Morgan had asked for breakfast, and Dad had quickly agreed. Now things were happening that hadn't happened before. Mom was walking slightly behind the two of them, the *clomp-clomp* of her black suede heels muted by the carpet. Morgan glanced back at her, just once, to confirm she was there. Was this how other people always felt? That their mom would be right behind them?

The three of them sat at a round table near the waffle maker and coffee cups. Mom put her purse up on the nearest table and looked around, like she didn't know what happened next at a buffet. *Used to people serving her*, Morgan thought. She glanced between Morgan and Dad like she was waiting for a line from a director. *End scene*, Morgan wanted to shout.

"Blueberry muffin?" Dad asked. "Butter?"

Zoe smiled. "Sure."

"I'll get yours, too, Morg," Dad said.

Without a task, Morgan felt a lurch in the base of their throat.

She'd seen so much crying. Of all the time the two of them had spent together, what percentage of it included Morgan crying? The TV announced another shooting, people scuttling out of a large brown building with their heads ducked, and Morgan tried to keep their gaze cast down, but it was too late. *Don't forget, you could always die*, the news cooed.

"Hey, Morg?" Mom asked. "Do you want to...tell me what happened?"

They checked their phone to see if Sadie texted, but no. In Oregon, Sadie didn't know anything about this. They felt weary, and aged, and embarrassed by how warm Mom's attention felt, like a sunlamp. She laid her hands out on the stained tablecloth and reached for Morgan. Her skin was so soft. They'd never felt such soft hands.

The whole faltering story poured out. Once they started, they couldn't stop.

"I'll kill that motherfucker," Zoe said. She said it like you might say *I'll take the dressing on the side*.

"What?" Morgan asked.

"The audacity," she continued. "Weaseling into your...Internet... to watch everything you do, just because he can? And now your dad felt like he had to take you *here*?" She gestured around them, the beige walls and '70s-patterned carpet. "Because of that guy, threatening you. It's unbelievable. And I want you to know," Mom said, lowering her voice, "that I'm not going to stand for that."

"What do you mean?"

"I know I have a lot to make up for. The least I can do is make someone else sorry for trying to hurt my kid." Pawing through her purse, she quickly swallowed a pill without any water. "Don't worry, okay, Morg?"

"I think there are a lot of things to worry about," they said, trying not to look at the news.

Dad returned with wispy, daffodil-colored eggs; a blueberry muffin hacked in half, a pat of butter broaching either side. He fumbled with the chair, with putting the plates on the table gently, and Morgan felt the checklist in their head start to tick. Dad couldn't look at either of them and wasn't talking up his usual flurry of facts. It was Mom who chattered away: the last time she'd been in a Super 8; a story about a car breaking down on the way back from a lake house. It would have been interesting but for the pull of the news, the pull of Dad's eyes starting to get that frosted glass look that said *It's been too much and I'm almost completely undone*. Mom kept talking: other stories about the lake house, friends carting smoked salmon and bagels from Russ & Daughters to spend the weekend, and did Jules remember the time that they drove up and almost hit a deer?

Dad said quietly: "I need to go lie down. Okay? You can stay with Morg."

"That sounds good, Dad," Morgan said, over her. Their voice felt like someone else's. This happened, not uncommonly, when it was time to care for Dad. They wondered if it meant they needed Dad to be in bad shape in order to be a better self.

"Take your toast," Morgan said, lifting the plate up to him.

Dad's face was blank, and his voice was blank, and his hand shook with the plate. "Okay."

Mom was quiet until he was out of sight. "I forgot what that was like," she said. "Watching him just go out"—she snapped—"like that."

"It's more of a fade than a snap," Morgan said. "You have to know what to look for." In their peripheral vision, they could see a toddler in its high chair, plunging empty half-and-half containers onto the ground like tiny bombs. *Thp*, the containers went as they hit the floor.

Mom chewed a chunk of honeydew. She was watching the news, all those miniature people fleeing the scene, and it didn't touch her. The news didn't *happen* to her, just like motherhood didn't happen, just like coming home didn't happen. Zoe had dreamed their driving lesson and at the end snakes consumed her. *Look at me*, Morgan thought. *Tell me you're sorry. Tell me you'll never stop being sorry.*

"I know what you're thinking," she said, waving her fork through the air. "Let me promise you. He's the one who'll be very fucking sorry, Morg."

"I still don't understand why you didn't have an abortion," Morgan said.

She didn't seem surprised by the conversational swerve. She reached for their hand. "Because I thought we'd be best friends," she said. "Like *Gilmore Girls*. I thought we'd never stop bantering. You'd be brilliant and raise yourself, and I'd be beloved and I'd know everything by instinct, and we'd never stop eating pancakes." Mom cleared her throat. "And, of course, I'm . . . afraid of needles."

Morgan swallowed. "You're afraid of needles?"

"That's why I didn't have one. They have to put you under."

That's a stupid fucking reason for me to be alive, Morgan thought.

But, of course. They were born out of inaction. They were born out of fear.

"I'll make it right," she said, standing. She fumbled with the strap of her purse, caught in the netting of the chair. She looked determined. Morgan knew the look.

"Where are you going?"

She slid an envelope across the table as she readied to leave. "Take this," she said. "I owe you this much, at least. My handwriting is terrible," she called over her shoulder, scurrying toward the door in her heels. "Did you inherit my bad handwriting?"

"No," they said, watching her go. "I didn't." They stared at the fruit salad remaining. A single watermelon cube had a spot in the center where there had once been a seed, and now there was nothing.

Inside the envelope was a check for eight thousand dollars. Each little zero like a pearl on a chain. Under note, she'd written nothing. Morgan stared at that nothing for a long time. They'd imagined a long letter, one that meandered through all the little moments of her life that she'd fumbled. They imagined a blistered apology that veered into poetry. But no. That would be too much effort.

It felt too soon to disturb Dad with their presence—to conquer logistical questions about what the rest of the day might hold. Morgan ambled. Through the chain-link fence, they could hear something hitting. They saw Mom's dented Mazda was at the front entrance of the hotel, and she was pounding her fist against the steering wheel.

They stood, watching. Her face, pinched with red, and the box of Teddy Grahams in the passenger seat next to a bottle of vodka. Through the glass the sound of a song. It took them a second to realize it was Mitski's "A Pearl," the same song that they'd listened to with Mom before the gala. It was blasting, the kicking up of Mitski's voice as she sang: *You're growing tired of me and the things I can't talk about.* The horns swept up, and grew quiet again. *There's a hole that you fill, you fill, you fill,* and Morgan could hear her crying, the sob of someone who couldn't stop. The song looped. She reached for the bottle with her eyes still closed, that hand that had reached for Morgan's across the table and now it had what it wanted, all along.

As they went back toward the hotel, they felt their phone start to buzz. Through their jean pocket they saw the home screen light up. *I need to talk to you right away*, Sadie said. *I have to come home. Who is Peter???*

32.

This was the opening Zoe had always needed: a bully goes after her child and she reacts with X. Solve for fucking X! She'd spent years waiting for this moment, however unconsciously, and now it was here. She'd never threatened anyone before. She needed help, or courage. Maybe both. She'd had her daily cry, letting Mitski wrangle out the emotions from her body; now she was ready for someone else to be sorry for once. At home she shed her clothes, took three shots, and waited for the warmth to clear her face.

She wore an ivory romper and heeled dusty pink boots. She draped herself in a mink shawl that had been her grandmother's. Back then, you had to wait until you were married before you got a mink. Zoe loved thinking about the moment when Grandma Lucie sauntered into the community center with her signature red lipstick and the other bitches realized they'd been wrong to underestimate her. Grandpa Stewart worshipped her. A diamond for every finger. That was her blood; it glittered.

At the bar, Zoe ordered a martini. It was the last dive standing in the neighborhood; Zoe was both too young and too old for the bar. She recognized some patrons: the guy with the port-wine birthmark; Ellie and Chantelle, the sisters who owned the old-school diner across the street. She chatted with the bartender, who was from Louisville. He had a horse at home named Chocolate.

She told the bartender about Peter, listening to her own promise bouncing around her ears: *I'll take care of him. I'll make sure.* Louisville poured her another.

"What would you do?" she asked. "If you wanted to hurt someone that fucked with your family." Zoe had hurt plenty of people, but she'd never plotted it out before. It was kind of exciting. Zoe sucked an olive. Salt cleansed her.

"What do you know about this guy?" Louisville asked. "Besides what he did."

"He's a film student," she said. "He's written some kind of...Brooklyn dramedy. Everyone's wearing a sweater. The character based on Peter has a mice phobia."

"Bad city to be afraid of mice," Louisville said. "Those fuckers run rampant."

Zoe agreed, brightening. "They do run rampant."

"You can buy mice at any pet store, baby," Ellie said. Who knew she'd been listening? "My boyfriend has a snake. It's like the nature channel. I hear that thump, I know to steer clear of the kitchen."

"So I buy myself some mice," Zoe said. She bought their next round. "What's the best way to break into somebody's apartment? It's probably a dorm."

"Easy to find out," Chantelle said.

Premeditated, a little voice inside of her chimed, but fuck that voice, it was just her mother. How much of a crime was it, really, to want to feed your imaginary pet snake? Chantelle was good with Google. She reversed-image searched Peter and found him on Facebook. He had a distinctive last name, German. Lived in a building that was owned by his grandfather, a rent-controlled apartment in Alphabet City. Chantelle wrote down Peter's address on the back of a receipt.

"What you want to do," Ellie said, "is open a jar of peanut butter and hide it under the bed. Mice love peanut butter. You let a few loose in the room, uncap the Skippy, and wham!" Ellie clapped her hands like a rocket launching. "You've got yourself a pest problem."

"That's sick," Chantelle said in admiration. "You know, with those old buildings—usually somebody's home. You just pretend to be delivering breakfast to some rich asshole. Oh, sir! I've got your biscuit with marmalade right here! Bam. You're in."

"You don't look like a Postmates driver," Louisville said. "Got to get a different outfit. Jeans, T-shirt." Nobody acknowledged his comment.

Although she hadn't intended to invite Chantelle or Ellie, there they were, piling into a cab and asking the driver to take them to the nearest Petco. They bought ten squirming gray mice in a bag with the word LUNCH on the front in a serial-killer scrawl. "I'm not touching that," Zoe said, giggling. When they arrived, it was getting dimmer before a rainstorm, the sky flushed with dark, Matisse clouds. Zoe bought a jar of peanut butter and then three more to meet the credit card minimum at a bodega.

Just pretend they're not alive, she thought, but they were squeaking vociferously. This was turning out to be disgusting, which was why it would be worth it, but a gag fluttered in the back of her throat.

She rang each buzzer, but nobody answered. Chantelle and Ellie stayed in the cab for a while, but then they got either anxious or bored, and soon they were out of sight. The mice were undeniably, wildly alive inside of the bag. Zoe eyed the fire escape—maybe that would be the best alternate plan. She tried to climb up in her heels but then she dropped the bag and the mice skittered every-where, and when she tried to run, she found she couldn't; she found herself on the ground with those mice, the sidewalk scraping her skin clear off. Her palms bled. She'd chipped a tooth and she could feel its jagged edge digging into the side of her cheek.

33.

Sadie called as soon as she got back from the airport. She was crying. Morgan hadn't realized, right up until the moment they answered the phone, that they had never heard Sadie cry.

The police had swarmed her family's apartment and now Robbie was in jail for three tabs of acid and a half ounce of marijuana, and it wasn't his first offense and he was fucked. "They have *everything*," she sobbed. She'd spent years working to have something for herself. Now it was gone. Now her brother might go to prison. Now she didn't have *any* money left in her savings account because she had to buy a plane ticket for the *next flight home*, because somebody named Peter wanted to make *absolutely sure* that Sadie "never felt safe again."

"I didn't know what this dude was talking about until he sent a transcript of him talking to . . . *me*," she said, her voice wilting. "On Twitter. It looked like hours of talking to *you*, Morgan, pretending to be me."

"I—"

"What I really don't understand," she hissed, "is why you would talk to some total *stranger* about all these issues you were having with your mom, and how scared you were to be close to somebody, how scared you were to have *sex with me*," she said, shouting now, "when you could never tell me that stuff. What was it about me that you didn't trust, exactly?"

"It wasn't— You didn't do anything wrong. I wanted to be—"

"All those guys that I've dated before you, they might have been shitty, but they never kept a barricade of giant secrets from me and then let loose an army of trolls to terrorize my *family*. Now my mom is afraid that she's going to lose her job because all these assholes are calling to make complaints against her as part of a campaign against *me*. Do you know what that feels like?" She waited, but Morgan could only breathe, one rickety breath after another.

"I wish I had never met you," Sadie said, and hung up.

34.

"Can I offer you some champagne?" the flight attendant asked.

"Yes. I mean . . . I mean no. No. I'm an alcoholic," Zoe said.

The person next to her, a business-suited man with a thick neck, squirmed.

"Perhaps a club soda? Lime?"

"Okay," Zoe said. "Thank you."

She could do this. She was doing this. Club soda. Lime. The chipped tooth scraped against her tongue every time she forgot to avoid that spot in her mouth, which was often.

Before the plane took off, she checked her phone. She had two alerts: one was a reminder about her flight to Lisbon. The other was a text from Julian. *Please be safe*, Julian had said. 4:04 a.m.

It surprised and comforted her, how fast she could delete herself from a life.

She awoke with a jolt. As the plane's wheels reached the ground, the businessman next to Zoe exhaled loudly in relief. "We're alive," he said, as breathless as if he'd been the terrified pilot and not a passenger who slept through 75 percent of the flight. He introduced himself: Barry. He was in Lisbon for business, a restauranteur.

"Business or pleasure?" he asked.

"Neither," Zoe said. He laughed; then his face grew serious. He pulled out a card.

"About earlier," Barry said. "Ah...the club soda? I...well, you might want to stop by this address. On Tuesdays, at seven p.m., more specifically. Abroad, you know, it's not as..." He shook his head. "You abandon your routine, you never know what else will fall. I've got ten months now," Barry volunteered.

Zoe looked at the time. "Nine hours for me," she said.

Barry folded a napkin in half and wrote: YOU DID IT. He handed it to Zoe.

"That's magnificent," he said, and for a moment, she believed him.

"Tuesdays at seven," she repeated. Even as it was happening, she could feel the acuteness of the urge to make this history. A turning point.

"Have you lost everything, too?" she asked. She realized, as Barry unclipped his seat belt, that she didn't want to disembark. Here, inside, Zoe knew every mechanism, every possible delay or consequence. The in-flight magazine. The vomit bag. But out there, there were a million variables that she couldn't control.

"Yes and no," Barry said. "I kept my childhood baseball cards."

Zoe laughed. They waved goodbye.

A cab whizzed her from the airport into the city. Lisbon, with its grand palm trees and candy-colored buildings on wide main streets, felt like settling into a warm bath after a long run. The sugary scent of *pasteis de nata* filled her mouth, and for a moment all she could remember was eating here. And the wine. It had been several minutes since she'd thought of it, her sobriety. She felt the business card in her pocket again, dug its edge underneath her fingernail until it ached.

Zoe got out at her corner. Her old corner. The building was smaller than she remembered. She realized with a now horrible burst of clarity that she didn't have a key. The key was with Morgan.

Her suitcase flipped on its back.

"Fucking—*God*—fuck," Zoe said.

She'd regroup. With every step, every pull of the suitcase now sending a rippling ache through her arms, she wondered what the fuck she was doing. (Eleven hours.) What would Brigid say when she saw Zoe? *Even in New York, even though I was only there for one night, I still had to save you.*

(Eleven hours and one minute.)

She found herself traversing a familiar street, one that she and Brigid had loved. There had been a store that sold herbs; Brigid and the woman who'd owned it, Patrice, had been friendly. Patrice's storefront was different now. The front window was inviting: soy candles in mason jars, dried flower bouquets. It was the kind of store where you'd buy accessories for a new life.

Inside, Zoe parked her suitcase in a corner and examined each object on the front table. An ivory vase felt just the right weight in her hand; a fluffy peony made of paper sat inside. She felt stupid but she couldn't help lowering her nose to the flower's face. All those dead plants, she remembered, and when she looked up, she was looking at Brigid.

Zoe cleared her throat and said, "How are you?"

"How *am* I?" Brigid repeated. She was unflappable. There was a pause in which Zoe watched Brigid evaluating her: perspiring, bloated with new soberness. Zoe watched Brigid decide to be kind. She tucked a piece of gray hair behind her ear. She was wearing earrings that Zoe didn't recognize, tiny gold slivers, like staples.

"I'm well. And you?" Brigid said.

"Excuse me, Ms. Holm?" a young employee asked. "Did the essential oils come in from—"

"They're in the back, Nicola. Thank you," Brigid said, not taking her eyes off Zoe.

"Is this your store?" Zoe asked.

"It is. Patrice sold it to me before she moved back to Greece." Zoe couldn't tell if she was supposed to already know this.

"It's lovely," Zoe said.

Brigid eased, telling her about the store. "We're thinking of expanding into next door. Opening a sort of...bakery space."

"We?" Zoe asked. She felt an arrow sink between her ribs.

"My sister Isobel is a co-owner."

"I know Isobel is your sister," Zoe said. She looked at the floor so Brigid couldn't see her eyes puddling. She remembered meeting Isobel's daughter, Matilda, the day after she was born, how she writhed with effort that Zoe assumed was pointed.

"Have you thought of a tearoom?" Zoe charged ahead. She felt manic with the desire for the conversation to proceed normally. "I feel like, there's coffee all over, but no tea shops around. With all of your herbs, it would be great, don't you think?"

"That's a good idea," Brigid said. Back when things had been better, she wouldn't have been so surprised that Zoe had a good idea.

As long as they talked about herbs, they could avoid anything else. So it went: chamomile, peppermint, cardamom. "I thought you weren't interested in herbs," Brigid said.

"I wasn't," Zoe said. "But I'm trying to do better."

"Ah." Brigid's line of vision traveled to the suitcase. "And am I involved in this plan for betterness?"

"That's not really for me to decide." Zoe's brain swirled inside her head. She wished she could lift up her scalp and let some air in. "I didn't know you'd be here. I would've been more prepared about what to say."

For the first time, Brigid smiled. "Yes?"

"That I'm sorry. I guess that's where I would've started, ideally." Zoe felt her eyes fill with thick, unstoppable tears. "Brigid, I'm so sorry for everything."

She never used the whole name. Always Bridge, sometimes B. The *d* felt like a judge's gavel. If ever there were a time to be serious, Zoe knew, it was now. Her throat felt lacerated.

"Let me look at you," Brigid said. Her eyes were wide and light gray. Up close, they seemed to wiggle. "How long has it been?" she said.

"Almost twelve hours." It sounded paltry and embarrassing.

Brigid said, "I'll buy you a coffee, but you can't stay with me."

"Deal."

The meeting was everything, all at once. She recognized no one's face but all of their bodies: pillows for torsos, matchstick arms. Defeated, sluggish energy that coexisted with frenetic self-consciousness: darting eyes, fingers preoccupied with tearing napkins into piano keys, crushing paper cups into statues. When the others spoke, some in English but mostly in Portuguese, Zoe thought, *I'm not you, I'm not you*, but she knew it wasn't true.

She knew it wasn't true because she was the tattooed man whose son wouldn't talk to him anymore and she was the tall woman who had accidentally let her dog eat chocolate and die a gruesome death and she was the woman who'd almost gotten into a car accident with her baby because she was too drunk to drive. She was all of them, an addict who'd pillaged different cities and careers and relationships all in the name of getting what she wanted and that need was bottomless.

Her turn. The silence was enormous; it quivered with all of the possibilities of her misdoings. She didn't know how to begin. "I guess...what I want to say is...I've hurt everyone I've ever loved. I did it because I only thought about myself. Fuck, even now—still—someone's come here to be there for me, but I'm just...circling my own drain. And I don't know how I'm going to do this," Zoe said, after a pause. "So...okay. Thanks."

She imagined the audience, the confessors, congratulating her. *You finally did the right thing. We knew you could; we never doubted you. Have a cookie. Have each of the cookies.* The jagged edges scraped Zoe's gums. Brigid watched her, her lips parted slightly as if she were panting, or praying.

35.

August wrapped around their neck and bit. Without Sadie, Morgan's life was a bleached, shrunken version of what it had been: shelving econometrics books in the library, microwaving cheese shavings on stale chips. They counted the days until summer was over. A clean black X on every calendar day. A kiss for every increment of time that passed.

What was Sadie doing? What was Sadie thinking?

I wish I'd never met you.

I wish I'd never

I wish

I wish I could go back in time and make myself understand how fucking good I had it, Morgan thought, *how Sadie was the best thing that would ever happen to me and for some reason I wanted more instead of appreciating how it was to want a hug and have someone, right there, who would wrap those strong field hockey arms around me. I should've never stopped looking over my shoulder; I should've known that danger would swallow me as soon as I settled into a false sense of calm. I should've never fucked it up by getting involved with Mom. Sadie said I should be careful and I was the opposite of careful, I was a fucking flotilla of ships sailing right into the Bermuda Triangle. And Peter . . . Peter was the Bermuda Triangle itself.*

Morgan wanted advice, but couldn't approach Dad for advice unless they knew how to explain their feelings, which they could not. For days the silence between the two of them had been thick, as viscous as the last globs of maple syrup slugging from the bottle. They ate sandwiches in front of the TV and Dad asked if Morgan wanted to talk and Morgan said no. Then it was time for bed, and another maple syrup day.

They'd already decided to give Sadie the check that Mom had given them. Eight thousand dollars; it was more money than Morgan had ever seen in their life. Morgan imagined picking out clothes the way that Mom did, all silks and furs, fabrics that sang against their fingertips. But they snapped out of it—that money wasn't for clothes; it was for college. And they knew it was for Sadie. She deserved all of it.

They knew it wasn't enough. *I wish I had someone to ask, someone who would actually give me good advice on what would help,* they thought, picturing a Disney-sketched fairy godmother. Then they heard Sadie's voice: *I always hate when a fairy godmother swoops in and says, "Hey, Sadie, want a better life?"*

Maybe Brigid would know. She seemed to know everything else.

At last Morgan rolled over, opened their laptop. It was easy to find Brigid's email; her business's website was minimal and bright, with a friendly looking *contact us!* page. It was, Morgan guessed, easy to find anyone. They thought of Peter.

Hi Brigid, I'm sorry if this is weird and I know I was rude to you when we met, and I'm sorry. I have to ask you a favor. Can you help me? they typed. Tears wriggled down their cheeks. *I think I need your help.*

36.

That evening Brigid was glad to be alone. Surrounded by her replacement plants, Brigid tried to process the unexpected afternoon and evening with Zoe. Her windows were ajar and people were just beginning to clomp their way to restaurants and clubs, the sounds of boisterous prattling wafting in.

So she'd shown up. It wasn't entirely unexpected; Zoe had a way of finding her way back to Brigid in moments of tranquility. Brigid had been glad to return from New York, glad to put the entire fiasco behind her. She had her work, and her sisters and nieces, and in the mornings she ran down to the sea and listened to the seagulls clattering. She had a routine in place, and the routine was just starting to feel organic rather than a list of items she forced herself to do each day.

When Zoe returned, wide-eyed and anxiously circling, Brigid wanted desperately to take her home, to kiss her clavicle and tell her yes, I can take care of you. Brigid knew better than to do any of this. Instead, they went for coffee, and Brigid found herself, despite how many times they'd done this particular waltz, hoping for a different outcome. Hope wasn't the thing with feathers. Hope was the latch that, when unlatched, led you right back to your old, stupid life and said, *Welcome back.*

She ran a bath and filled it with her own recipe of bath salts: lemon, rosemary, magnesium. In the bath her brain flipped back to a memory at cousin Georgette's wedding, how Zoe laid her hand right at the small of Brigid's back and whispered, *I think we should go look at the stars,* and the two of them snuck out like teenagers, Brigid straining to remember constellations while Zoe listened raptly.

Brigid wondered now if she had been drinking then, that night when Brigid finally found the big dipper and Zoe rested her soft cheek on Brigid's shoulder and said it was perfect here, wasn't it? She seemed so *present* and loving. Brigid felt a flare of frustration; couldn't she just leave one memory, one quite nice one at that, and not taint it with speculation? And what had she signed up for, putting Zoe up at their favorite hotel, waiting for the whole painful cycle to play out once more?

She yanked the drain and the healing waters slurped out of sight.

It was then that she checked her email and saw the message from Morgan.

How long, how long, how long she had waited for this email. *Can you help me?*

Of course she could.

That desire to be a mother that Brigid always tried to shelve was always right there, underneath her skin. At first she was touched to be considered a source of wisdom. Then, like a sinking stone, she thought how much it would crush Julian to know that Morgan had turned to her, instead of their only parent, for advice.

Still. She couldn't very well turn them away, could she?

Brigid wrote back immediately. *Skype?* she suggested.

Morgan didn't look at her as they spoke. Brigid knew the gist of what had happened with Sadie, though she'd had to look up the term *doxxed*. She let Morgan talk. She saw this chrysalis of a person and wanted to protect them and to teach them what a gibbous moon looked like in the sky. Instead, she cleared her throat, using her business-strategy voice.

"First," she said, "let's come up with an action plan."

Brigid loved solutions. Solutions included a lawyer, Zoe's brother Albert, who would be all too happy to do Morgan a favor if it meant confirming that their families would have no contact whatsoever. Albert could explain the situation to Sadie's mother's employer in terms of harassment, and could probably sway a judge to get the brother out of jail and into an aggressive community service program. Solutions included mailing Sadie the check as soon as possible. Solutions included, Brigid waded slowly, seeing a therapist.

At this Morgan looked up. "Why would that...help?"

She watched Morgan peel a cuticle and wondered if they'd always been a cuticle peeler and again felt the pang of having lost so much time with them, and wondered how much wider and unpalatable that mass of regret sat right under Zoe's sternum.

"It'll show her that you want to make changes. And," Brigid ventured, "even if she doesn't forgive you, it'll be good for you to understand why you did this."

"I know why. It's because I fuck up everything good that comes my way."

It was like hearing Zoe, transported inside a different person's body. Brigid shook her head. "I reject your hypothesis. You're seventeen. You've made a mistake. There are things that you don't know about yourself yet."

"We can't afford it."

"I'll pay for it," Brigid said, over their protests. "I insist."

"I don't know why you'd want to do that," Morgan said softly. "But okay. Thank you."

Brigid felt a heat creeping up her forearms. "Morgan, why did you want to talk to me about this, rather than your dad?"

Morgan took a long time to answer. "Because you've let her come back, after she's hurt you. You keep the door open. I need to know . . . how to keep the door open."

She couldn't have predicted this response. How dexterously they'd flipped from sweet and grateful to unknowingly cutting. Brigid knew how to rip every bit of that sadness into a tiny, manageable shard and then swallow them all whole.

Morgan said, "Hello?"

"Morgan . . . you need to talk to your dad. Does he know that you and Sadie broke up?" Brigid asked. "Does he know the extent of all this?"

"I don't know," Morgan said, barely audible.

"You need to. This is going to be very painful for him, knowing that you'd approach me for advice but not ask him as well. Let's say that that conversation is my one request."

"I don't know how to talk about this stuff with him."

"I'm quite sure he doesn't know how to talk about this with you, either, but that doesn't mean you can avoid it," she said sternly.

Morgan was quiet for a long time. "Okay," they said. "I guess you're right."

"Yes, I usually am," Brigid said, thinking of the door, and how long it had stayed there, open. There she was, suspended in pixilation. The woman who left the door ajar.

37.

In the morning Zoe thought, *It's another day*, and all of its nothingness chiseled her into a statue. She tried on new outfits: a maxi dress breezed with coral perennials, a leather jacket with gold zippers. She started to text Julian but stopped herself. She thought of those mice, scuttling into the street from the paper bag. Maybe one of them had gotten the message and wrangled its way upstairs. Maybe he was feasting on a glob of forgotten food, loving every minute of life in Peter's apartment. Maybe she hadn't let that one lowly mouse down.

She rummaged to find Barry's number, the businessman from the plane. "Hi," she said, after reintroducing herself. "I could really use a friend who doesn't hate me."

"What about one that doesn't know you enough to hate you?" Barry said, and she laughed. Barry asked if she wanted to meet at a food hall for an early lunch. She was so glad to say yes to something that didn't deluge her in shame that she would've tweezed every hair from Barry's head if he'd asked.

* * *

She didn't really know who she was looking for. In her mind, Barry was just a man who bore some resemblance to a toe. In real life he wore a navy blue polo and a baseball cap and ordered three tiny ham tarts. Zoe got a latte, lofted by layers of foam.

Barry asked if she wanted to talk about anything and she said, "Anything, just not that."

"But that's why you called me," he said. "I mean, isn't it?"

"That is why I called you," she said.

"Let me get you a tart, too," Barry said. "No fun in eating alone. When I get back, you can tell me about it."

She looked at Barry. She wondered how hard it would be to seduce him. No ring. She saw it all: a tangle of denim dragging around his ankles, Zoe's mouth full of an inoffensive penis. Maybe this was what she needed, a fresh start with someone who found her bewitching. Maybe everything she needed was right here, with Barry, and all she had to do was stretch her foot a few inches longer than she would normally stretch it, and it would be on.

"Here you go," Barry said, sitting, and there it was: the decision.

"Thanks," she said, reaching for a napkin. "It looks good."

After the lunch there was a meeting. This time Zoe told them a story about her father, how she'd been drunk when he died, drunk during the time when she would've needed to buy a plane ticket for his funeral, drunk during the time when his funeral proceeded and her brother had never forgiven her. She wasn't even sure where he was buried, whether it was in the sun or the shade.

When the leader thanked her for sharing, she wanted to crawl on her knees and beg him to absolve her, to tell her she was a good person after all, or that she could be. She shook in her chair as the next few people rose to divulge their thorny, shameful pasts.

She resolved: she could be better. She was here, wasn't she? If these people, these crunchy cookie eaters, were doing *the work*, couldn't she?

Besides Barry, a few faces looked familiar from last time—a woman with a hummingbird tattoo, a man with a hearty mustache. It comforted her, recognizing them. "See you tomorrow?" she asked, and Barry saluted her with a cookie in hand.

Outside, Brigid waited by a tall, gnarled tree. Zoe spotted her right away, carting a leather handbag with a bouquet of lavender tucked in its side. Zoe waved first.

"You're here," Zoe marveled.

"And you're here, too," Brigid said. She was marveling, too, in her own way.

"I made an AA friend," Zoe said. "He likes baseball hats and ham."

"Both important," Brigid said. "I bought the ingredients for a carbonara. Should we have dinner together? I can incorporate ham, but not hats. Or, wait—" She dug into her tote, finding a floppy magenta beanie. "This was an ill-advised gift from my niece. Now we have it all."

"We really do," Zoe said.

38.

It took Morgan three weeks to dredge up the courage to talk to Dad. Brigid's voice pinballed through Morgan's thoughts: *That doesn't mean you can avoid it.* They creaked downstairs with heavy steps. Dad had spread his five-thousand-piece puzzle out on the dining room table with a plate of discarded crusts. Despite his headphones, he looked up at Morgan as they approached. Morgan stood awkwardly in front of his puzzling, draping a hand over the top of a dining room chair that no one had ever used, and tried to appear casual.

"I want to talk to you about something," Morgan said. "I . . ."

Dad squirmed under the weighted blanket. "How bad is this going to be, on a scale of one to ten? One being pure bliss. I guess there's no reason you'd come down here to tell me about a situation that ranked at a one."

"Maybe a four," Morgan said, their voice starting to waver. "In the grand scheme of things, I guess. To me it's a ten."

They started to outline all of the happenings that they'd herded carefully underneath their cone of silence: Sadie breaking up with them, Sadie's brother in jail and her mom's dialysis center being inundated with complaints. By the time they had arrived at asking Brigid for advice, Dad had started jotting down notes on the inside of the top of the puzzle box so that he didn't lose track of any of his questions.

Brigid's name seemed to plunk Dad into a different conversation altogether. "That doesn't make sense," he interjected. "Why would you— You said you hated her. Okay. Okay, so you called her. What did you talk about?"

"I wanted to ask her how I could get back together with Sadie."

Dad processed this. "Because she's a queer woman like Sadie?" he asked.

It wasn't, but Morgan was relieved for an out. "Yeah," they said. "I thought...she might have a good perspective. And she knows things but isn't *in* the things."

"It's true that I've never been a seventeen-year-old girl," Dad mused. "So, okay. What's the plan?"

Morgan didn't start with therapy. Instead they began with Mom's check.

"I'm going to give it to Sadie," Morgan rushed. "I don't think I should keep it."

Dad nodded. "All these years, I've never taken money from your mom. Your grandma would've hated..." he said. "Well, I'm glad that you...see what that money is used for."

Morgan continued eagerly into Brigid's suggestion of using Uncle Albert as a lawyer for the harassment complaints. Dad kept writing things down, billowy smears of ballpoint. Morgan rushed through the word *therapy*, keeping their head ducked.

"Brigid insisted she'd pay for it," Morgan muttered. *Insisted* indicated that the matter was closed. Tears stood at salute, ready for Morgan to blink.

"Okay," Dad said. "I'll ask Dr. Gold for a recommendation."

Morgan looked at him. Was that the end of the conversation? He didn't want to know what was so infinitesimally fucked about Morgan that needed professional assistance?

"Dad . . . I'm so sorry. For everything."

"This is part of a normal developmental phase in which you question authority in order to assert yourself as an autonomous individual," Dad said quickly. He picked up a puzzle piece and put it back down. "This might be my own issue, but I . . . I miss when you were my friend."

The tears plumed. "I'm sorry, Dad," Morgan said.

"I know. You just told me that." Dad reached for Morgan, uncharacteristically, and wrapped his fingers around the width of Morgan's arm. "Your mom . . . she left her car here. We should give that to Sadie's family. When you leave for college, you can take mine. I don't think I'll be using it too much without you."

It was the first direct mention of Morgan leaving that felt real.

"But what if you need to go somewhere?"

"I can figure that out." Dad cleared his throat. "Or maybe you won't need it, if you're in a city. Public transportation is the single greatest contribution that we can make for the safety of the planet."

Their thoughts filled with images of what this gift would've looked like in a different, alternate world, one where Sadie still loved them and would've clenched Morgan tightly and whispered thank you in her tingly, ASMR voice.

"Do you want to stay for a while and help me with the puzzle?"

"Sure," Morgan said, and got up to sit in their regular seat.

* * *

The next day Dad asked if Morgan wanted to learn to drive, and Morgan said okay and carefully pretended to learn each skill anew. *This is an act of kindness, not a lie,* Morgan convinced themself, adjusting the mirrors with exaggerated caution.

After twenty minutes, Dad said, "I feel okay about you driving to Sadie's tomorrow and bringing this to her. Do you feel okay about it?"

"Besides the Sadie part, I feel okay about it," Morgan said. It was peculiar, being in Mom's car together. Dad had rooted through the car and thrown everything away. Still, they couldn't help but feel Mom there, decapitating crackers, cranking the window open so she could reach her fingers outside.

"I don't think she's going to forgive me," Morgan said.

"Probably not." He paused. "Was that the wrong thing to say? I can lie. Morgan! Forgiveness, straight ahead." He used his *Titanic Iceberg, straight ahead!* voice, which softened it a little. Morgan hit the blinker. They weren't ready to go home, just yet.

Two weeks later, Sadie met Morgan outside in the YMCA parking lot, with a whistle around her neck and a red one-piece. Seeing her, Morgan thought they might throw up, which would've been fitting. Sadie watched with her arms akimbo, squinting to see if Morgan was the driver of this strange Mazda.

"Hi," Morgan said, wiping their hands on their basketball shorts. They took a step toward Sadie, then stopped. Then changed their mind and took another step, but wobbled. It was like they had never interacted with another person in real life. Sadie bit down on her lower lip. She hadn't taken any steps.

"Hi," she said after a long pause. "Whose car is this?"

"Um . . . yours," Morgan said unceremoniously. "Sorry. I meant to say that in a way that was more . . . dazzling. This car was my mom's and she's gone now." They took a loud breath in and out. "She left this and . . . you should have it. After everything."

Sadie's expression was stony. "I got your money," she said.

"It's my mom's money," Morgan muttered. "Did it, um . . . cover everything? Until you figure something else out?"

Her face was completely impassive. "Yeah," she said. "Until I figure something else out. Lifeguarding pays pretty well, actually. If I have a car, maybe I can do it year-round somewhere." She peered at the car, allowing herself a small smile, and then back at Morgan.

"That lawyer," Sadie said. "He got my brother into a 'community service betterment program.'"

"Yeah. He's my uncle, apparently." Morgan couldn't maintain eye contact. "Did your mom . . . Is her job okay?"

"Yeah. They filed some kind of Yelp complaint about harassment and had the reviews removed." She paused. "So your mom's gone? What's that like?"

"Quiet." They didn't say anything for a few beats. "It sucks, actually, but maybe it sucks in a way that's going to be better later on."

"I'm not ready to talk to you yet," she said.

"Yeah, I get that," Morgan said. "Here, I don't want to forget to give you the keys."

"I'll give you a ride home," she said, and couldn't help the grin that spread across her face afterward at her new car. An automobiled room of her own.

After Morgan left Sadie with her car, they waited every day to see the blur of the red Mazda weaving around the blocks between their homes. They punched their time card at the library, Ragúed bowls of spaghetti for rowdy, babysittable children.

Rosemary, Morgan's new therapist, suggested they try acupuncture. The acupuncturist pressed her fingers deep into their muscles. Needles unzipped into pressure points. Morgan thought of Mom, how afraid she would be in Morgan's position. *I'm braver than you*, Morgan thought, and it felt sad. Afterward they felt peeled, like the inside of an orange.

In therapy they started to realize how they could be so cloistered in their own anxieties that a stranger would be the only safe haven for secrets. How, even with Sadie, Morgan's brain spooled constant possibilities of violence—a stranger brandishing a brick and slamming it into the back of Sadie's skull, a movie theater attendant firing at the crowd. Morgan found themself going for long bike rides on the shoulders of the parkway, foliage painting leaves the color of egg yolks. Morgan listened to audiobooks to fill their ears with somebody else's voice, though they never stopped comparing the rhythms, the tiny mouth sounds, of those voices to Sadie's.

Then it was senior year. Tiana and Aiden asked if Morgan wanted to sit with them at lunch, if they didn't have anyone else to sit with, and Morgan felt grateful and depressed by their invitation. They watched the back of Sadie's head from across the cafeteria; they felt her laugh carry and hit them in the stomach like a dodgeball. Sadie had thoroughly arranged her schedule to avoid Morgan. On Tuesdays they caught a glimpse of her hair as she left Spanish, flanked by the field hockey girls. Morgan sent their college application at the beginning of October to Brown—early decision. Which would put them within an hour's distance of Sadie at MIT. Just in case.

Two weeks later, Sadie left a note taped to their locker. She wrote: *Ready when you are.* It was both a question and an answer.

Sadie picked Morgan up to go to Baskin-Robbins, a neutral location. She honked for Morgan to come outside, though they had been peeking through the blinds for a full hour. Sadie had never looked more natural than she did behind the wheel of her very own car.

"Hey," they said, trying desperately to sound casual. "Thanks for—"

It had been a long time since they talked about anything besides homework or trauma. Sadie hadn't unlocked their side of the car. She gestured for Morgan to return to the driver's side and pressed a button to roll the window down.

"I'm going to ask you some questions," she said. "Part one, is your mom still out of the picture? And part two, have you been up to any self-destructive shenanigans with or without her?"

"No mom. No shenanigans. I've been in therapy," Morgan said, reaching to rub the back of their head so they'd have something to do with their hands. "I think I'm...doing better." They paused. "Rosemary thinks I have PTSD."

"Yeah, no kidding," Sadie said. "Rosemary's powers of observation are *magnificent*." She dropped her hands from the wheel. "That's good," she added, her voice softer. "I'm glad you're going."

"Thanks." Morgan let the pause hang. "Are there more questions?"

"No more questions." Sadie paused. "So, I was talking to my mom, and...she said that you've been respectful of my boundaries, and trying your hardest to make this up to me and my family, and that you've been dealt a hard hand in your life, and...that if I'm this miserable without you, it might be worth one last shot." Sadie clenched the steering wheel.

"I couldn't be more sorry, Sadie," they said. "I hope you know."

Sadie paused, saying nothing about Morgan's apology either way. "I think we can get some ice cream," she replied finally. "Let's take it one ice cream cone at a time."

"Let's hit the rocky road," Morgan said.

"I'm still going to unlock the door, but that was a horrible joke, Morgan Flowers."

"I promise I'll do better," Morgan said, and it hung there for a second. Sadie twisted her hair into a knot at the top of her head, a few strands of blond fluttering down the nape of her neck. Then Morgan heard the distinctive clink of the car unlocking, and they got in.

39.

Zoe started out slow. Every morning, she propped all of the windows open to spy on the people sauntering through Restauradores. Every day there was a different variety of juice, different fruit sliced into pieces. Every day, a different meeting, where Brigid would often be waiting for her. On Tuesdays, Thursdays, and Sundays, Brigid cooked pasta and sometimes tiramisu. She wondered if Brigid had rearranged her schedule to be here, with her, but didn't ask. Pasta and occasional tiramisu were enough.

God, grant me the serenity, Zoe recited, along with the others. God, grant me wisdom.

An excerpt from Natalie's book was published in the *New Yorker*. Zoe scanned it, recognizing herself instantly. *Flailing through her life like a blindfolded ballerina on center stage. Slicing through the evening dress with a knife, she only barely avoided shearing her own flesh in the process. Every life the woman touched was indelibly altered, thrown in an infinite collision course.*

She cried and cried. She stood in front of a bar and counted to 365 and walked home with her shoulders hunched.

In the end, Zoe didn't want to rely only on herself. Brigid made her an appointment with a doctor who prescribed her a medication that made her violently ill if she relapsed. She took the pill in the morning. The horror stories she'd read online about the months of insomnia, anxiety, and depression that would follow any "slipping up" scared her. She had been doing everything right, but still the guilt of the past shrouded her, a fog that never felt as if it would clear.

One Sunday Brigid made a pasta with butternut squash and mint, little knobs of feta. Brigid poured seltzers with lime, asked questions about Zoe's day. She was not flirtatious but not *not* flirtatious, either, loaded pauses emerging and neither one of them moving, hoping that the tension of past intimacy would pass. Some moments were easier to paddle past than others. Tonight Zoe complimented her cooking an extra time, trying to summon whatever rusted-up courage remained.

"I want to talk to you about something," Zoe said, as Brigid chased a husk of squash across her bowl. "I've been thinking about... forgiveness," she said. All of her words felt trite and gristly. "About Morgan and Jul."

Brigid stabbed the squash and chewed it thoughtfully. "What were you thinking?"

"I was thinking... I could invite them here for a trip. Maybe for Thanksgiving? I want to... I feel like... I owe them something. Something big."

"Well, they might not care to see you," Brigid said flatly. "Or hear from you. Are you prepared for that?"

Zoe moved the prongs of her fork lightly against her plate in a figure eight, unable to eat but equally unable to keep still. "I want to try," she said.

Zoe wrote Julian an email. She watched the cursor dance in place, reminding her of the infinite combinations of words and phrases that existed, and how all of them would be inadequate for what she'd put Julian through. She wrote: *I've been sober since I got here, three months ago. If you would like to come to Lisbon for a visit, I would like to have you. It would be my treat. You don't have to see me much, or at all, if that's what you want. Every day I am so sorry, Jules. I know it doesn't cover the half of it. What I want is to do something nice for you both, because you deserve it. I hope you're well. I hope you're beyond well.*

Julian wrote back, an agonizing seventy-two hours later: *What would it mean to be "beyond" well? Is there a spectrum of wellness, in which well is in the center, and excellence is on one end, and suffering on the other? I have questions about your rubric.*

It would be nice to take Morg somewhere special for their eighteenth birthday. Here are my criteria: a) your continued sobriety, b) we stay somewhere that is neither with you nor Brigid, preferably somewhere with a balcony/outdoor space, c) no time alone with Morg unless it's approved by me beforehand. It's up to them, though. If Morg says yes, then yes, we'll be there.

40.

The airport was in New Jersey. On the way there, Dad narrated facts about logistics: construction, accessibility, how dramatically air travel had changed since 9/11. Beneath the sky, which was as thickly blue as Morgan had ever seen, like tarpaulin, Morgan couldn't stop staring; thinking that in less than three and a half hours, they'd be catapulted into that sky.

Morgan dug their fingernails into their palms. It was real; they'd parked in long-term parking and it was time to take their shoes off and have their bodies scanned by a horrible machine and a man with a mustache burrowed his hands across Morgan's body, agreeing *we are both the same*, but they smiled because they wanted it to be over and when it finally was, they stood in front of the two bathroom choices and, defeated, went into the choice that meant they were invisible.

Dad and Morgan laced their shoes back up, reconfigured their belongings.

"Dad," Morgan said. "I . . . I'm kind of scared about this."

He looked at Morgan for a long beat. "There's only one thing you need to know. When the airplane lifts off, and when it lands, you'll have horrible pain in your ears. So you'll want to learn the Valsalva maneuver. You close your mouth, pinch your nose shut, and then exhale hard, like you're blowing up a balloon. That's key."

"What about...not the plane stuff?" Morgan said. "What about after?"

"I'll be right there with you," Dad said. "We'll be there together."

It was late when they arrived in Lisbon, but it was also not a time. It was a dream. Everything felt surreal—the two of them waited in line, other tourists chatting in languages Morgan didn't recognize, a stranger ushering them forward and then holding a hand tightly up to say *STOP!* while Dad answered terse questions about the purpose of their visit. *Pleasure* seemed to be far from the right word, Morgan thought.

"I think I see a palm tree," Dad said after they exited the airport. "See?" Morgan had never seen a palm tree before. They'd associated palm trees with Beverly Hills; Hollywood starlets with tanned limbs. Here the palm trees looked vampiric against the gloamy sky. Soon they would reach the front of the cab line; then the check-in desk at the grand, gold-adorned hotel up a colossal hill.

The next day, the two of them went to Brigid's apartment for dinner, where she'd made a tagine, whatever that was. She asked whether Dad wanted to hug, which he did not, and whether Morgan wanted to hug, which they did.

"I saw the woman selling cherries," Dad said to Brigid. "She *does* have a leonine face."

Brigid brightened. "Doesn't she?"

"You were right about the pretzels on the flight. Strange texture."

"Gritty," Brigid said, and Dad nodded enthusiastically. "Did I tell you Nicola finally called me Brigid yesterday?"

"At long last!" Dad said. "It's been, what, six months? Seven?"

Morgan looked between the two of them. All those details, exchanged. They'd been friends for fifteen years and only stood in the same room twice.

Brigid's apartment was filled with plants, leaves that spindled across the main wall, and a decorative fireplace doubling as a display for thick art books. Morgan pored over her fruit bowl, which housed a plastic box of figs with little slits for the fruit to breathe through. She offered to make tea. "Peppermint," she said, before Dad could ask, and they smiled at each other.

"Brigid, could I . . . lie down for a second?" Dad asked. "Suddenly I'm feeling very . . . wobbly."

While Brigid showed Dad to a guest room, Morgan watched trams amble up the steep hill through the large window by the sink. Miniature pastel houses and steeples of faraway churches sat like an impressionist painting come to life. Again they felt a surreal, where-am-I-ness, where Morgan was sitting alone in their mom's ex-partner's house, drinking tea. Maybe this had been Mom's mug. Maybe she'd burned her tongue on this very tea, too.

When Brigid returned, she cradled her cup of tea carefully, then placed it back down into a marigold-colored saucer before she said, "I imagine there are many things you might want to know."

"Is Mom okay?" Morgan rushed out. It wasn't what they meant to ask and they wanted to take it back immediately.

Brigid paused for a long time before answering. "It may sound naive, but I think . . ." She swallowed. "It's better, for right now.

I also know better than to say this is the time it will be different forever."

"You do sound naive," Morgan said. It felt so good to call another person that.

"Having hope and being naive are different," Brigid said. "You'll learn that."

Then she reached forward into the fruit bowl and handed Morgan a small handful of cherries. Morgan ate them quickly. They imagined growing up here with Brigid as their other mother, handing them dark cherries with breakfast to stall having difficult conversations. Sitting on airplanes, knowing exactly how much pain to anticipate as the vessel pierced through layers of frothy clouds.

"I'm all mixed up about how to feel," Morgan said. "Should I be happy that she's better, for now? Even though it might not be for very long?" Brigid didn't answer, just watched Morgan with her wide, gray eyes. Morgan reached for the grapefruit in the basket and held it in their quivery hands. "I wish I could just turn my brain off," Morgan said to the grapefruit.

Brigid scooted her stool closer to Morgan. The legs squawked against azure tiles.

"Listen," she said. "I want to tell you something quite seriously. When you run from your feelings—I mean, when you reach a point where you would do anything not to think about how you feel—that's when you're in trouble."

But what do you do if you stop running? Morgan wanted to ask. Morgan expected her to continue in this vein but then she began to tell Morgan about the night that Brigid and Mom had met, in Copenhagen, when Morgan was a toddler and Mom was sleeping on the floor in her cousin Ingrid's dorm room, next to a gas station.

"She came back to my apartment, and I had a pineapple and she said she didn't know how to cut it, that she'd only ever bought presliced pineapple. Can you imagine?" Brigid asked, but Morgan could. That Zoe was the mom they'd always imagined, clean hands, clean space underneath her squared fingernails.

"Why did you leave Copenhagen?" Morgan asked.

Brigid tilted her head with a sad smile. "Because trouble would find her everywhere. She could be in a city one day and have found a terrible new friend who had a brilliant idea, and...so on." Brigid shook her head. "I wasn't innocent, either. I got bored everywhere. I could never find a profession that held my interest. We fed off each other."

"I thought you were blissful nomads," Morgan said.

Brigid laughed. "Why would you think it was blissful?" she asked, and Morgan wasn't sure if they should answer.

"What may look like a joy ride," Brigid said, "is actually someone fleeing the scene. I'm not saying that you need to forgive her. It's your grudge to carry if you want to keep it with you. But you can empty your baggage whenever you want," she said. "You can let go."

Morgan sucked their upper lip underneath their teeth. *But I don't want to let it go*, they thought desperately. The animosity was the only thing that they had that seemed stable, permanent. They reached for something else to say.

"But you stayed...entangled with her," Morgan said hesitantly.

"Yes. We're not exactly back together," Brigid said. "But not quite *not* together."

"That's confusing."

Brigid nodded. "I thought, for sure, if I saw her again...it would be gone. That old feeling. But with her sobriety...there is still a part of me that wants to think, yes, this is the time. Maybe we'll move to the country like gentle old ladies. Drink tea in the garden." She shrugged. "We'll see what the next few months bring."

"Do you think I should see her?" Morgan asked, after a heavy pause. "And please, don't tell me to look deep within myself, et cetera."

Brigid nodded. "I think you want me to give you permission to say yes."

"Yeah," Morgan mumbled.

"Your dad can set that up, then. And, Morgan?" Brigid said. "I think you're a lovely person. And . . . it's been quite nice for me to get to know you."

Morgan ducked their head. "I don't know. I don't feel lovely."

"I'm quite a bit older than you are, and I'm very wise," Brigid said. "So it's mandatory that you accept my judgment of your character."

"Okay, but I have to tell you something. I don't know what tagine is," they confessed, and Brigid paused before laughing and pulling them up by the elbow to show them the Moroccan pot and the cubes of lamb and all of those spices, swirling together to make something wonderful.

⚘

The train station was noisy, bustling with people. Morgan caught their reflection in a mirror by the ticket counter—their twiggy legs and their floaty black T-shirt—and felt as if they were fluorescent. "Your mom is by the vending machine," Dad reported after a quick survey. "She's wearing a sunhat and a blue dress. Do you want me to stay? I'll stay, if you want me to."

Morgan wanted so much to say yes. "It's okay," they said. "See you in a few hours."

She looked different. It wasn't just the bleached hair; her face seemed a different shape than they remembered. She was wearing espadrilles, tall ones that laced up her calf. Her toenails were painted red. Morgan observed her, cataloguing every detail as if it were a clue. *Are you sure you're not drinking again?* they asked the espadrilles, the nail polish. They raised their hand.

"Morg," she said, and she put both arms outward as if she were impersonating a mummy. She waited for Morgan to fill the space between those arms. She smelled like spicy roses. "I didn't think you'd want to see me," she said into their shoulder. "Are you taller?"

"A little."

"Do you like Portugal?" she asked. She had their arms in a lock. In some ways they hated this embrace and how long it had gone on for, but in another way it saved them the discomfort of prolonged eye contact.

Morgan tried to think of something horrible to say. "It was rainy when we got here."

"It can be rainy," she agreed.

Morgan's mouth went dry. A blur of people continually walked past them, and Morgan felt their attention being pulled toward the strangers' swimwear, their tote bags, their laughter.

"Why did you want to meet me here?" they asked.

She released them from the hug. "Because we've never had a *real, proper* adventure together," she said. "I brought olives! And raisins." She rummaged through a leather bag. She held out the little box of raisins as if it were a treasure.

"I'm allergic to raisins," they said quickly, which was a lie.

Zoe leaned forward then, a conspiratorial smile on her face that Morgan recognized from the gala, the sparkle that made them feel like the only person in the room. "Then fuck them!" she said, raising her voice a little. "Fuck these raisins!" and she dumped them into a trash can.

***

She didn't remember the name of the stop. "It sounds like couscous. Or Quetzal," she mused. Morgan leaned so far into the window that they may as well have fused with the glass. "I'll know it when I see it."

"How did you get us tickets?" Morgan asked.

"I paid to go to the end of the line," she said. Of course she did.

Morgan gritted their teeth. All around them, people seemed entirely relaxed, splitting their headphones and lightly dancing, reading thick novels, sleeping languorously across their loved ones' laps like pets. *She doesn't even know where the fuck we're going.*

"You're quiet," she observed. "Is it . . . because you hate trains?"

"Trains are okay."

"Is it because . . . you hate . . . *me*?" she tried, raising her eyebrows.

"I just . . . like to know where I'm headed."

"Nobody knows where they're headed," Zoe said. "It's a metaphor. Oh, that's it," she said. "Queluz. Get up, get up!"

"Why didn't you say we were close?" Morgan said, scrambling. Very few people got off with them; only a smattering of stern-faced men, some wearing dark baseball caps that shielded their faces. Mom led, weaving toward an underpass and then on a long pedestrian path flanked by a highway.

"Where are we going?" Morgan asked.

"It's a surprise, but it's going to be excellent. I promise."

They walked. Across the not-highway, a clot of men in work shirts toasted their green-necked beers together. Shards of glass were scattered across the narrow pedestrian path, as if they were bits of bread meant to feed the ducks.

And then, suddenly, the palace came into view. It was strange, how wandering through this mostly empty suburb, you could stumble upon an enormous fountain, a tall, buttercream-colored building with royal statues guarding the doors. The grass was cut into neat squares, dotted with orange blossoms. The adjoining houses were shabby, watercolored by age and poor maintenance. Zoe gestured to the first one on their left. "This is the restaurant," she said. "Then we can see the rest of the grounds after."

"Okay."

"Are you surprised?" she asked, smiling for the first time since they'd debarked the train. "It's a *palace*. You've never been to one before, right? History happened in there. Carlota Joaquina of Spain tried to overthrow the Portuguese monarchy! So then she was under house arrest and maybe killed herself. It's very exciting."

Morgan stooped to pick up a discarded euro. The coin had a pleasing weight in their palm. She looked at them quizzically. The moment passed between them. Surrounded by the buildings that housed royalty, Morgan was still the kind of person to pause their life for a chance at an extra dollar. If Sadie were here, she would have understood. But not their mother.

"Lunch?" she said.

❧

Morgan tried to remember the sentences that echoed in their head late at night. Those sentences were symphonies, by the

time the clock's hands stretched to one, two in the morning—
the resentment and the confusion and the anger all knotted and
inconsolable. Most nights they felt they could fill an entire note-
book with things to say, but now they couldn't begin.

"Some wine?" a tuxedoed waiter asked.

Morgan's eyes were glued to hers, watching this, the first test.
Zoe shook her head. "Take the glasses, please," she advised, and
the waiter whisked the possibility away, at least for now. She put
her sobriety chip in front of her on the table and looked at it as
she spoke. "We'll both have the lamb-tasting menu, please."

"Very good, miss."

As the waiter left, Zoe glared at Morgan. "Stop looking at me
like I'm a grenade somebody threw in your lap." She dug into her
bag and shimmied some olives into her palm. "Olive?"

Morgan shook their head as the first course of lamb was set in
front of them. Stalks of artichokes stood like a forest, crisped and
browned.

"I want to know what happened," Morgan said softly. "When
you left the first time. I want to hear about it from you."

Zoe nodded. "I knew I wasn't . . . having the normal experience,
being pregnant. I knew something was missing. When you were
born, I hoped . . . I'd hold you, and I'd be transformed."

"And you weren't," Morgan said.

She looked up, as if surprised to see them there at all. She'd
never looked so sad. "I was," she said, throaty. "Just not in a good
way. When I first held you, I loved the shit out of you. But I
also wanted to run. Do you ever get that way? When something
happens, and it's too much, and you just—"

"Run," Morgan said. "Yeah. All the time."

She sawed the lamb into tiny shards with her sharp knife.

"Family trait, I guess." She chewed. "I can't tell you how scary it is, knowing that you're responsible for someone else's life. And your dad, from the very beginning, he was so much *better* at it than I was. I thought, he hates noise and smells and disturbance of routine—we'll be in the same sinking ship. But he was doing it, somehow, and I really, really was not.

"I'd wake up crazed, trying to remember something tiny, like . . . a scene in a TV show where they were reciting the lyrics to Pearl Jam or . . . this Turkish chicken I had once near the Museum of Natural History . . . and it was like my brain had just caved in on itself." Mom shook her head. "One day I thought, my brain doesn't work right, and I'm going to ruin your life. And I saw, all around you, the life that you were going to have. I just felt . . . *unhinged*. And then it was your birthday, and I came back from my run and you had your dad on one side and Cheryl on the other, and she'd made you this beautiful fucking carrot cake from scratch, and I hated her because you were this perfect little family without me, and I . . . I knew you'd be better off."

Zoe crimped her lips together. "And then I started drinking, to get away from what I did, and I couldn't stop. So I was right, and you were better off," she said, her voice breaking. "You were better off."

"Rack of lamb with pearl onions and potatoes," the waiter announced. Morgan and Mom both said thank you. Morgan tried to cry discreetly, bringing their chin down into their neck's cave. The lamb's bones created a canopy over the white plate.

Morgan's voice shook. "How do you . . . How can you say that?"

"Because it's true, Morg. You're so young, you know?" she said. "I know it fucked you up, and I'm sorry. But you're not thinking about how fucked up you'd be if I'd stayed. Sometimes every choice is a shitty choice with shitty consequences that hurt everyone around you."

Morgan thought then about Peter, how much damage they'd caused without ever meaning to, and they thought for a moment that they understood her, now, for the first time. The two of them chewed their lamb under glimmering chandeliers. Morgan fought the urge to clear the air between them.

When they were finished, and the plates were cleared, another group came in, older ladies with oversized glasses around their necks. Their entrance, for some reason, felt like a new beginning.

Morgan looked up at Mom. She had been clandestinely crying, too, pretending to look for something in her purse. But Morgan knew a fellow crier when they saw one.

"So you got your chip," Morgan said.

She sniffled. "Eight months now. That's almost as long as I carried you for, so . . . it's not such a short time, I guess. Without Brigid, I don't know where I would be right now. I don't know how she forgave me." She paused. "What about you? Do you think you can ever forgive me?"

Morgan paused. "It's not that hard to forgive you when you're right in front of me. But I don't know . . . what happens when we aren't right here, together." They looked at her expression, which was both searching and somehow inert, resigned. "I want to try to hold on to it."

She smiled gratefully. "Morg," she whispered. "Do you want an olive?"

"Okay."

"I'll pass it to you under the table."

"Okay," Morgan said, and extended their hand to hers.

"Sorry I cried in there," Morgan said once they were safely out of the restaurant. Ahead, the palace glittered. They crossed a fountain, filled with statues of gods with weapons and bewildered-looking women who stared into the sky.

"It's just . . . too much to take in." Morgan gestured around them, the wide girth of the palace with its rococo finishes and ornate hedges. "Like, how a few months ago, I was with Dad, wondering if I'd ever see you again. Now I'm at a castle, and I just ate lamb ice cream, and you're right here. It feels like I'm dreaming. Why did you want to come here? You never said."

"I'll show you when we get to it," Mom said.

"Mom," Morgan said, and the word took on a different timbre. "Do you remember . . . that pigeon that used to live outside of your window? That summer you were back in New York? I forgot its name."

"Frederick," she said.

"Frederick," Morgan repeated. "That's right." And for a minute, it felt just like Sadie talking to her mom, just a normal conversation, a forgotten fact that was possible to fact-check with the person who was by your side, and they tried to lose the rest of it, all of the tumult that trailed after them like a cat's tail.

Everything around the palace was so ornately painted and decorated that Morgan didn't know where to look: the heavenly figures reclining on crowds of clouds, gold filigree domes and mirrored walls and chandeliers that dipped low into the center of the room like they might plummet into the floor at any moment. They were alone; no other tourists followed. Still they walked in silence, trying to imagine a time when people lived like this, in places like this, to read or eat soup or fall asleep in the middle of a humid day.

"This is what I wanted to show you," she said. She gestured to a canal, lined with elaborate blue tiles showing images of the seascape. The area around the canal resembled a tiered cake, many-layered, with a coat of arms in the center. The shape looked like it had to have some function; a tall, tomb-like structure with steps leading up to a flat precipice. It was beautiful, like everything else here, but Morgan didn't have any idea why it was meant for them to see.

"Last time I was here," Mom said, "you could help restore it. They had all these materials and people were helping to clean up the gardens. Anyone could just wander over and help." She looked around, as if the memory would materialize behind her. "I thought it was so bizarre, that a royal palace was basically coming undone and any strangers could grab a . . . thingy to spackle over whatever or help clean off some grime. I thought it would be . . . meaningful. Or something." Her face clouded over. "But I missed it."

A familiar orb of anger filled Morgan. *You missed it like you've missed everything*, they thought, but then it was gone, and she was their mother.

"Do you still have the olives?" they asked. "And a tissue?"

Mom stared at Morgan in wonder. "A tissue," she repeated, as if Morgan were the most brilliant person alive, and she smiled.

In one life, Morgan had already decided she was gone. In one life, they'd spent the day with Dad, wedging their fingers into the thick, warm sand at the beach. In one life, they'd never come here to begin with. In one life, they'd never chatted with Peter, never been afraid, never followed Sadie out of the parking lot. In one life, they were learning what it meant to know you were careening toward a blackout and never want to stop. Morgan saw the other paths for their life, folded outward like a fan. Then those other paths receded into a bog, and they were left dipping a tissue into olive juice, scrubbing a tiny square of tile to mark the spot where they'd once been.

Acknowledgments

First, thank you to my wonderful agent, Stephanie Delman—I feel so lucky to be represented by you. Thank you for your sharp eye, endless support, and honest feedback. To Iwalani Kim, whose wise feedback also helped shape this novel and distaste for pineapple on pizza brightened my editing process considerably.

Thank you to my brilliant editor, Maddie Caldwell, and to Jacqui Young, for all of your help sculpting this book into its final form. Working with the Grand Central team has been a dream (I would say this even without the joy of rhyming!) and I feel so grateful to be in your hands. Thank you also to Anjuli Johnson, Roxanne Jones, Alana Spendley, and to Grace Han for the gorgeous cover art that, upon receipt, made my face hurt from smiling too hard.

A special thank you to my friend Jen Wilde, who gave so much of herself in sharing her experience of what it means to move through the world as an autistic person, and pointed me toward autistic educators and activists. You literally saved me during this process (to borrow your phrase)! Thank you for your work in educating allistic people about autism and for creating community for neurodiverse folks to connect: Agustina CM (@TheAutisticLife), Eden, Leo, and Laurel (@TheAutisticats), Sara Jane Harvey (@AgonyAutie), Sarah Kate Smigiel (@justsaysk), and Nicole Cliffe, whose Twitter threads on neurodiversity were incredible to read while I was working on this project. I am also grateful to Sarah Kurchak, whose essay in *Catapult* ("When the Way You Love Things Is 'Too Much'; or: Why I Went to Portmeirion") is a wonderful piece of writing. I have learned so much from all of you.

I began working on this novel, albeit in a very different form, way back in 2010, when I was a senior at Vassar. I have so many people to thank for reading early drafts of this book, which has gone through so many radical shifts over the years. Thank you to everyone in my senior experimental writing seminar at Vassar College in 2010, especially Victory Matsui. I kept Morgan's affinity for the pigeon for you. Thank you to Jose Nieto, who helped me craft an early version of the arc with Peter and Sadie, and to Larissa Belcic, who generously read this before I applied to graduate school. Thank you to the Jasper Collective, including Jessica Lanay Moore, Jessica Kashiwabara, Jessica Espinoza, Stephanie Jimenez, and Isabel Pichardo, and to Alexander Chee and the workshop group at Disquiet literary seminars in 2015. To Dana Nield— thank you for reminding me that my characters can be kind to each other, too.

Thank you to the editors and staff of the *Missouri Review* circa 2017, who selected an excerpt of this novel ("Clean") as a finalist for the 2017 *Missouri Review*'s Jeffrey E. Smith Editors' Prize in Fiction. It meant so much to me, and buoyed my confidence in this project through many months of editing.

To my MFA friends and teachers at Columbia University, I am endlessly grateful for your continued wisdom, generosity, and support. To Heidi Julavits—I think all the time about being the person in the room that never quits. To Angelica Baker, Cory Leadbeater, Kerry Cullen, Breanne Reynolds, Emil Ostrovski— thank you for carving out time in your lives to read and give feedback on this project, I am so appreciative. Thank you, Julia Drake, for everything.

Thank you to my family, biological and chosen. To my parents, Allen and Susan Feltman; and all of the Feltmans, Greenbergs, Rosenthals; to my Leonians, who have seen me through; to the Barcellonas, Guillorys, and Dalton Shively. I am incredibly lucky to have your support. To my friends: Sara Lyons, Paul Treadgold, Kelli Trapnell, Jillian Tomlinson; Caroline Moran, Emmett Martin, Addie Guiliano, Damien Martin; Allison Castelot, Sophie Beckwith, and Paige and Elisabeth Plumlee-Watson. Thank you to my *Poets & Writers* family, especially Rachel Britton, Melissa Faliveno, Dana Isokawa, and Kyndal Thomas—how lucky I am to have found you all.

Thank you to the artists whose work percolates all the way through my heart: Leslie Jamison (especially *The Recovering: Intoxication and Its Aftermath*), Denis Johnson's *Jesus's Son*, and Julie Buntin's *Marlena*. I could not have written this book without the music of Warpaint, Lucy Dacus, Wilsen, Foals, Lemolo, Fiona Apple, and of course, Mitski.

To Christine Barcellona: without you, I'd still be shuffling index cards around on the floor, trying to understand what plot is. Thank you for loving me incandescently.

About the Author

Amy Feltman graduated with an MFA in Fiction from Columbia University in 2016 and is now the Assistant Director of Advertising at *Poets & Writers Magazine*. She is the author of *Willa & Hesper*, which was long-listed for the National Jewish Book Awards' Goldberg Prize for Debut Fiction. Her writing has appeared in *Cosmonauts Avenue*, *The Believer Logger*, *The Toast*, *The Millions*, *The Rumpus*, *Lilith Magazine*, *Slice Magazine*, and elsewhere. She lives with her partner in Astoria, New York.